PRAISE FOR RISQUÉ

Red Light Special

"So realistic that you better have either a lover nearby or a cold shower to jump into . . . Risqué has successfully made her mark in the erotica genre." —Urban Reviews

"The new queen of erotica has entered the building. You'll need a tall glass of water and an industrial-strength fan to cool you off while reading this steamy page-turner!" —DE'NESHA DIAMOND, co-author of *Desperate Hoodwives*

The Sweetest Taboo

"With the passion of Zane and the gut-wrenching emotion of Noire, Risqué takes the erotic-fiction scene by storm." —DANIELLE SANTIAGO, author of *Little Ghetto Girl*

"A sexy drama that will have you lusting for more." —ANNA J., author of *The Aftermath*

"Nothing is off-limits in Risqué's tantalizing and intensely stimulating debut novel. Prepare to be entertained, enthralled, and scandalized!" —CRYSTAL LACEY WINSLOW, author of *The Criss Cross*

"Rough, raw, and riveting! Passionate, fiery prose blazes across every page. Risqué captivates the reader from the very beginning and never lets go." —ALLISON HOBBS, author of *A Bona Fide Gold Digger*

"With so much to tell and feel, this knock-out, drag-down erotica love story will have you dripping by the last page . . . one of the best e_____ r Zane; there's a new sheriff in _____ y, crazy, sexy, and exhilarat_____ l to stay up all night!" –_____ ook Club

ALSO BY RISQUÉ

Red Light Special

The Sweetest Taboo

Smooth Operator

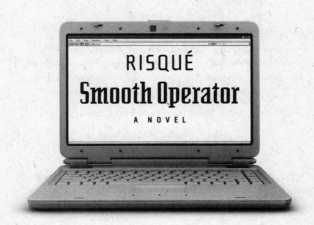

RISQUÉ

Smooth Operator

A NOVEL

ONE WORLD TRADE PAPERBACKS

BALLANTINE BOOKS   NEW YORK

A One World Trade Paperback Original

Copyright © 2010 by Risqué

All rights reserved.

Published in the United States by One World Books, an imprint of The Random House Publishing Group, a division of Random House, Inc., New York.

ONE WORLD is a registered trademark and the One World colophon is a trademark of Random House, Inc.

LIBRARY OF CONGRESS CATALOGING-IN-PUBLICATION DATA
Risqué.
Smooth operator : a novel / Risqué.
p. cm.
ISBN 978-0-345-50432-6 (pbk.) — ISBN 978-0-345-52312-9 (electronic)
1. Single mothers—Fiction.   2. African Americans—Fiction.   I. Title.
PS3618.I736S66 2010
813'.6—dc22   2010032069

Printed in the United States of America

www.oneworldbooks.net

2 4 6 8 9 7 5 3 1

Book design by Laurie Jewell
Title-page photograph: © iStockphoto

To my husband, Kevin,
who I finally convinced that people
would believe that this is fiction
and not our life!

"You've been misled;
money is *not* the root of
all evil. Pussy is."

— RISQUÉ

Smooth Operator

California

The platinum moon over Holmby Hills, California, left streaks across the marble floor as Payton stepped through the French doorway of her husband's home office. Her Angel perfume announced her entrance and seduced him to close his eyes; anxiously awaiting her arrival. He sat facing his computer, his back to the doorway, and the smoke from his Cuban cigar danced a tango toward the vaulted ceiling.

The Mary Jane Girls' "Candy Man" played in the background as Payton began her cat walk. Once behind him she gently ran the tip of her tongue over the muscular curves of his broad shoulders; and that's when it clicked; the song playing on the radio was apropos because he was *definitely* candy. At six foot two, he bore the physique of a lifer pushing hundred-pound weights, with sensually forbidden yet highly desired rips and bulging muscles. His skin was the color of a smooth and sweet Sugar Daddy, complimented by the milk chocolate eyes of a Zulu king: strong, regal, and serious. He wore a low and sexy well-lined Caesar, and framing his succulent lips was a delicious shadow-box beard.

He was polished and powerful. Articulate yet able to bring it to whomever, whenever. Confident but not arrogant. He was bilingual but Hood was his native dialect. He was perfect but always willing to expound upon his perfection. And all of this is why Payton loved him—or maybe not.

Her feelings for him were more erotic; no, more adoring. But then . . . perhaps her feelings were actually quite simple: she felt as if she owned him, that he belonged to her in every way imaginable—from the spinning waves in his hair to his large feet that lived up to the myth. All belonged to her.

Payton felt she'd raised him, though she wasn't his mother—she was definitely his wife. And she wasn't a cougar—they were both thirty. However, Payton deserved the credit for finding him five years ago, when he drove a UPS truck and delivered packages to her corporate offices. She was the one who'd asked him out to dinner, compelled by the way his eyes smiled when he looked at her.

Though she could've had any man, she chose to save him from the trenches of Crenshaw and deliver him into the golden-gated community of Holmby Hills, California, because she wanted him—not because she had to have him. After all, she was not only swanky rich but was wickedly beautiful: a slender size six, five eleven with perfect posture and a Naomi Campbell saunter. She had eyes like brown marbles and skin the deep amber of the evening sun.

He'd become one of the talented tenth because of who *she* was: a strong black woman who pushed him to become *the* man among men. For all intents and purposes, he should've worn *her* last name. After all, Payton was the one who'd come from great stock, not him; his father was a mystery, and his mother died of a heroin overdose. His sister had too many babies, and his brother drove somebody's garbage truck. Needless to say, he didn't have a name until Payton gave him one. "Mr. Lyfe Phillip Carrington," Payton said, tracing his shoulders with the tip of her index finger, "I was thinking that a good boy like you deserves to have his fantasy fulfilled."

Lyfe opened his eyes and slowly turned in his burgundy

leather wing chair. He stared at his wife, who stood before him in a cupless, glow-in-the-dark latex suit, with a slit that ran from her wet and warm pussy lips to her luscious ass. And on her feet were six-inch, extremely spiked heels that made her look as if she were walking on nails.

Lyfe attempted to contain himself, but he couldn't. His cock was so hard that he had to unzip his pants and allow his ten-inch endowment more room to expand. He stood up to drink Payton in full view.

She licked her lips and ran her hands from the latex hood that covered her hair to her breasts, where she toyed with her hard nipples. "You sit back down, baby," she said, and he complied. "I have a surprise for you."

Payton placed one of her legs at the side of Lyfe's thigh, revealing her swollen and dripping pussy lips. "I want you to sit here," she eased his cigar from between his lips and mashed it in the ashtray, "and watch this." She turned her head to the side and called over her shoulder, "Come to Mama."

An unknown and completely naked voluptuous woman stepped across the threshold, glowing in neon yellow body paint. Her E-cup breasts swayed as she placed her hands on her hips and headed over to them. She stopped at Payton and kissed her. "Now serve your purpose," Payton whispered. The woman then slid between Lyfe and Payton and kneeled. She dipped her glowing hands into Lyfe's already unzipped pants, removed his cock and began licking her way around the curved tip and taking him into her mouth, until she had deep throated all of his inches.

For a fleeting moment Lyfe wondered why Payton was really doing this, but as soon as the glowing woman placed a tongue vibrator in her mouth and electric sensations forced his body into a trance, he was no longer conscious enough to care.

Payton stroked the woman's long and silky auburn hair. "You're doing well, honey. A good job. Damn," Payton moaned, "you're sucking that dick real good. You know it's candy in there. Get that candy, baby, and find out how many licks it takes to get to the center of a Tootsie Roll pop."

Lyfe couldn't figure out if he needed to scream or to pinch his arm and see if this was a wet dream, because hands down this had to be the chick who invented sucking dick; he had never, ever, *ever* had brain like this. "Shit . . ." he moaned, entangling his fingers with Payton's as they both ran their hands through the woman's hair.

Payton looked in Lyfe's face and knew he was about to cum. "The candy is for me, baby." She tapped the glowing woman on the shoulder. "I just wanted you to get the candy to the center." Payton kneeled before Lyfe as the glowing woman moved behind her and ran her wet and heated tongue through Payton's sticky butterscotch and around her clit.

Payton moaned as she blew Lyfe's throne, seducing his cream candy out the tip. She could feel the glowing woman's tongue licking her pussy and pushing into her wet valley like a dick. All Payton could do was scream and moan, and moan and scream as the woman ate her pussy with extreme intensity, even as Lyfe's cum filled Payton's mouth.

Once Payton was satisfied, Lyfe rose from the chair and she lay in missionary position on the floor, allowing his member to expand her walls and force her body into complete submission. He stroked Payton with all of his might, tossing one of her legs to the side of his neck, causing her to scream his name in octaves.

The glowing woman kissed Payton from her bottom lip down the neck of her latex suit to her nipples, where she coddled her tongue around them. After sucking her breasts as if she were waiting for milk to come she lifted her body into the airplane position where she was breasts to breasts with Payton, tossed her legs over Lyfe's shoulders, and pointed her sweet and silky pearl directly in Lyfe's face.

For a moment Lyfe didn't know whether he was coming or

going. He was working his dick one minute and his tongue the next until he was finally able to maintain a balance, between licking and stroking, stroking and licking, until they were all cumming, creaming, and screaming in delight.

This went on until the wee hours of the morning, from both women gracing Lyfe with the best neck he'd ever had, where one sucked his dick and the other tea-bagged him—to the glowing woman riding him while Payton sat on his face and he feasted from her garden.

Once they were all done, Lyfe went to their master suite and fell asleep while Payton saw to it that the glowing woman left as easily as she'd come.

Afterward Payton slipped into the bed beside Lyfe and admired him, like one does fine art. She was happy to have him, her own personal reincarnation of Adonis, or better, Zeus—because as she traced the outline of Lyfe's muscular pecs down to his deliciousness, which had grown hard again, she knew that he had to be a gracious gift from the god of all gods.

New York

Flickering lights crowned the twenty-four-hour bodega's sign and illuminated the rusted fire escape outside of Arri's Brooklyn bedroom window. Vanity 6's "Nasty Girl" flowed from the CD player on the nightstand and into the cool winter's breeze, mixing in with the orchestra of nonstop traffic. The bass line of the eighties throwback set the mood and steadied Arri's focus. She peered through the eyes of her vintage Mardi Gras mask and into her gentleman's face and said, "I hear you've been a bad boy."

He didn't respond. He was too busy watching her beautiful D-size breasts that sat upon her chest like tasty melons with ripe chocolate peaks, thirsting to be sucked, licked, and played with. Arri's curvaceous hips swayed like an ocean's wave as she flicked the red leather whip in her hand against the hardwood floor and repeated herself. "I hear you've been a bad boy," she said sternly.

He still gave no response; his eyes were too busy molesting her size twelve hips and wondering how he would save himself from becoming addicted once her thick hips rode the dick and creamed all over it. He studied how her thong rested between her luscious ass cheeks, the same place where his tongue longed to be. His eyes moved down her voluptuous thighs to her French manicured feet, covered by pencil-heel knee-high boots.

The clicking of her boots sounded like wind chimes as she flicked the whip again and said one last time, "I hear you've been a bad boy!" She peered into his eyes.

"I have," he said, entranced by the way her hair fell over her shoulders in coils of ebony curls that hung to the small of her back.

"I want you to punish me," he said, unzipping his pants and stroking his rock-solid cock.

"And what punishment do you deserve?" Arri demanded to know.

"Submerge my face; open your pussy lips and torture my tongue as it travels through the rivers and streams of unending, heated, and silky cream. Then you should kill me. Force me to drown in your overflowing sea of vanilla."

Arri placed her right foot on the edge of the bed and pulled at the sides of her thong. "You don't have to take your panties off." He stopped her. "Just move 'em to the side."

Arri gave a sinister laugh. Who the hell was this slave to tell the Goddess what to do? After all, he had no will. So, to remind him who had the power, she untied the strings on the sides of her thong and let it fall to the floor, completely revealing the slither of pubic hair that ran down the center of her vagina. She turned her ass—shaped like a perfect set of twin bubbles—toward him, slowly bent over, and revealed all that lay between her succulent cheeks.

He wrapped his massive hands aggressively around the shaft of his dick, squeezing, and holding it tight, highlighting the pre-cum that shone like the morning sun on its swollen head.

She turned back to face him. "You are to obey my commands," Arri said evenly, as she opened her silky mine, massaged the diamond glaze from inside and over the tiny gold hoop that hung from her clitoris.

He moaned in sweet agony and Arri knew his dick was due to explode. He bit his bottom lip, practically drawing blood.

Afterward he eased his hungry tongue from between his full lips, and though his eyes were closed he could clearly see her hard clit coming toward him.

Arri slid her finger over her silky pearl and felt his tongue run a marathon up and down her lava mountain, working its way through her milky sea as if it were a water snake caressing the cherries of her forbidden shores, forcing chills up her spine, and taking her body to the banks of, "Damn, baby!" "Eat it up!"

Arri's legs trembled as together they forced her clit to become the hardest it's ever been and then suddenly she panted, short of breath, and just as he'd asked for (and as he deserved), she drowned him in her sea of thick and sticky vanilla.

He wasn't dead long. After all, this type of reincarnation was a quick bitch, leaving Arri with no choice but to ride and suck the life out of the dick. "Are you going to behave from now on?" She flicked the whip diagonally across the bed.

"Yes." He licked his wet lips. "So does my punishment end?"

Arri paused and stuck her index finger suggestively in the corner of her mouth; her Cherries in the snow lipstick coated her fingertip. "Apologize," she said, "for questioning me."

"My apologies."

"Not accepted. Now grant my wish to see that big dick."

He removed his hands from his shaft. "What are you going to do to it?"

"I'ma suck it and then I'ma fuck it, the way I want to." She eased one inch at a time into her mouth, licking each vein and bulging ridge like a maze of rock candy. The slurping sounds drove him wild, forcing him to scream, "Goddamn, I need you to ride me!"

"I will ride it," she said coldly, "when I'm done making it cum." She continued making music with her mouth and within a matter of minutes the liquid evidence of his pleasure skeeted out.

Arri knew the dick would take a few moments to recharge, so

instead of waiting she grabbed hold of the cold metal retractable pole in her bedroom, wrapped her legs around it, and embraced it like an Alvin Ailey dancer—poised and freakishly graceful. Arri clapped her ass and simultaneously climbed to the top of the pole. Once at the top she spread her legs into a spilt, slid down, and eased toward the floor; landing perfectly on the fully recharged and awaiting dick. Her pussy creamed like warm butter as she rotated her hips on the dick.

Arri knew there was no way he wouldn't be pussy-whipped when she'd completed her mission. "You will learn," she swerved her hips, "how to behave, or this big juicy dick will continue to be served with my punishment!"

"But you already know I'ma fuckup," he moaned.

"Swear you're going to behave or I'll stop right now," she said wickedly, "and I will not let you cum!"

"I promise. I fuckin' promise!" He grunted and she grunted, both of them holding on for dear life. And within an instant they returned to their realities, where his cum oozed like sticky gum over his fists and her thick wetness ran over a loaded flesh dildo and onto the floor.

Arri eased the dildo from between her legs and tossed it onto the bed. She sat up and looked around her bedroom; for a moment she'd lost sight that she was actually masturbating and performing for her client via the Webcam. She stared into his exhausted face and a sly smile ran across her lips. Mission accomplished.

Arri walked over to the computer and checked her account to be sure his credit card had been charged the fee for his fantasy. And just as he said, "Tell me—," Arri turned off the computer and headed for the shower. After all, she didn't have shit to tell him and she wasn't running her erotic site, A Smooth Operator, to chance a relationship with one of her clients.

It was all bullshit anyway: love, trust, commitment, faithfulness . . . and A Smooth Operator had nothing to do with being a man's better half. This was about making a way out of no way, about preparing an escape from this godforsaken building and ghastly apartment she lived in, a dire need to get away from too much damn traffic, too much fuckin' pollution, cabs, dollar vans, dope fiends, Bloomberg, the damn economy, memories upon memories, and from being a struggling, black, single mother who fell into the can't-win-for-losing category on the census. It was about just getting some sort of freedom, redemption, breath of fresh air, away from flashbacks and haunting regrets of what her life should've been like.

A Smooth Operator was about survival, about letting each and every motherfucker know that though she may have pleased their pleasure palates, at the end of the session she was simply handling her business.

I never intended

California

The sultry sounds of a twenty-piece jazz orchestra resonated throughout the W Hotel's ballroom as Payton softly graced Lyfe with a kiss and they slow-danced across the floor. They were at their company's annual black-tie New Year's Eve gala; amid their employees, investors, high-powered executives, A-list entertainers, lobbyists, and politicians.

Most people were either dancing, networking, bragging, or becoming inebriated courtesy of the bartender's top shelf.

The orchestra's rendition of Nina Simone's "I Put a Spell on You" seduced Payton to place her head on Lyfe's tuxedo lapel and whisper, "We should be daring and fuck right here. No one would even notice."

"They would notice," Lyfe said while easing Payton's hand from his crotch and placing it back around his waist.

Payton held her head up and looked into Lyfe's eyes; their reflection didn't reveal her standing before him in a black, Vera Wang halter dress but instead revealed thoughts a million miles away. "What are you thinking about?" she asked him.

Lyfe ran his hand over his shadow-box beard; the tip of his thumb and index finger met at the center of his chin. "Why did you arrange for me to go to New York without speaking to me first?"

"What?" Payton said, taken aback. "I brought it before the board, we voted, and then I advised you." She waved at a few of their guests.

"I should've been at that meeting." He grew increasingly aggravated.

"You were with clients."

"You should've discussed it with me first."

"Why would I do that?"

"I'm your husband."

"Which is why you should be celebrating." She grabbed two champagne-filled flutes from a passing butler's tray and handed one of the glasses to Lyfe. "As well as appreciate the fact that I allow you so much power within the company."

"Allow me?"

"And that I recognize your talents." She stroked his cheek. "So, just accept that you are going to the New York office to bring in new clients, secure bigger deals, and to assure our existing clients that, yes, the Dow and the NASDAQ may be south, but there is no need to worry because, as the board says, we are wealth builders." She clinked the tip of her glass against his.

Lyfe sarcastically clapped his hands. "Who wrote that speech? Robertson? Dave? Raymond? Or was it Patricia, or one of those other motherfuckers on the board who should really be going to New York instead of me? How about this: I go with my gut, do an audit, and follow up on *their* asses."

"Don't piss me off."

"And don't be so trusting."

"Would you stop throwing a tantrum? It's not attractive. And besides, the board and I are fully capable of making decisions. Not to mention the majority of them don't just have their MBAs, they also have their DBAs."

Lyfe looked at Payton, perplexed.

"Please don't tell me you're confused." She sighed. "Would you follow me here, it's a doctorate in Business—"

"I don't need you to explain shit to me."

"Well you looked as if—"

"Looked as if what? I wasn't impressed?"

"Would you stop cutting me off?"

"Then say something I want to hear," he said tight-lipped, as a few guests passed by them, "and maybe I'll let you speak."

Payton was so taken aback that she paused and withdrew from his arms. "Are you fuckin' confused? Did we switch places and you're suddenly *my* boss?" She chuckled in disbelief. "Let me remind you that the letters behind your name are G.E.D. Unless, I didn't check the mail the day your advanced degree came."

Lyfe paused.

"That's what I thought. Now, I'm going to ask you one last time to drop this." Payton pointed to the clock, which read eleven twenty-five. "Besides, this is not a meeting. It's New Year's Eve!"

Lyfe clinched his jaw. "You better watch—"

"No, you better watch *your* fucking post."

"And where is that?"

"Behind mine." She squinted her eyes. "I make the decisions around here, not you. Now, you have a choice: you shut the fuck up, stop acting like a li'l bitch, or you go back to Crenshaw and rep for a set. Now, like I said, it's New Year's Eve."

Instantly, Lyfe's chiseled jaw tightened and a road map of bulging veins ran along the sides of his neck. At that moment Lyfe knew he'd been too understanding, accepting, and too easily changed into the junkie she wanted him to be—addicted to rearing his shoulders back, perfecting his poise, and pretending to be the happiest man in the world, all while he felt the opposite. A counterfeit reality where Payton's prominence, stamina, and beauty all went in for the kill; and now the Lyfe he knew, the man the streets raised, who preached to his friends about what he would and wouldn't accept from anybody—especially a woman—no matter what, that Lyfe had died and been buried in this manhood-stripping bullshit.

"Let me put this to you real quick," he said evenly. "Whatever motherfucker you're used to dealing with and speaking to like that, you need to go and find him, 'cause I ain't that niggah. Now, unless you lookin' for me to completely spazz on your ass and act like the fuckin' goon that I can be, you'll step the fuck back." He paused and looked her over. "Now, don't push your goddamn luck. And I meant exactly what I said, in the dialect and the incorrect grammar that I said the motherfucker in, so don't try and restructure my sentences." He walked toward the bartender, leaving her standing solo on the dance floor.

"Let me get a Hennessy and Coke," Lyfe said, unbuttoning his black tuxedo jacket and loosening his bow tie. He leaned against the glass bar and the blue light that shone beneath the countertop reflected streaks of indigo on the side of his chocolate face.

"Lyfe," Quinton called out to him as he walked over and gave him a brotherly hug and handshake. "Wassup?"

Lyfe stroked his beard, a nervous habit he had when he was upset. He looked at Quinton and for a passing moment Lyfe thought it would be in bad taste if he told Quinton what had really pissed him off. After all, Quinton was their Chief Investment Officer, the one who—after Lyfe met with the clients and secured their business—maintained their corporate (and individual) wealth by making the hard sales, investing the clients' money into the most profitable stocks, and managing their portfolios.

But Quinton had also become one of Lyfe's closest friends. He accepted him without question when Lyfe became a part of the company. Quinton never snickered behind his back, never passed judgment, and he always seemed to understand that although Lyfe's higher education came from the streets, Lyfe was intelligent and capable of the career that everyone else had questioned.

Lyfe arched his eyebrows and a thousand creases ran across his forehead. "I'm mad as hell."

"Why?" Quinton sipped his Ketel One martini, lifting his eyes over his drink. "We need to go run up on somebody or somethin'?"

"Nah." Lyfe shook his head. "No shit like that."

"So, what's the problem?"

Lyfe squinted and his lips melted into a frown. "Did you know I was going to the New York office for a month?"

"Nah." Quinton sipped again. "Why are you going to the New York office?"

"To bring in new clients, secure bigger deals, and to assure our existing clients that although the Dow and the NASDAQ may be south, there is no need to worry because, as the board says, we are wealth builders." Lyfe shook his head. "I don't believe I just said that shit."

"And verbatim too." Quinton laughed. "That shit's been floating around the office like a Bible quote. But anyway, what's the problem with you going to New York? It's a new office."

"It's been operating for three years."

"Yeah, and upper management has yet to go and spend an adequate amount of time—"

"That's why we hired Thomas to run the office."

"Yeah, and his ass quit."

"He didn't quit." Lyfe smirked. "Payton fired him."

"Yeah, true. She did, but he also complained all the goddamn time. Said it was too much responsibility. And no one else besides you is qualified enough or trusted enough to go out to New York, handle business, and bring their asses back home without some type of catastrophe happening."

"Man, please. Bullshit. Robertson could've gone, Dave, Patricia, a number of people."

"You know you sound like a li'l bitch, right?" Quinton laughed.

Lyfe paused. "Don't make me whup yo' ass."

"Nah, seriously, I really don't see what the problem is."

"First off, the decision was made without my knowledge and finalized without my consent."

"Oh, so that's it." Quinton sipped his drink. "Your ego was fucked with. Understandable. But that's why I restrict Dominique to staying home."

"What did you just say?" Dominique walked over and placed her arms around Quinton's waist. "You restrict me to what?" She looked him in his eyes. "I'm listening." She smiled.

"You know I'm joking, baby." Quinton kissed her on the forehead.

"You better be," she said, pushing her shoulder-length hair behind her ears.

Quinton looked back to Lyfe. "Chill, it'll be fine."

"Excuse me." Payton came from behind Lyfe and grabbed his hand. "Honey, I want you to meet someone." She waved two couples, one white and one Asian, over toward them.

Still fuming, Lyfe thought about leaving, but Quinton's words made him question how bad it would look for him if he did.

Once the couples were standing before them, Payton made the introductions. "Lyfe, Quinton, Dominique, this is Mr. and Mrs. Raymond Cunningham and Mr. and Mrs. John Chin, and they are—"

"The CEO and Financial Vice President of the Public Employees Pension and Deferred Compensation Fund of New York State," Lyfe said with confidence. "I'm pleased that you all accepted the invitation."

"How could we resist?" Raymond smiled. "Especially since you sent us two sets of first class tickets and arranged hotel suites for the weekend. Our wives wouldn't allow us to refuse."

John Chin joined in, "Because if we did they would've been upset forever."

"After all," Mrs. Chin interjected, "hell knows no fury like a woman scorned."

All the women laughed and the men nodded in agreement.

Mrs. Cunningham looked toward Dominique. "Your dress is absolutely stunning."

"Yours as well," Dominique returned her compliment. "I do hope that while you're here you'll get to explore Los Angeles."

"We were hoping the same," John Chin said as he looked toward Lyfe. "And while we're here we'd like to arrange a business meeting."

"Well,"—Payton batted her extended lashes—"we aim to please."

"We certainly do," Lyfe assured them. "But I tell you what, like my wife says, this isn't a board meeting, it's New Year's Eve, so we want you all to party and have a wonderful time. Besides, you're here with your wives, so take the next few days and enjoy the City of Angels. I'm due in New York in two weeks and at that time we can discuss business, but until then let's enjoy."

Everyone agreed and after a few moments of light chatter, the New Year's countdown began. "Five, four, three, two, one! Happy New Year!" Everyone lifted champagne-filled flutes in the air for a toast and cheered. White and silver balloons and streamers fell from the ceiling, scattered over everyone, and drifted toward the floor like snow.

The jazz orchestra began playing a swinging tune and the dance floor quickly filled. In an effort not to draw unneeded attention to them, Lyfe wrapped his arms around Payton's waist and began to move slowly with her. Payton slid her arms around his neck and whispered to him, "Lyfe, I really don't want you to be upset with me. I'm sending you to New York because you're good at what you do. And, honestly, I hated to be so hard on you, but there are times when you seem to forget where you came from."

Immediately, Lyfe stopped dancing and looked down into

Payton's face. "I'm sick of you speaking to me like you have lost your damn mind."

"Well, honey, the next time—"

"The next time, I'ma sling your ass across the room." He released her from his embrace, walked out of the double doors, and onto the elevator.

"Lyfe—" Payton called as she walked swiftly behind him, only to be halted by the elevator doors closing in her face.

Lyfe was so pissed that when the elevator opened and he stepped off into the underground parking lot, where his kettle-black Range Rover was, he didn't notice Payton breathing heavily and leaning against the hood until she reached for him.

Lyfe jumped and once he realized it was Payton he stared at her; her heavy sighs revealed that she'd run down six flights of stairs in stilettos to beat him here.

"I can't let you leave," she said as she placed her arms around his waist and began kissing him on his neck.

He pushed her away. "If you don't get the hell away from me. I'm done with you and your bullshit. You know how hard it is to be with you? It's like you wanna be the fuckin' man. If I didn't know any better I would think you had a fuckin' dick and shit." He laughed in disbelief. "Yo', if you know like I know, homie, you'll get out my fuckin' face." He reached for the door handle and Payton placed her hand over his.

"Wait." She sighed. "Lyfe, honey, I'm sorry." She cupped his chin. "You know I love you."

"Payton—"

"And I know I need to change . . ." She wrapped her arms around his neck and locked her fingers. "And I will . . . I am . . . willing to change." She lightly kissed his Adam's apple.

Silence.

"Please say something."

More silence.

"I'm sorry, baby," she said, unbuttoning his starched white shirt and running her tongue through his smooth chest hairs; sliding her apologies over his colossal pecs. "Please forgive me," Payton said as her tongue led a wet trail down the center of his eight-pack to his right nipple, where she felt his heart thunder against her lips.

The cool breeze cut across their skin like razor blades, as the echoing of car engines, the slamming of car doors, and the lingering laughter of people in the distance turned Payton on even more.

For a fleeting moment she thought about how her company was ringing in 2010 a few flights above, and how embarrassed she would be if anyone saw her . . . but the risk of getting caught, and the challenge of soothing her man's bruised feelings while getting her erotic jollies off in public forced the freak in her to take over.

Payton unzipped Lyfe's tuxedo pants with her teeth and he grabbed her hair and yanked her head back. She looked into his eyes and said, "Let me do this."

She worked her tongue in between the sash of his boxers and pulled out his treasure with her mouth. She could feel his grip on her hair loosen as she rubbed the light glimmer of precum glistening on the tip across her lips like gloss. "I need you to forgive me . . . ," she whispered repeatedly as she licked the bulging veins and ridges.

Payton eased Lyfe's shaft from her mouth and sucked only the tip. This was a new trick and before Lyfe could wonder where she learned it from he was pouring rain between her full lips.

Payton swallowed and just when she thought he was going to leave her on her knees, wondering if their marriage had hit its bottom, he lifted her from the ground and roughly bent her over the hood of his SUV.

There were voices in the distance that became clearer with

each passing moment; but right now—at this moment—Lyfe didn't give a damn because he was still pissed, stressed, and confused about what to do with this beautiful bitch.

He ripped her panties off and spread her ass cheeks, ran his hard dick between them, and rammed his member through her wet and pasty pussy lips. He stroked her fiercely, taking no shorts, and showing no remorse. "Your fuckin' ass." He gritted his teeth as he yanked her head back. "Better learn how to act." He slapped one side of her ass and then the other, forcing her to scream out his name. "Lyfe!" she yelled, and he whipped her around toward him.

"Shut . . . the . . . fuck . . . up," he said in a low, even, and sinister voice as he entered her again. "I get," he said with every hard stroke, "so fuckin' sick of you." Lyfe pushed the tips of his fingers into Payton's neck, the tips of each digit almost piercing her skin. His dick grew harder with each struggling gasp that she took.

Car engines and voices continued to sing in the background as Payton felt as if she were floating above her body. This was a high that most people only spoke about, but were too worried about the possibility of death to experience.

Payton wanted to scream and tell Lyfe to choke her harder as he pounded her pussy with unspeakable force, but she couldn't—all her attempts were clouded by the small sips of air her body could take. Payton knew she was due to pass out at any moment and all she could do was sink her nails into Lyfe's back and listen to him as he said, "The next time you talk shit like that to me, I'ma whup your fuckin' ass. I'm not the fuckin' one—"

Lyfe stopped himself midsentence, because their bodies were having their own conversation and it was taking precedence over the words coming from his mouth. It had only been a few seconds, but the relief he received from wrapping his foot-ball player hands around the base of her neck made him feel renewed, and refreshed, as if he'd done his civic duty and made her understand that *she* was not the man.

Payton's cream overflowed and poured out in an arctic blast of putty that tangled into Lyfe's pubic hairs while his cum lined her collapsed walls.

Once Lyfe released his grip on Payton her shoulders slumped, and for a brief moment, as the distant voices were now upon them, Lyfe thought Payton was dead. He looked into her face and whispered, "Payton."

She opened her eyes slowly and smiled.

"Is everything okay?" floated from behind them.

Lyfe knew it was Quinton so he did his best to quickly fix his pants.

"Yes, everything is fine." Payton's voice was slightly groggy as Lyfe extended his hand and helped her slide off the hood of the SUV. She steadied herself on the ground and began to smooth the wrinkles out of her dress. "I was just a little light-headed." She slyly kicked her panties lying below the driver's-side door out of sight.

"Light-headed." Quinton said, suspiciously, "Really?"

"Yes."

"Well, there are a few people upstairs looking for you two." He looked Payton over. "A few bigwigs and potential clients."

"Okay." Payton caught a glance of her disheveled reflection in the neighboring car's window. "I'll be right there."

"I'll meet you upstairs," Quinton said, turning around and walking away.

Payton turned to Lyfe, once Quinton was out of sight. "Are you coming?"

He didn't respond and instead he slid into his Range, started the ignition, and left her standing there.

New York

"It's a pity you already have a wife." Tanya Stephens's, "A Pity," floated from Arri's CD player, as she eased the blunt loaded with purple haze between her MAC-covered lips and flicked her Bic to light it. She leaned against the moist windowpane in her bedroom and spoke into the air, "Happy New Year." She paused and took the pain that crept into her chest and released it with a hard toke of marijuana.

She felt slightly dizzy, being she hadn't smoked a blunt in over a year, but tonight, especially tonight—at the dawning of a new year—she needed this. She needed to escape the ache of her life teetering on the edge and hanging on to old and ridiculous shit. She needed a new start, and the coolness of the purple haze lifted the weight off her shoulders and made her believe that anything was possible.

Arri took another toke and smiled as she remembered what it felt like to live without a care in the world and how it felt to be back to herself, Arrielle Askew, a Brooklyn mami with Trinidadian roots. An Island girl, who was scared to love, because she'd lost too many times to count . . .

New Year's Eve, 2005. Sweat poured from Arri's brow as she wined on Ian's middle and he cupped her breasts and massaged her nipples with palms full of rose petals. They were in the tub, making love, splashing water over the sides and onto the floor. Ian ran his hands from Arri's nipples down to her thighs.

The water splashed against his shaft, some of it hitting him in the chin, as Arri squeezed her sticky walls over him. "You know I'm addicted."

Arri paused. "To what?"

"You." Ian wrapped his lips around Arri's chocolate nipples as she cupped water in her hands and cascaded it over his head and into his dreads. The water ran over his face, over his lips, and onto her nipples, where his soft, sensual tugs sent her to the moon and left her there. "Tell me you love me," Ian whispered.

"I love you."

"Tell me why you're marrying me."

"Because there's no one else for me." She flexed her inner walls repeatedly and their pelvises contracted uncontrollably until they were both short of breath.

"Happy New Year, baby."

A few hours later they were dressed for their intimate wedding ceremony with a small gathering of close friends, when the bell rang. Ian answered the door and an unknown woman stood there.

"Who is that, Ian?" Arri asked, looking the woman over.

"Oh, you don't know me," the woman pulled a .22 from her purse, "but he knows me."

"What are you doing?" Ian blinked, as Arri stood frozen.

"Tell her who I am," the woman spat at Ian. "Tell her!"

"Who is she?" Arri screamed, too scared to move and too scared not to.

"I'm his fuckin' wife!" the woman screamed as she pulled the trigger and everything Arri had ever known or trusted about love was left in a bleeding puddle on the floor . . .

• • •

Arri's cell phone alarm jolted her out of her flashback and into the present. She looked at her computer and remembered that she had a client scheduled for tonight. Quickly she mashed the blunt in the ashtray and wiped the tears pouring down her face. She could deal with life's bullshit later.

She quickly showered and dressed in sparkling body oil and her vintage Mardi Gras mask. It was easier to handle her blue business like this, undercover, without anyone knowing exactly who she was. She took one last look at herself before she turned the computer on, and for the first time she wondered when she knew her body was her greatest asset.

Was it after her mother abandoned her at fifteen and she had to war with the world to survive? Whatever it was, Arri knew she wasn't born with any extraordinary talents and she damn sure wasn't born with a silver spoon, so she had to do what she had to do.

From the time she was sixteen and up until last year, she'd been a stripper, dancing for dollars and clapping her ass before perverted men and down-low women who groped her titties and slid their fingers through her slit without her permission. But Arri didn't care, because she had a mission—to get the fuck out of Brooklyn—and she was almost there . . . almost, until her drug-addicted sister, Samara, pounded on her door, and when Arri opened it, she ran, leaving a hungry, badly bruised, and snotty-nose little boy behind. Soon after that, Arri stopped dancing.

There was no way she could raise her five-year-old nephew, Zion, be home with him at night, and make money on the sex stage to take care of them. And she couldn't take the chance that Zion would go back to wetting the bed and having nightmares when he was finally blossoming into a normal little boy. He'd been through enough, being dragged around in the streets by Samara.

But Arri had to survive, so she made the best of it: got her a nine-to-five during the day, and for the night she bought her a Webcam, set up a website, and the rest was today's history.

She turned the computer on and lay across her leopard chaise. "A Smooth Operator," she said seductively. "What's your fantasy?"

"I wanna see your pussy drip" was the client's request.

"Oh, you wanna see that pretty pink pussy make milk?" she purred, as she looked into the Webcam and smiled. She hit the computer's remote and allowed the Webcam to zoom in.

"Yeah," the client moaned, "I would like that."

"Well, how about this?" She reached for the silver ice bucket she had on her nightstand and pulled an ice dildo from it. The dildo dripped with water as Arri slowly worked it over her breasts, circling her nipples, and down toward her navel ring. The dildo left streaks of water behind like a cascade of shower beads. "You like that too?" She took the head of the ice dildo and licked it as if she were tongue-stroking a lollipop.

The client didn't answer, instead he unzipped his pants.

Arri gave him a seductive smile, opened her pussy lips and revealed the milk easing from the inside. She centered the dildo between her lower lips, lifted her hips, and twirled them. "You like this, Daddy?" She worked the dildo as if she were riding a dick.

Arri could see her client licking his lips and flicking his tongue as if he could taste her cunt, so she rotated the speed of her hips and the twirling of the dildo, until she felt her belly tightening.

"Cum all on my face," her client said, his face plastered in the Webcam. "Smear that fat pussy all over my mouth, my eyes, everywhere! Damn, I can taste it," he moaned.

Arri's hardened clit peeked through like snake eyes as the sweating water dripped from the iced member and slicked down the Mohawk of pubic hair she had, forcing her now frozen cherry to pop and explode.

Arri sat up and looked into the Webcam. Her client couldn't stop smiling as the cum, from him choking his dick, inched over his fingertips. Arri rose from the bed and checked her account to be sure he had been charged his fee, and before he could even say "thank you," she shut her computer down.

"I want my fuckin' baby!" jolted Arri out of her sleep. She looked around her bedroom. Other than her furniture all she could see was the blinding sun rays easing through her miniblinds.

Arri grabbed her goose-down comforter and raised it over her head, until she heard it again, "I want my fuckin' baby!" This time it was followed by pounding on the apartment door.

Before Arri could get up, Zion bolted into her room and into a spot on the corner of the floor where he tried to hide by folding his arms over his head.

Arri rose from the bed and looked down at Zion, who was the color of pecans, with almond-shaped eyes and a low-cut Caesar with two parts on the side. "What I tell you about hiding? Get up!"

Arri snatched her white terry cloth robe from the foot of her bed and wrapped it around her body like a cyclone. She looked back at Zion, who was slowly easing out of the corner, and said, "Come on."

Once Zion was behind her she sucked her teeth and dragged herself to the door. "This is bullshit," Arri said as she slid her bare feet across the cold floor. Standing in front of her door, she didn't even look through the peephole, she simply snatched it open. Her sister, Samara, who was five years her senior, stood there looking and smelling as if she hadn't bathed in days. She had a third-degree burn, from a butane lighter explosion, that covered her neck. She stood about five foot five, was frail, and wore a grease-spotted, black nylon jacket with the name of a bowling league on the front breast pocket, a stretched blue

T-shirt that fell off her shoulders, exposing her protruding collarbone, too-big skinny jeans, and an unknown brand of high-top sneakers. Slobber was caked in the corners of her mouth as she looked Arri over. "I want my baby back." As she said that, Zion took cover and hid under the coffee table.

"Well, obviously he doesn't want you back," Arri spat.

"What?" Samara frowned; her sunken lips appeared as if they'd run into the tight and scorched plastic-looking skin on her neck. "He don't have no fuckin' say. And you don't either. I'm his goddamn mother, so ain't no need for you to try and hold on to him no longer than I asked you to—"

"You never asked me, and furthermore, this isn't about you—"

"Yeah, you're right. This is about my fuckin' money. Now welfare is threatening to cut off my shit if I don't have this ma'fucker with me today when I go down there." She arched her eyebrows. "Get me? Now, I'm gettin' him." Samara pushed her way inside but Arri shoved her back into the hallway.

"You want me to fuck you up?" Arri pointed her right hand like a gun toward her sister's bloodshot eyes. "Huh? Is that it? Now, you try some shit like that again and see I don't whup your fuckin' ass for the old and the new. Now, get the fuck away from my door! Don't try me."

"That's my goddamn baby!" Samara screamed at the top of her lungs, causing a few of Arri's neighbors to peer through their peepholes and those passing through the hallway to quickly look before continuing about their business.

"Is everything all right?" Arri's neighbor and friend, Khris, stood in her doorway and yelled across the hall. She could see Arri's face and Samara's back in full view. "You need me?"

"I'm fine," Arri said to Khris, while looking her sister over.

"And what you gon' do, bitch?" Samara spat toward Khris, "this between me and my sister."

"What-the-fuck-ever," Khris snapped in her strong Brooklyn accent. "You try and run up in there again and it's gon' be between all of us." She placed her hands on her size-eighteen hips and twisted her lips. The freckles sprinkled across her nose and high cheekbones wrinkled as she tilted her head to the side for emphasis.

"Why you always doing this shit to me?" Samara spat.

"Doing what to you?" Arri looked confused. "What the hell are you talking about?"

"You always turning motherfuckers against me and shit! I don't give a damn about that fat bitch," she tossed over her shoulder toward Khris, "but my son? My child? First Mommy and now him?"

"Listen," Arri said, fighting back the tears she felt filling her eyes. She hated to see her sister like this, especially when all they had was each other. "It takes more than for you to squat down in some fuckin' dingy-ass alley and drop a baby from your pussy for you to be considered a mother. You clearly don't give a fuck about him! What you are is a dope fiend, a crackhead, a godddamn junkie! And as far as *our* mother, I really can't understand why you haven't run into her ass yet, being that you ended up in the streets just like her!"

"Who the hell are you talking to like that?"

"Yo' ass," Arri said matter-of-factly. "No need to be confused about who I'm talking to, 'cause I'm talking to you!"

"You don't talk to me like that!" Samara pointed into Arri's face.

"Bitch, are you demanding respect?" Arri said, taken aback, chuckling in disbelief. "And from me? Did you forget that you left me here in this apartment when I was only sixteen—alone, long after Mommy had been gone—so that you could go and be with some niggah that turned you the fuck out? Respect? When I was out there dancing for money to eat? When I had to finish high school between giving lap dances because you were too busy sucking on and getting burned up by a glass dick. And you want respect?" Arri could no longer hold her tears back and they streaked down her cheeks. "When are you going to have some respect for me?" She pressed her index finger into Samara's chest. "When the hell will I get to be the baby of the family? When do I get the luxury to be irresponsible and not give a fuck? You ain't shit, you know that? You're supposed to be my big sister, Zion's mother, not some fucked-up and fucked-over nothing. Respect? Bitch, please, kiss both of our asses, and after you do that get the fuck away from my door!"

Samara's face was wet with tears and red with rage. She walked up close to Arri and spat, "You gon' give me my baby!" She pushed her way into the apartment and Arri slapped her so hard that she fell back into the hall against Khris, who had taken up a spot directly outside Arri's door.

Samara struggled to stand up. "You put your hands on me?" She raced toward Arri, who picked up her steel crowbar—which served as her burglar alarm—and said, "Come on." She held the bar in the air, halting Samara in her spot. "Please, bring it, so that I can show you just what the fuck I've been threatening you with!"

"That's my child!" Samara shouted, and pointed to a visibly shaking Zion, who was still hiding under the coffee table.

"And you left him here!"

"I just wanted you to babysit!"

"For a year? Bitch, please. Be clear, as long as you are like this, you will never get him back. Ever. Zion," Arri yelled over her shoulder, "come here!"

"No," Zion said, long enough to uncover his eyes and then shield them again. "I don't want her to see me."

Arri looked at Khris. "Make sure she doesn't bring her ass in here." Arri turned around, stormed over to Zion, and pried him from under the coffee table. Once she was able to get him to stand up, pee ran from the bottom of his pajama pants. Arri looked at the puddle of pee on the floor. "Oh, my baby," she said as she hugged him. "You don't have to be scared. I'm not going to let her take you."

Zion's eyes lit up as he grabbed on to Arri's waist and she turned back toward Samara. "Until you have yourself together, do not come back here or I will be calling the police on you. This is my child now; I take care of him and I will not let you come into his home and have him hiding all over the damn place. Now, get . . . the . . . fuck . . . on!"

"Yeah," Zion said, peeking his head from beneath Arri's housecoat, "move on before we see you at three o'clock." He balled his fist and held it before his eyes.

Arri looked down at Zion, and though tears wet her face, her lips curled into a smile. She snorted, and wiped her cheeks with the back of her hands. She almost fell out laughing, but she contained herself. "Be quiet," she said.

She looked at Samara and started to say something else, but figured Zion had pretty much said it all, so instead she slammed the door in her sister's face.

Samara started banging on Arri's door, and Arri could hear Khris saying, "I'ma call the police on your li'l ass, 'cause I see you like to play too damn much. And it's too early in the morning for this bullshit! Stand right there since you think bitches is playing with you." She pulled out her cell phone and a few moments later Samara's pounding stopped.

Arri untwisted Zion, who was still holding on to her from behind. She stood him in front of her and said, "You don't have to run through here like a bat outta hell, you understand me? You are not going anywhere. I love you as if you were my own child and I don't care who comes in here, you don't ever have to hide. You hear me?"

Zion held his head down. "Yes," he said softly.

"Hold your head up and say it like you mean it."

"Yes," he said, and started to smile, revealing his dimples in his round face. "But Auntie . . ."

"Yes?"

"I might have to run just one more time." He bit his bottom lip.

Arri looked confused. "Run where? Why?"

"To my room, so I can get dressed for school, or I'ma be late. It's after seven o'clock."

"Oh my God." Arri looked out of her living room window at the school and saw the children gathering in the playground. She looked back at the clock: seven twenty-five. "When did you learn to tell time?" She grabbed Zion's hand and they rushed into the bathroom. "Come on, let's get you cleaned up. I can't believe this; I'm not even dressed for work!"

New York

The train shook feverishly as it rattled over the underground tracks from Uptown to Midtown, the echoes of iPods, conversations, leafing of newspapers and magazines, and the hissing of the train's metal wheels filling the air.

Lyfe sat in his seat flipping through the pages of the *New York Times*, wondering if he would be able to stand Manhattan's winter.

"Fuck it," he mumbled to himself as he placed his steamy Starbucks coffee to his lips and concentrated on an article about investments. A few minutes later he felt a hard bump, which caused his coffee and newspaper to slip from his hands to the floor. He watched his coffee cup roll along the aisle, leaving a wet zigzag trail behind it, while the newspaper lay drenched on the floor beneath his feet. "What the—?"

"I'm soooo sorry."

Lyfe looked up. He didn't know what pissed him off more: his day being off to a fucked-up start or that the woman staring at him and handing him napkins was absolutely breathtaking. From the apple-butter color of her skin to the thick ebony curls that fell over her shoulders, to the way her three-quarter-length, gray wool car-coat lay perfectly on her defined hips, her whole package was stunning.

Lyfe took the napkins from her hand and lightly dusted the

specks of coffee that had splattered on him. "As big as I am, you didn't see me?" he snapped.

"I'ma try this one last time." She arched her eyebrows. "I'm sorry," she said matter-of-factly. "The train *is* moving, in case you missed that. I've walked through three cars to find a free seat and this was the only open one I saw. Trust me; had there been somewhere else to sit, I wouldn't be here." She plopped down next to him.

"And you still gon' sit here?" He laughed in disbelief.

She paused and looked directly in his face. "Hell yeah, but you're free to move."

Lyfe stroked his chin. "You know what," he said in an attempt to lighten the mood, "you owe me a cup of coffee."

"Umm-hmm." She curled the right corner of her upper lip. "Yeah, you wait on that."

Lyfe cleared his throat and pushed the thought of checking her ass to the back of his mind. "You look really familiar."

"Oh . . . my . . . God," she said, clashing gazes with him. "Are you serious?"

Lyfe looked baffled. "About what?"

"Are you trying to pick me up or some other bullshit?"

"Pick you up?" he said, taken aback.

"Pick . . ." she said slowly, "me . . . up. Because, seriously, I am not in the mood. I had a fucked-up morning and since I've been on the train it seems to have gotten worse." She looked him over. "And I don't know where you're from, but understand this: we don't do all of this random chit-chattin' out here. Okay?" She stroked her hair behind her left ear, revealing a discolored birthmark that ran down the side of her neck. "And I don't have the time nor the patience to be sitting here and wasting my time on some tired-ass suit-and-tie. So please save that for one of these other li'l bougie tricks that apparently you like to meet and greet on the train."

Lyfe sniffed as his nostrils flared. "Apparently you have a li'l habit of getting out of line"—he stared at her birthmark, and then back to her face—"so let me put you back in place. If I wanted to pick you up, I would simply tell you how beautiful I thought you were until you opened your nasty-ass mouth. Now, I don't know what kind of morning you had, but it probably doesn't top the shit I got goin' on, so chill." He paused. "And another thing, don't let this suit and tie fool yo' ass."

"Whatever," Arri sighed dismissively, as she sat on the train, running late for work, and next to a fine-ass brother who despite his sexy-ass swagger, had just told her off and was working the hell out of her nerves. She felt guilty about knocking his coffee from his hands but that's where it ended. She didn't care that he was pissed because she'd messed up his morning caffeine fix, and she was doing her damndest not to care about how beautifully black and pretty he was. Fuck him. Besides, she had a million "why mes?" of her own. And she hated sappy shit, and shit that made her feel grim, and dull, and depressed, and sorry for herself. She couldn't stand wondering when her circumstances were going to change, because the reality was, this was her life.

Arri turned away and looked out the train's window. The tunnel whipped by in blurry snippets as an unexpected vision of the last time she'd seen her mother danced before her eyes . . .

"Run them goddamn pockets!" Darlene's voice rattled with aggravation as she peered at twelve-year-old Arri. "And hur' up. I'm tryna be nice 'bout this shit." She spat as she flicked a loose string of snot that slid from her nose and over the corners of her cracked lips.

Darlene repeated herself, "I *said*, I'm tryna be nice 'bout this shit, but you pushin' yo' luck, Arri."

Arri watched Darlene stagger closer to where she sat on a dingy white mattress in a sea of sunflower seeds and Swedish Fish, with a mouth full of Lemonheads.

"I know you got some money," Darlene continued, " 'cause I saw you outside in them niggahs' faces, so give it to me right now!"

The Lemonheads in Arri's mouth stuck to her teeth and bathed her tongue in yellow as she watched her mother's mahogany face dance in the flashing streetlamp's reflection. Arri's eyes traced the black extension cord that snaked across the floor, running electricity from the neighbor's apartment into theirs. She studied the withered sunshine of the wall's dingy yellow paint, and thought about the furniture that once sat sporadically around the room—at least until James, Darlene's boyfriend, and dope, Darlene's best friend, moved in and slowly the furniture moved out.

Arri's eyes ran across her mother's sagging jawline, protruding collarbone, frail arms, and sticks for thighs. She rolled her eyes, sized up Darlene's small frame again, and figured that this time—on everything she loved—she was gon' rock wit' Darlene's chicken-ass if she pushed her to it. As far as Arri was concerned, this time—out of all the times her mother had shaken her down—she wasn't having it. To hell with this dumb shit. Today, if her mother's hand called for it, it would be on and the fuck poppin' in Brooklyn tonight.

Darlene cleared her throat. "Arri," her tone softened, "Mommy need you to help her."

Arri swallowed the Lemonheads, tasting only slightly more sour than the sounds of Darlene calling herself Mommy and letting that name fall effortlessly from her lips.

Arri wondered, was a mother supposed to love you and care whether or not you went to school, or did a mother get mad because you wouldn't suck dick, turn tricks, and support her habit? Did a mother actually do some shit, other than spread her pink pussy lips, push you through, and then let the streets nurse you until you were old enough to understand that didn't nobody owe you shit?

Arri twisted her lips and cracked open a sunflower seed. "Puleeze."

Beads of sweat ran down Darlene's forehead. "I want that money. And Samara told me that she saw some li'l niggah out there hand five dollars to you."

"So? I got the money 'cause I braided his hair," Arri snapped. "He gave me money for me and *I* spent it on candy."

Darlene snorted and scratched the side of her neck. "You spent it on candy?"

"That's what I said." Arri cleared her throat and did her best to push the fear she felt rising in her chest back down to her stomach.

Darlene looked surprised. She studied Arri's face and said, "You lyin'." She looked at the water lining Arri's eyelids. "James said you was a ho, and I believe him. So since you a ho and this is your stroll, you gon' pay me to live here. I want that money and I want it now." She stood over Arri and stared her down.

Darlene hated staring at Arri because it was like looking at her own reflection. "You know what? I'm sick of lookin' at you!" Darlene grabbed a fistful of Arri's hair and dragged her to the floor. "Always thinkin' you better than me!" She slapped her. "Always thinkin' you so much!"

"Stop it!"

WHAP!

Arri felt everything inside her skull thump. She wondered why she couldn't take Darlene down like she'd planned. Her body may be frail but her strength was unmatched. "Get offa me!" Arri screamed and her voice drifted into the other room, where her sister, Samara, rushed to the doorway.

"I don't have no money!" Arri screamed, doing her best to squirm out of her mother's grip.

"You lyin' . . . and you lyin' because you think I ain't shit!" *WHAP!*

"Mommy, *please*!"

"Don't Mommy me now, 'cause if I ain't shit,"—*WHAP!* Spit flew out the side of Darlene's mouth—"then you worse than that, because you came outta my pussy!" *WHAP!* "So ain't neither one of us shit and don't you ever forget that! Now I asked you for that money and I want it!"

"I don't have it!"

"Yes you do!" Samara screamed. "I saw Ahmad give you five dollars. And Mommy, five dollars is enough for a bag of smack."

"You need to mind your business!" Arri responded, trying to grab Darlene's hands.

"You need to tend to yours," Samara said. "Give up that money and stop gettin' yo' ass kicked. You too damn grown!"

"Shut up!" Darlene yelled as she slammed Arri against the wall, causing her to hit the back of her head and slide to the floor. "I want that goddamn money and I want it now!" She started ripping Arri's blouse, "Where is it, I know you ain't spend it all on candy!" She yanked her pants down and before she could pull at her underwear loose change fell from Arri's pocket, some of it spinning on its head and others rolling across the floor. "Lyin' ass!" Darlene snorted, wiping loose snot from her nose again. "Samara, pick up that money." She scratched her neck.

Samara hurried to collect the change.

Street noises drifted in from the open window. "Darlene!" someone shouted from outside. Darlene huffed her way over to the window and looked. It was James, holding a taxicab's door open. "Move ya ass," he yelled, "you know this goddamn meter runnin'! Hell, whatcha waitin' on?"

"Hold it a motherfuckin' minute." She walked away from the window, collected the change from Samara, slipped it into her pocket, and snorted again. She straightened her clothes and fluffed her aged weave. "You gon' learn not to fuck with me!" she said while catching her breath. "Now, look." She stared at Samara. "I'll be back in a few weeks."

The room fell silent and Samara asked, "Whatchu mean?"

"Listen," Darlene said as she walked to the closet and started packing what little she had in a worn suitcase, "it's a job I need to see about. Some bidness I need to take care of."

"Ma . . ." Tears rolled from Samara's eyes. "And when you gon' come back?"

"You questionin' me?" She set her suitcase on the floor.

"Ma, I don't want you to go. I'll turn tricks. I'll take care of you."

"You sound stupid, Samara. Shut up. You will not be turning no damn tricks!"

"Ma . . ." Samara wiped tears from her eyes.

"Shut up. I'll be back."

Samara looked at Arri. "Why you just ain't give her the money! Now she leavin'!" She flew on top of Arri and Arri hit Samara so hard that she slammed into the wall.

"It ain't my fault she's leavin'," Arri cried.

"It is!" Samara retorted, standing up. "Ma, what you need me to do?" She ran over and blocked the doorway. "Whatever you need I'll do."

Darlene walked toward the doorway with her suitcase in her hand and stood before Samara.

"Mommy, please." Samara folded her hands in a prayer position.

"Don't beg. You know I can't stand no beggin'-ass niggahs. Now, listen, I'll be right back. Right back. I'm just goin' to the store."

"You goin' to the store?" Samara asked for assurance.

"Yeah, to the store."

"You gon' come right back?"

"Uhmm-hmm." Darlene walked toward the front door, with Samara following her. "It's gon' take me some time but I'll be back." Darlene stepped into the hallway and Samara scurried behind her.

"Ma," Samara called, but Darlene didn't answer. She could

tell James was pissed by the look on his face. "I had to say good-bye," Darlene snapped.

"Ma!" Samara cried.

Darlene ignored her and threw her suitcase into the back of the cab, then she and James slid in. She closed the cab's door, looked up, and saw Arri staring at her through the window, with tears streaming from her eyes, waving 'bye. "Get yo' ass back in that building!" Darlene yelled repeatedly until the cab blended into traffic and Samara's image faded.

"Excuse me." Lyfe tapped Arri on her shoulder. She didn't answer him and he could tell that she was in a daze. "Miss," he called out to her again, and she turned toward him. He looked into her eyes and could tell that a story sat on the brim, but shit, he didn't know her and she damn sure didn't know him. And besides, this wasn't California, this was New York, and these motherfuckers tended to their own affairs. "This is my stop."

Lyfe wasn't sure if she heard him or not, as she exited the train and blended in with the crowd.

Arri walked around Midtown for an hour to clear her mind. She hated to be late for work but she had to get rid of the aching feeling that sat between her breasts. She caught a glimpse of her reflection as she walked into the office building she worked in and boarded the mirrored elevator to the twenty-fifth floor.

Once in the office she waved at a few of her co-workers and attempted to make her way to her cubicle, which sat outside the office of the vice president, for whom she was the direct secretary. Arri softly sucked her teeth as she remembered the VP was due in town today and her being late was not a good first impression.

"Shit." Arri sucked her teeth again as she attempted to sneak past Khris's cubicle and ease to her desk. "Arri?" Khris said in a loud whisper, rolling her chair into the center of the aisle, "Where are you coming from? I left yo' ass at least three hours ago."

Arri sighed, walked over to Khris, and mumbled, "Would you shut the fuck up?"

"Where have you been? I been lying for you like crazy. You knew the HNIC was coming today and this mofo came in trippin' this morning."

"I forgot he was coming today, and besides, he doesn't know me, so he couldn't be looking for me."

"He knew he was missing a damn secretary. And that would be you. Anyway, I told him a buncha ski-masked motherfuckers ran up on the train and held ya'll asses up at gunpoint. I told him they were feeling you up and shit."

"What?" Arri said in disbelief. "Khris, I know damn well you didn't tell him no shit like that."

"I had to tell him something. Besides, I told him you were a freak, so that shit was cool with you."

"Oh . . . my . . . God . . ."

"Shame, y'all just a cussin' early in the morning," Mare-Hellen, one of their extremely religious and nosy co-workers, tossed across the cubicles. "Ya need Jesus, that's what ya need."

"And you need a man," Khris snapped.

"Whew, my Jesus, the devil is a liar!" Mare-Hellen panted, turning up her radio and allowing the gospel music she played in her cubicle to float into their space.

Khris waved her hand dismissively and turned back to Arri. "She just mad 'cause the pastor stopped tappin' dat ass. Anyway, back to you and Mr. Boo. I didn't tell him anybody ran up on the train. I started to, but changed my mind." She laughed. "I just told him your train was stuck in the tunnel and you called a few minutes ago to say that it was moving now, and you were on your way in."

"Girl, you were about to make me have a damn fit. Thanks,

Khris." Arri sighed with relief. "And by the way, thank you for being there this morning."

"Anytime."

"Is he as ugly as we thought?" Arri laughed.

"Hell to da nawl, honey." Khris blinked. "All this time, we were looking at the wrong goddamn picture. The nasty-looking one is somebody named Paul, who used to be VP a few years back before we got here."

"So he's cute?"

"No," Khris shook her head, "he's not cute. He's so fuckin' fine it don't make no"—she let out a breath—"goddamn sense."

"Don't put Gawd's name in y'all's mess," Mare-Hellen snapped. "And yeah, I said it." She sucked her teeth and beat the tambourine on her desk. "And what?"

Arri rolled her eyes, ignoring Mare-Hellen. "Khris, you are so animated."

"No, I'm so serious with you," Khris continued. "I have called him boo, quite a few times already, gurl. Like when he asked where his secretary was, you know yo' ass"—she pointed—"I was like 'Oh she's running late, boo. I mean, boo-boo. Gurl, I been hot, bothered, and sweatin' since I got here. Not even another round with Samara could undo how horny I am around this man. My God."

"Buncha raunchy heathens" floated from Mare-Hellen's cubicle.

"Anyway," Khris continued, "go unload at your cubicle and then make your way in there."

"I will," Arri said as she tiptoed to her seat. She eased her coat off and peeked into the VP's office. He was sitting with his back to the door, facing his computer. Arri picked up the small mirror she had on her desk, made sure her hair was in place and her makeup was intact. She ran her hands over her teal knee-length skirt and fluffed the cowl neck of her cream-colored and sleeveless sweater.

Her heels clicked as she entered his office and pretended to be utterly exhausted. "I am so sorry, Mr. Anderson," she said, "but I just had the worst train ride over here. I was trying my best to be early but we were stuck in the tunnel at first and then we had to come out and change trains; it was terrible."

"Anderson Global is named after my wife's family, I'm Mr. . . ." Lyfe said, turning around, and to his surprise he was staring at the same woman he had a round with on the train. ". . . Carrington."

Arri practically lost her breath. *This motherfucker again* immediately ran through her mind. She shook her head. This had to be a dream, but the longer she stood there the more she realized this was reality. "I didn't . . . why are you . . . Oh I didn't, *hmph*. I don't even know what to say."

"Well, you can either finish your train-being-stuck-in-the-tunnel story, which was starting to sound really exciting, or we can kill the tension in the room and talk about the last time I saw you."

Arri was silent for a few moments and then she said, "I just want to do my job. Nothing more, nothing less."

"I can respect that," Lyfe said.

"So, how do we start again?" she asked.

"We can start right after you get me that cup of coffee you owe me."

Arri fought off a smirk she felt easing onto her face. "Yes, sir."

"Oh," Lyfe snapped his fingers as if he'd just remembered something, "and pick up another copy of the *New York Times* while you're out there." Lyfe smiled as Arri sashayed out of his office to her cubicle for her coat. Afterward, he leaned against the door frame and inauspiciously watched her ass move like a gazelle as she disappeared into the distance. "Damn," he said, feeling a hard-on building in his pants.

California

From the first time he hit it from the back, they simultaneously came, bit their bottom lips, and grunted out the other's name, their plan of a one-night stand disintegrated.

Four years ago they'd agreed to satisfy curiosity and dead the wonderment of their unspoken attraction by seeing what the extra glances, lingering gazes, and soft kisses on the cheeks— that were nearer to the ear or the neck—were about. And they planned to fulfill their conquest only once, because they swore that that would be enough to shake the undeniable magnetism between them.

But it wasn't.

Payton lay in the center of her king-size bed, watching him slowly unbutton his dress shirt and pull it from the waist of his Versace suit pants. He placed his ringing cell phone on the nightstand and said, "I've been thinking about that ass all day."

Payton stuck her index finger suggestively in her mouth. "Oh, you missed this pussy?" She took her thumbs and show-cased her swollen pearl, the face of it radiating with glaze.

"That pussy *better* have missed me," he said.

"Oh, really?" Payton stroked her clit at the sight of his hard and luscious dick. Instantly, she salivated, as her heart traveled down to her heated sex and made creamy water between her thighs. She crawled to the foot of the bed, where he stood before her, his hard and swollen cock pointed directly in her face. Payton smiled as she grabbed his dick with one hand, made a fist around it and massaged his balls with the other. For a moment she thought about Lyfe's dick; his was definitely an inch or so longer, but they were both the same width, like fat, hand-rolled, bursting sausages with muffin tops at the tip. Both of their dicks screamed "choke!" "gag!" and "throttle!" whenever she contemplated blowing them. But the challenge of it all was worth the pleasurable punishment.

Payton's full lips suctioned his balls completely into her mouth, as he swirled his shaft into her face. Her tongue skated from his scrotum to the tip—a trick he showed her how to do specially for him—before Payton ventured on to deep-throating him. A few moments after rolling her tongue over his member, he lifted her onto the bed and placed his dick between her double Ds.

Payton loved it when he tittie-fucked her until he came and laced her neck and her nipples with one-of-a-kind pearls.

Afterward, as he nibbled her nipples and fingered her clit, Payton reached her hand into her nightstand drawer and removed a few toys: red metal handcuffs, shackles, and a red leather noose.

Hearing the metal clinking together caused him to look toward the direction of the noise. "What's that about?" he said, giving her a devilish grin. "You want me to handcuff you?"

"No," Payton said, "I'ma handcuff you."

"I don't want to be handcuffed."

"Yes you do," she said as she ran her tongue over his middle as if it were her favorite flavor. "And you wanna be choked too."

"No." He moaned as he fought to keep his eyes open. "Lick it right there, baby." He slipped his dick out of her mouth and pointed to the side of the head, "Right there."

Payton stuck her tongue out and licked him as if the fudge

from his dick were melting. She ran her tongue from the side to the tip, back and forth and back again. He rolled his eyes to the top of his head, grabbed the back of her neck and stuck his dick back into her mouth.

"Payton—" he moaned as she took him to places he'd never been. His knees began to shake and "Goddamn" was all he could say. He took his hands and ran them up and down her back, as her lips continued their symphony and his mouth shouted their song's bridge of "Shit, baby, wait."

He cupped her chin and she wiggled her head free and bit his fingers, quickly resuming her dick-sucking masterpiece. "You ready to play?" She swallowed him whole again.

Unable to speak, he stretched his long arms across Payton's curled back and shot off down her throat. "I don't give a damn what you do to me!" he said with exhausted excitement.

Payton stretched his arms across the bed and handcuffed his hands on their respective sides. Then she shackled his feet. Once he lay restrained to the bed, she placed the noose around his neck and eased her creamy trenches onto his cock. She pulled the rope tight and rode him like a G.I. Jane headed for war. She flexed her inner walls, causing her sugar to pour from within and make a vanilla cone between them.

"Payton!" His eyes bulged out and he moaned, "Harder!"

A menacing smile ran across Payton's face as she tightened the noose as far as she could around his neck. His hands flagged hysterically and his feet twisted. His dick was as hard as a boulder. Payton wrapped the end of the noose around her fist and yanked it as if he were runaway cattle. She could see the rope marks burning a way onto his neck, as she rode his dick into space, and just when she thought being choked was the best nut, she remembered that choking someone else was even better. Quinton's chest heaved up and down, his cock exploded, and his unconscious head dropped to his chest.

Payton stared into his face as she convulsed into a double orgasm, drowning his long, fat, succulent pipe with more of her vanilla cream. Just as she thought about sucking her stickiness off of him and bringing him back to consciousness with her tongue, his cell phone rang.

She loosened the noose and whispered his name, "Quinton."

He slowly opened his eyes and as he said, "You're a beast," his cell phone rang again. Payton faked a smile, but she really wanted to scream; the wet spot had barely begun to dry before his wife was steadily calling. Payton rolled to his side, flipped his cell phone open and placed it on speaker. "Please make this shit short," she mouthed as she uncuffed and unshackled him.

He shot her the evil eye. "Wassup, Dominique?" he dryly answered the phone, his throat parched.

Dominique's voice rattled as if she were loosing her breath, "Where are you, Quinton?"

"I told you I had some things to finish up at work," he said, agitated.

"But . . . I just called your office and your secretary said you weren't there."

"Dominique," he sighed seriously, "you're about to make me hang up on you."

"What? Are you kidding me?" she asked in disbelief.

"Does it sound like I'm joking? You're getting on my nerves with this shit." Before Quinton could continue Payton straddled him and said in a low tone, "You need to wrap this up."

Caught off guard, Quinton snapped at Payton, "Are you fuckin' crazy?"

"Quinton," Dominique called for his attention, "who are you talking to?"

He paused. "I'm . . . ummm . . . talking to you. Look, Dominique, I really don't wanna go through this. I gotta go. I'll be home in an hour."

"Two hours," Payton mumbled, and held two fingers up.

"You know, Quinton," Dominique cried, "I'm really trying not to nag you . . . but it's really important that you come home now. I need to talk to you."

"I told you I will be home in a while."

"I need you now, dammit! I swear I'm married to you and feel lonely as hell!"

"Can we please," Quinton stressed, "talk about this later, when I get home?"

"But—" Dominique went on to say as Payton snatched the phone from Quinton's hand, snapped it closed, and tossed it to the floor. A few seconds later it was ringing again.

"Have you lost your fuckin' mind?" Quinton grabbed Payton by her forearm, tossed her to the side of the bed, and pinned her down. He held her tightly by both of her wrists and her body shook as he spoke. "Don't ever do no shit like that again. That's my fuckin' wife!"

"And when did you remember that, before or after you came while calling my name?"

"What," he said, sternly, "matters is *what* I just said to you. And another thing, don't ever in your life come at me like that again, 'cause I'm not Lyfe."

"No, you just suggested that I send him to New York."

"*The point is,*" he stressed, as sweat formed on his forehead, "you can talk crazy to him all you want to, but don't try that shit with me, 'cause that's the quickest way for you to get fucked up and left alone." He roughly let her wrist go and stood up.

Payton sat up, crossed her legs, and gave him a half smile. "Aww . . ." she said, "that was cute you were trying to take up for your wife. Isn't that sweet." She snapped her fingers. "You better work it, boy. Now, seriously," she lifted her eyes and locked into his gaze, "don't you ever come out the side of your neck at me again, 'cause I will have you out on your ass before you can even think to apologize to your fat-ass wife. So, let me remind you of Payton's rules again: I'm in charge, and along with making me money you need to play your position, which is on your knees."

"I don't have to take this shit." He snatched his clothes from the chair.

"Then leave." She lifted her glass of merlot off the nightstand and sipped. "But if you do, consider this your pink slip."

"One thing has nothing to do with the other."

"Well," Payton lifted one leg on the bed, spreading her pink lips, "I don't separate very well." She flicked her hand. "Now go on and get your things, because I have work to do." She fingered her pussy with her index finger, stirred her finger into her drink, and licked off the drippings. "Unless, of course, you're rethinking your behavior."

Quinton didn't respond and Payton could tell that a million thoughts were running through his mind as he looked down at how her pussy dripped. She knew he hated that he was attracted to how much of a bitch she was, but she also knew that it kept his dick hard.

"This shit is going to be the death of me." He slid to knees.

"I knew you couldn't resist." Payton moaned, throwing her legs over his shoulders.

California

Dominique sipped her third glass of wine and held a lit cigarette between her fingertips. She sat on the edge of her bed and fought like hell not to stare at her reflection in her vanity's mirror. Yet, no matter which way she turned there she was, beneath the crystal chandelier, looking into the reflection of her eyes and wondering how despair, bankrupt feelings, and fucked-up thoughts had etched their way onto her brow.

She was supposed to be fly at all times, high on life, not wearing misery on her face. After all, she was never content with being a plain Jane from New Orleans. She always knew she was destined to have more, which is why she couldn't contend with her first boyfriend, Harry Johns. Hell, she didn't even like his name. He was too boring, too safe, had never been outside of Louisiana, and yeah, he had a big dick and a mouth filled with tongue tricks, but nothing about him satisfied her fantasy.

Then there was Sheldon Lewis, the assistant pastor she dated. But after six months she'd had enough. All he wanted to do, in between screwing her, was keep her in church all day, preparing her to become his first lady. There was no way in hell that she wanted such a responsibility. She believed in God, but being the head of a church was a whole other level. And she didn't want to settle, because ever since she was a little girl she knew exactly what she wanted in a man: wealth, power, a ruler of men, Super Man . . . Obama'esque. A real man, who, when she strolled her size-fourteen hips down the street with him on her arm, every bitch in her path hated and salivated because they weren't Dominique, the baddest bitch of them all.

Dominique knew that sluts may have had more fun, but meek and mild women always won, because men chose them to be their wives, to have their babies, and to stay by their sides. So she placed herself in a position to quietly be noticed. She moved from Louisiana to Hollywood, where she became a real estate agent. Worked her way up the ranks until she finally landed the right client—the Chief Investment Officer of Anderson Global.

She'd sold him his house and on the day of his closing he asked her on a date. She accepted and six months later they were married. Finally her fantasy had come true; she rubbed elbows with the stars, befriended all the Hollywood wives, and quickly became pregnant; striking gold the first go-round: twin boys.

She had only one problem: Quinton's affairs.

He'd gone from late nights, to overnights, to two and three nights out of the house. He treated her as if she were at the top of his shit list and he barely interacted with their now four-year-old twins.

Dominique knew that the only thing left for Quinton to do was pack his shit and never come back again . . . but there was no way she could let that happen. Not when she'd wasted the last five years of her life loving this man; and she'd done everything to keep him, from searching through his things, to hooking up a surveillance camera to see what he was doing when she wasn't around. She was desperate for anything she could find that would give her a clue of what she needed to do to get her husband back where she needed him to be.

Dominique heard Quinton's keys jingling in the front door and she quickly mashed her cigarette in the ashtray, stood in front of the mirror, and ran her hands along the sides of her white lace negligee. She hoped Quinton would find it appealing, since in the last year he hadn't touched her much.

She heard his footsteps coming closer to the bedroom door. She hurried and lay across the center of their oval king-size bed.

Once Quinton entered the room Dominique pushed thoughts of where he'd been out of her mind and pressed forward. "Quinton." She did her best to give him a full smile. "I've been waiting for you, baby."

Quinton stared at her lying across the bed and she could tell by the look in his eyes that she drained him. "I've had a long day." He sighed.

"I know, baby." She forced herself to smile, her eyes tracing the redness of his neck. She wanted to ask him what had happened, but she didn't want to give him any excuse to turn away. "And it's okay," she rose from the bed, "because I know exactly what'll make you feel better." She walked over to him and began kissing him. "I just want you to know that I love you so much. And no matter what, I will always love you." She placed her hand on his crotch and began to rub his dick through his pants.

"Not tonight, Dominique."

She ignored him and led him by the hand to the bed. Though he was obviously reluctant, he allowed her to undress him.

"Quinton," Dominique whispered in his ear as they now lay on the bed and she straddled his lap, "I just want us to work this out . . . please."

He looked at Dominique and she knew he was turned off. Tears of desperation streamed down her face. She felt like she was having sex alone. Quinton's hands were folded behind his neck, as he watched her bounce up and down on his dick.

Dominique placed his hands around her waist and they simply rested against her skin. There was no gentle guide of "Go 'head baby, work that pussy," or "Whose pussy is this?" Just the sound of her desperately climbing up and down on his erotic log, and for a moment she wondered if it was even hard.

She knew that continuing to make love like this was useless, so she slid off of him and he immediately rose from the bed. She watched his defined back as he walked out the bedroom door, and in between bouts of shock and a flooding of tears, the faint scent of perfume oozed from the heap of Quinton's clothes that lay on the floor.

New York

Lyfe worked Arri's last fuckin' nerve. And she didn't give a damn about how fine he was, how much she found herself attracted to him, or daydreamed about him; all she knew was that he was a demanding and arrogant motherfucker that she wished, sooner than later, would take his black ass back to California.

"What he needs," Khris whispered to her, as they stood at the copy machine, "is some pussy."

"I don't know what the fuck his miserable ass needs," Arri snapped, "but in a minute he will need a secretary."

"Why?" Lyfe walked over and handed Arri a file. "You plan on quitting?"

Arri looked at Khris—they were shocked and surprised. "I hear everything." Lyfe looked Arri over and glanced at Khris. "So the next time you wanna talk about what my miserable ass needs you may wanna make sure I'm not in earshot." He nodded his head for emphasis. "Understand?" He paused and they each faked a smile. "I need you to copy this," he said as he walked away.

"Damyum!" Khris whispered.

"What?" Arri said. "He's nerve-racking as hell, right?"

"Nope, that's not it." Khris picked up the papers she'd copied. "He wants to fuck the shit outta you."

"Puleeze."

"You act as if you're getting some. Those little freaks on your website don't count."

"It doesn't mean I have to give it to my goddamn boss!" Arri placed the papers from the file into the copy machine.

"Live a little."

"Oh, please."

"You didn't die with Ian."

Immediately Arri felt frozen in her spot. "The conversation is finished, Khris."

"Arri—"

"What did I say?" She snatched her papers from the machine and walked away. She placed the copied file into Lyfe's in-basket and walked out of his office before he could say anything.

For the next hour Arri busied herself with as much work as she could to avoid thinking about the remark Khris had made. She knew that Khris meant well, but there was no way in hell that she was dealing with somebody else's husband, no matter how fine he was.

Arri could see into Lyfe's office from the locker-size mirror that hung in her cubicle and Lyfe's massiveness filled her cubicle, causing her clit to disregard her mind and palpitate. Despite what her mind said, Arri's eyes knew that Lyfe exceeded eye candy. From his deep and sensually brown skin to his strapping body . . . She could only imagine rocking against him as he sat her on his dick and made her ride it.

She knew by looking at him that his unending inches would initially hurt going in, but that would be okay, because she knew he would be gentle. Or maybe he wouldn't. Maybe he would be rough, and sweat would pour from both of them like an Amazon rainstorm as he whispered to her, "Take this dick and get used to it!" Perhaps instead of sensual sucks she would welcome hungry tugs, pulls, and pops from between his lips as his tongue fucked her nipples. And maybe he'd suck her clit as she sat on his face and filled his mouth with erotic taffy.

"Arri," Lyfe called her name and snatched her attention away from her daydream. She looked up and realized that his reflection filled her mirror because he'd been standing directly behind her all this time, staring at the reflection of her hard nipples.

This motherfucker. "Yes," she said, turning around and standing up, where Lyfe stood so close to her that air struggled to get in between them.

"I um . . ." Lyfe paused and for the first time in two weeks, since he'd been at the office and established that he was serious about his business, he fumbled over his words. "Umm." He cleared his throat and Arri boldly took her index finger and lifted his chin, bringing his gaze from her hard nipples to her face.

"Yes?" she said.

"Damn." He looked slightly embarrassed. "I was . . . ummm . . ." He stepped back and collected himself, straightening his tie. "Listen, I hate to do this to you, and I know it's close to five o'clock, but I need to prepare for an internal audit. So this is going to be a late night. I'll need you and accounting to stay behind."

"Stay?" she said, taken aback as visions of Zion and her Smooth Operator clients ran through her mind.

"I don't mean to impose, but I really need you to pull some hard copy files, scan them into the computer, and take some notes for me. If that's okay?"

Arri knew what he'd said may have come across as a question, but she also knew he was far from asking. "Sure." She forced her lips to form a crescent moon. "No problem."

"Thanks." Lyfe turned and walked toward the accounting department and Arri overheard him telling them about staying late. She walked over to Khris's cubicle, where Khris was putting her coat on, and leaned against her desk. "I need a favor," Arri said as Khris placed her purse on her shoulder.

"Gurl," Khris frowned, "it's five o'clock and you know my boo is coming over to rock da spot. So ask me the favor on the way to the train."

"You just a nasty freak," Mare-Hellen interjected into their conversation, never leaving her cubicle. "Where you need to be is on your way to church." She shook her tambourine.

"I really am not in the mood for this." Arri rolled her eyes, and looked at Khris. "Listen, I have to work late and could you please, please get Zion from aftercare for me?"

"It's cool, gurl," Khris assured her. "Plus, he can play Wii with Tyree while my boo and I cook dinner."

"Thanks," Arri said with a sigh of relief and headed back toward Lyfe's office, where he sat behind his desk, writing out the list of files he needed her to copy and scan. His usually cuff-linked sleeves were flipped at the wrists, his tie no longer hung around his neck and now lay at the side of the desk, while the top two buttons of his shirt were undone, giving her eyes quickies as she fucked him with her gaze.

Thankful that he couldn't see her wet panties, she rapped lightly on the door frame. A look of frustration lingered on his face as he stroked his beard and looked up.

"Whatever it is," Arri said, "you'll work it out."

His eyes smiled. "What are you talking about?"

"You. Whenever you stroke your beard you're upset about something."

Lyfe gave a sexy chuckle and half a grin. "And how do you know that?" His eyes drifted down over her hips and back up to her face again.

"Because I noticed it . . . I guess," Arri said, her eyes settling upon his wedding band. "Is that the list you're preparing for me?"

"Yes," he said, walking over and handing it to her. "There will be a few others tomorrow, but this is it for now."

"Okay," Arri said as she took a step back and he took a step forward. "Umm . . . you said this is it?" she nervously asked again.

"For now." He nodded, as they continued her step back and his step forward dance, until the door frame halted Arri in her spot and they stood there, with her pussy creaming and his dick dreaming of connecting them. He brushed her hair behind her shoulders and she warred like hell not to kiss his hand.

Arri spoke softly, her lips a breath away from his, "A Mr. Glenn Peters called wanting to discuss his portfolio. I placed his message on top," she pointed to a mountain of handwritten messages she'd placed on Lyfe's desk earlier that day.

For a moment Lyfe looked at Arri slightly confused and then he walked back toward his desk. He sorted through the messages and said, "You should've forwarded these, including Peters's call, to California and had him speak with Quinton King—that's his department."

"I did," Arri said, standing up straight, "but Mr. King hasn't been in all week."

"Yeah," Lyfe said as if he were speaking to himself, "I haven't been able to reach him either."

"And most of the clients," Arri pointed back to the stack of messages, "are calling here."

Lyfe paused. "All right, I'll reach out to them in the morning." He picked up his legal pad and pen and said, "I'm going into the conference room with the accounting team; when you're done, join us. I'll need you to jot a few things down."

As Lyfe stepped out of his office, Arri let out a loud sigh and closed her eyes.

Once she collected herself she went to the file room, pulled what she needed, scanned, copied, and put the information back in its place. Afterward, she joined Lyfe and the accountants in the conference room, where he stood before them, explaining what he'd found, and what he expected them to do.

It was spellbinding, watching him walk before the overhead projection screen, point to a graph, and speak about millions of dollars in investments, buying stocks, selling them, Roth IRAs, 401Ks, deferred compensation, and a zillion other financial textbook terms that turned Arri's panties into a wet cloth.

She could tell by his ability to mix "you feel me and you see what I'm saying" in with proper English that he was the best of both worlds: smooth and mellow, but if pushed far enough, his street sense would come out, and he would go the fuck off.

Arri placed her hand onto the side of her hair and looked him over. She loved the way his tailored Armani pants swayed over his wing tips as he walked toward her. And the way his platinum TAG Heuer watch slid down his wrist as he stood over her, pointed to her pad, and said, "Tomorrow, I want you to pull the last three years' financial reports."

This was simply too damn much, and if Arri had ever wanted to leave so she could go home and masturbate via her Webcam, it was now, because then she could pretend that he was her client and bust this pinned-up nut for him.

I have lost my damn mind, Arri thought. *I'ma mess around and get fired . . . and I need my job. Besides, he's not that fine . . . or that smart . . . and my pussy isn't that wet . . .* She sighed. *I need to shut the fuck up, 'cause I'm lying to myself.*

"Arri," Lyfe called out to her, "did you get that?"

Arri blinked. "What's that? I'm sorry, I didn't hear you."

"Chinese food?"

"What?" she said, put off. "Chinese food?"

"Would you like Chinese?" he asked her, his eyes pulling weights not to roam all over her. "I figured it's the least I can do for having you all work so late."

"Sure." She rose from her chair. "If everyone tells me what they want, I'll place the order." Everyone passed around a menu, selecting what they wanted to eat, and as they resumed the meeting Arri placed the order. Once the food was delivered everyone dug in and between the orders of lo mein and fried rice, they continued their conversation and preparation for the audit.

Before long it was ten o'clock and Lyfe was concluding, "All right, good people, let's wrap this up and resume in the morning."

As the accountants said their good-byes and hurried to leave, Arri stood up and looked down at the conference table, which was littered with paper.

Lyfe moved his hand toward his beard, but before he could reach it, Arri said, "Don't worry, I'll stack the paper for you."

"Are you sure?" Lyfe arched his eyebrows. "I mean, it's late and I wouldn't wanna make your man upset by staying any longer. Feel me?"

"Don't ask me shit about feeling you," Arri mumbled.

"I didn't catch that," Lyfe said. "What did you say?"

Arri paused. She knew, if nothing else, he heard everything. "I said," Arri paused, "that you're right . . . it is late."

"Yeah, that's what I thought." His eyes drifted to her breasts.

"Do I have something on me?" she said, lifting his chin again, wanting desperately to kiss him.

"Nah," he said as the phone started to ring. "You're perfect."

"I'll ummm . . ." Arri said, "get that." She walked toward the double doors.

"Where are you going? There's a phone right here." He pointed to the center of the conference table.

"It's a little cooler out here." She walked quickly out the doors and picked up the phone at her cubicle, "Anderson Global, Arri Askew speaking."

"Oh . . . this is Payton Carrington," the caller said, taken aback. "I was trying to reach my husband. He hasn't been answering his cell phone . . . is he still there?"

"Yes, Mr. Carrington is still here, we were just finishing up a meeting for the internal audit. Would you mind holding so that I can get him for you?"

No response.

"Hello . . . Mrs. Carrington?" Arri said, and then realized the line was dead. She placed the phone back on the cradle and returned to the conference room.

"Who was it?" Lyfe asked.

"Your wife."

"My wife?" he said, as if for some reason he'd forgotten he had one.

"Yes, your wife. She was surprised that we were still here. I told her we were finishing up a meeting for the internal audit and she hung up."

"Shit," Lyfe hissed and Arri could tell he was slightly annoyed.

"I'm sorry, did . . . I . . . do something?"

"No," he said, his smile reemerging, "I'll handle it." He flicked off the light switch. "Are you going to be okay getting home?" They grabbed their coats. "I could get a car for you."

"No, it's fine," Arri said, walking backward out of the room. "I could use a nice train ride."

"Sure?"

"Yes." She smiled.

"All right. Well, good night," Lyfe said. "I drove in today, so I'm out back." He pointed to the elevator bay farther down the hall.

"Okay, see you in the morning." Arri slid on her coat, placed her bag on her arm, and left. Once she stepped into the all-glass lobby she watched as buckets of rain fell from the sky. "Stay dry," the doorman said as she walked out of the building, and stood under the overhang, wondering how wet she would be by the time she ran the two blocks to the subway station. "Get in" interrupted her thoughts as she looked up and saw Lyfe in a Black

Escalade in front of the building. "Get in," he repeated. "It's late and it's raining. I won't kidnap you; I need you at work tomorrow. I promise."

Arri looked up and down the block and rain washed over everything in sight. "All right," she said, sliding into his truck, "I live in Brooklyn, on Church Avenue."

"That's no problem, I'm staying right off the West Side Highway," Lyfe said as they pulled off.

"Really?" Arri said, taken aback. "Where at?" She playfully twisted her lips. "Because I know you're not in Harlem."

Lyfe laughed. "What is that supposed to mean? I can't be in Harlem?"

"Of course,"—she fought like hell not to give him the world's biggest smile—"but I just expected you to be in . . . I don't know . . . the presidential suite at some five-star hotel on the Upper East Side."

"Well, for your information," Lyfe said as he blew the horn at a cab that cut in front of them, "I'm not in Times Square."

"So where are you staying?"

Lyfe paused. "Downtown . . . the W Hotel . . . but still."

Arri snickered, "It's okay to be a yuppie."

"I am far from that."

"Okay, honey, if you say so."

"Don't try and patronize me, it's after five o'clock."

"Ha-ha," Arri said sarcastically, "is that so?"

"You think I'm an asshole of a boss, don't you?"

"You? Oh no, honey." Arri did her best to keep the lie she'd just told from burning her mouth.

"Why you playin' me?" he said, feeling relaxed and allowing his sexy and street Compton accent to sneak into his words. "When I'm at work I don't mean to be hard-nosed, but I have to be about my business."

"I understand."

"But I'm off now."

Silence.

"What? You don't have anything to say?" Lyfe quickly looked at Arri and then back to the street. "Don't be shuttin' down on me."

"I don't shut down."

"Yo', you do and you know it."

"Look at you tryna be hood."

"Now you wanna change the subject, it's cool."

"What you want me to say?" Arri joked, throwing up the West Side symbol, "West Side." Arri laughed and once she looked into his face she was caught between a blush and a flush of embarrassment. "I didn't mean to be so silly," she said, feeling self-conscious.

"A woman who can handle her business in the day and let herself go at night is sexy as hell."

Silence.

"Plus," Lyfe said, breaking the troubling monotony, "you're a li'l hood yourself."

"Umm-hmm, whatever." Arri waved dismissively. "Now, where exactly in California are you from?"

They stopped at a red light and Lyfe said, "Compton, baby. Crenshaw, to be exact."

"What the—?" She whipped her neck toward him. "Your ass is hood as hell. Don't go doing no drive-bys while I'm in the car, Dough Boy. And what are you doing with an Escalade; where's your seventy-six psychedelic-blue Impala?"

The light turned green. "Oh, you got jokes," Lyfe chuckled, "and it wasn't an Impala. It was a hunter green and black ragtop deuce and a quarter with spinners on it. And the sound system"—Lyfe's smile lit up the night—"was knockin'."

Arri laughed so hard that tears filled her eyes. "And what did you have, Snoop, a perm? Oh wait, Ice Cube, a curl?"

"None of the above, pretty girl. I had the same Caesar that I have now."

Arri paused; hearing him call her pretty girl made the butter-flies in her stomach jump. "You are so corny." She tried like hell not to blush. Arri pointed to the building she lived in and Lyfe pulled over.

"Me, corny?" Lyfe went on, "Ai'ight, well then . . . show me how not to be corny."

Arri was silent. She looked at the dim and damp Brooklyn street that was ironically named Church Avenue, lit only by streetlamps and the headlights of never-ending traffic. She could see people walking up and down the block and some con-gregating on corners.

She wondered why she'd sat here this long, entertaining something that she knew was bullshit. Not only was Lyfe her boss but he was her married boss. She'd been through enough bullshit with married men, but then . . . honestly, him being married really didn't slice her. No, what fucked with her was the fact that she was comfortable around him, and though she was sitting on the other side of the SUV from him, she really wanted to slide next to him and sit with her head on his chest, or in his lap . . .

And she wanted to tell him her wildest dreams and her fucked-up memories. She wanted to explain to him that she one day wanted to love again but that she was scared as hell, be-cause the one time she let herself go there, he was shot dead. And she wanted to share with him that the prostitute pacing the cor-ner up ahead wasn't just a fiending crackhead, but was her sister.

She felt protected sitting here with him and she'd never ex-pected to feel anything like this ever again, which is exactly why she was going to get her heart, her horniness, and her common sense in check and get the fuck out of here, go inside, get Zion, put him in bed, and perform for a client or two. She needed to get back to her life and sitting here feeling giddy with some ran-dom motherfucker wasn't cuttin' it.

"What's the silence about?" Lyfe interjected into her thoughts.

"It's just . . ." Arri voice trailed off and her words became dead in her mouth before they could reach the air.

Lyfe gently turned Arri's face toward him and said, "True story, no game, and no politics. I'm enjoying being myself around you, and not having to hear about what we made last quarter. I promise you I haven't laughed and shit like this in a minute. But if you feel funny, or awkward, or maybe you have a man peeking out the window, it's cool and I'll see you in the morning, no harm, no foul."

After a moment of deciding to toss caution to the wind, Arri said, "I hope you like to dance."

Sounds of live singing and steel-pan playing eased onto the street as Arri and Lyfe parked in front of Dextra, a small club on Flatbush Avenue, surrounded by twenty-four-hour West Indian restaurants and apartment buildings. Though Dextra sat in the heart of the hood, people from all walks of life loved the atmosphere and frequented the club like it was a tourist spot.

Dextra was nothing fancy; it was a simple storefront with a hand-painted Trinidadian flag on the front door. A banana tree sat by the entrance and people poured shots of rum punch onto it for good luck. The walls were covered in electric-teal paint and decorated with only two pictures: one of a bowl of fruit and the other, a large map of Trinidad. The map provided the backdrop of Dextra's makeshift stage, where the world-renowned Wild Head, a reggae and soca band, performed every night. Small card tables and folding chairs littered the room, and most people were either drinking, eating, or working the dance floor.

"Let me know," Arri said sarcastically, "if this is too much for you. If so we can leave and five-star dine at Mr. Chow's."

Lyfe smiled, "Too much for me? Whatta gurl like you know 'bout dis?" He put on a fake and extremely unbelievable West Indian accent.

Arri chuckled, and released an authentic Trinidadian accent. "But what de bumbeclot dis yankee boy call heself doin'?" She sucked her teeth long and hard. "Leave de Trini to me and you just be ye self."

"And who's that?" he looked into her eyes.

"A rude boy."

"You like rude boys?"

"A little too much." She relaxed her Trinidadian accent and returned to her natural flowing American one.

Before Lyfe could comment the bartender asked what they were drinking. Lyfe looked at the bartender and said, "Give the lady—"

"A Shandy," Arri said.

"And I'll have a Guinness."

The bartender handed them their drinks and as Lyfe slid backward onto the bar stool, Arri eased between Lyfe's legs and he placed his left arm around her waist. "Ah"—he smiled as the stroll lights hanging above their head illuminated the shape of her ass—"an Island girl. No wonder."

"No wonder what?" Arri said as Lyfe took a swig from his beer.

"No wonder you're so beautiful."

"Plenty of all-American girls are beautiful too."

"I never said they weren't. And stop that," he said seriously.

"Stop what?"

"Stop tossing back my compliments," he said, as he completed his hold on her waist, placing his right arm on the other side of her hip.

Arri became silent and Lyfe said, "And stop that too. Think tomorrow at the morning meeting, not tonight."

"You're right." Arri placed her Shandy on the counter and grabbed Lyfe by the hand. "Let's dance."

Arri and Lyfe moved to the center of the dance floor and started to groove. They melted into each other as Arri fit her ass perfectly against Lyfe's shaft as she wined, making it all too easy for him to imagine her screaming while he tossed it up doggy-style.

Lyfe moved to the West Indian beat, but he was no match for Arri's movement—and he didn't really want to be. He wanted to watch her throw her voluptuous hips with a gracefulness he'd never seen.

He knew she could feel his hard dick pressed against her slit because the harder he became the deeper she thrusted into him.

Arri pushed everything from her mind that told her she was having too good of a time. Hell, she hadn't even called home and checked on Zion. Although she knew he was safe, that wasn't the point. She didn't need to be here, but then again she did. She turned around and faced Lyfe, slid her arms around his neck, and daringly, she kissed him—a soul-stirring kiss, the kind that made them feel like, even if only for the moment, they were the only two in the room.

"Damn," Lyfe said as his hands roamed freely over Arri's ass, "I don't think"—he sucked her bottom lip—"that we need to be doing this."

"Why not?" Arri said, continuing to kiss him.

"Because I'm married," Lyfe broke their kiss, "and I didn't come to New York to fuck around on my wife."

Arri swallowed the embarrassment creeping into her throat. "I didn't ask you to fuck around on your wife." She could feel her heart hardening while her mind screamed, *This is exactly the bullshit you didn't want to deal with!* Nevertheless, things were better this way, because Arri knew that the longer their tongues intertwined, the more likely she was to get addicted to the taste of him, the look of him, and the feel of him. "I have to go." Arri stepped out of his embrace and turned to walk away.

As if they were making a dance move, as quickly as she turned away was as quickly as he twirled her back toward his chest. He massaged his temples with one hand and held her around the waist with the other; "Wait, just wait."

"You want me to wait for you now?" Arri said with sarcastic disbelief.

"That's not what I mean."

"Listen,"—Arri patted Lyfe on the chest—"it's been real." She backed out of his embrace again and moved quickly and to the side so that he wouldn't be able to pull her back.

"Arri," he called through gritted teeth, careful not to cause a scene, yet she kept going, disappearing into the heavy rain-drops.

Watching the door swing behind her, Lyfe pounded his fist against the bar and briskly walked out. "Arri," he called out to her, spotting her halfway up the block. "Arri." When she didn't stop or respond he slid into his Escalade and crept along the side of her. "Arri," he called out again, as the heavy rain seeped in through the open window and drenched his passenger seat, "get in the car. It's raining, it's dark. You don't have to talk to me if you don't want to. I just wanna make sure you get home safe."

Silence. She ignored him and as he continued behind her she walked the three short blocks to her apartment building. Once she reached the stoop, she turned around, looked into his face, and then quickly turned back toward the door and walked in.

She heard Lyfe pull off as she walked upstairs to Khris's apartment. She rapped on the door and a half-asleep Khris opened it, wiping her eyes. "Gurl, where the hell you been?" She looked at Arri suspiciously. "You know Zion and Tyree fell asleep playing Wii. Just come and get him in the morning."

"I'm sorry I was so long."

"Why do you sound like you just ran up on a niggah with a li'l dick?" She sniffed her and said, "You been fuckin?"

"I wish," Arri dragged, avoiding eye contact with her friend. "Listen, I'll come first thing in the morning to get him. Good night." She walked to her apartment and closed the door be-hind her.

New York

"Good morning, everyone," Lyfe said with a slight edge to his voice, doing his best not to let on that he was still aggravated from the night before. He looked around the conference room and fought like hell not to stare at Arri, who sat before him holding a legal pad and a pen.

Lyfe owed her an apology, that he knew, but now wasn't the right moment to offer it to her. Besides, he'd already crossed the line of fucking up business with pleasure, and in order to redraw the line, he would have to wait until after five to correct his actions—at least that's what he'd planned, but it was clear that his mind had a different agenda, because the mere sight of her made a flashback of last night creep into his thoughts.

Lyfe could feel his dick getting hard as he remembered how she felt in his arms, and nothing was worse for him than standing before a room full of people and having to cautiously shift his dick so that the mountain rising within wouldn't be noticed. He stood closely behind his black, oversize leather wing chair, slid his hands into his pockets, slyly moved his dick, and continued on with his meeting. "As we discussed last night we will be pulling files and financial reports over the next couple weeks for an internal audit—"

"Oh, hell no, you won't," caused everyone to turn toward the double mahogany doors, which had flown open and revealed

Payton standing there in a blue sable fur coat that draped to the floor and four-inch stilettos that made her the same height as Lyfe. Her presence filled the doorway as she stormed in with one hand on her hip and the other slamming her signature Hermès clutch onto the conference table. She stood opposite Lyfe as she looked him directly in the eyes, and said, "Everybody, get the fuck out!"

Each of their employees were stunned and sat in complete silence, forcing Payton to slam her hands onto the table and demand at the top of her lungs, "Now!"

Everyone darted to their feet and quickly left, the last person closing the door behind them.

Lyfe folded his arms across his chest and stroked his box beard twice. This had to be a nightmare, so he blinked, yet Payton was still standing there.

"Have you lost your fuckin' mind!" Payton stood up straight and peered at Lyfe. "Pulling some shit like this without my permission! When I told your fuckin' ass to leave it alone—"

"You . . . better . . . lower your motherfuckin' voice," Lyfe said through gritted teeth, the veins in his neck and along the side of his head exploding.

"You up in here flexing and shit"—Payton pointed her hand in Lyfe's face—"showing your ass like you're the goddamn CEO out this bitch, oh hell no!" She waved her hand dismissively and continued, "Get your shit. Your flight has been arranged and a car will be here to take you to the airport in the next hour. Robertson McDaniels is coming out here to take over and you're coming the fuck home!"

"What Robertson McDaniels is gon' get," Lyfe said confidently, "is his motherfuckin' lung collapsed if he comes the fuck up in here. I wish the niggah would." He shook his head. "You are really out of order."

"This is my company!" Payton pounded her fist on the table with every point she made, causing the stacks of paper to topple over. "And this is my goddamn money! What the fuck is on your mind? I swear you are ungrateful as hell. I gave you this motherfuckin' job and you're doing everything other than what you suppose to be doing! If it wasn't for me you would be adding to the recidivism rate or busting out a goddamn Crip walk and locking down one of Crenshaw's raggedy-ass corners! You acting like you walked up in here with some motherfuckin' qualifications. I gave you a chance, niggah, and this is how you repay me?"

"Hold it—"

"No, you hold it!" She pounded between each word for emphasis. "I tell you what and you better begin to understand this— you're my goddamn man and you do what the fuck I tell you to! And I didn't tell you to do no shit like this, motherfucker. I'm the queen bitch." She yelled into his face and specks of spit whipped from her mouth like a wet wind. "And I don't know who's been gassing your goddamn head up or what the fuck you been running around here telling these people and shit, but this ain't your goddamn spot, Mr. Compton. It's mine!"

"I'ma ask you one more mother . . . fuckin' . . . time," Lyfe said, backing Payton into the corner of the room, gripping her by the collar, and lifting her off her feet, "to lower your motherfuckin' voice. Because I ain't afraid to catch a case; and I will toss yo' ass out this fuckin' window before I let you come up in here embarrassing me! I ain't that niggah! Motherfuckers have dropped for less than this. Now you tryna be murked?" His eyebrows arched into the shape of Vs. "You wanna be raked down the motherfuckin' street? Sprayed? You got a death wish, is that it? 'Cause if you think," he spat with his eyes squinted and his lips unshakably stiff, "that I won't land your ass out there on that concrete, then say one . . . more . . . mother . . . fuckin' thing."

Payton moved her lips and before anything could come out of her mouth, Lyfe whipped her around toward the window so hard and fast that the thick glass vibrated and waves of fear caused tears to fall from Payton's eyes.

Lyfe pressed the side of her face into the glass and her eyes frightfully scanned the street below, where the people resembled action figures and the cars looked to be toys.

"You see that shit," Lyfe forced Payton's head to nod, "you see it? You want me to splatter your ass all over it?"

In the midst of Lyfe's grip Payton struggled to shake her head no.

"Then don't you ever in your life come up in here, or anywhere else, speaking to me like you snortin' insanity. 'Cause I will whup your fuckin' ass to a pulp. This is the last time I'ma tell you—that fuckin' wit' me ain't an option. And I'm not your fuckin' man, I'm your *goddamn husband* and you will fall your ass back, do you understand? And you better not say a word more than yes."

"Yes," Payton tearfully whispered.

"Now what you gon' do is get your sick ass back on the plane, go back to L.A., and stay the fuck out my face!" He roughly walked her to the door and as he opened it people scattered and scrambled to their seats, some of them falling and tripping over one another.

"Jesus!" Mare-Hellen yelled. "Y'all 'bout to stomp all over me! I'm tryna get out the way too!"

"Would you shut up," Khris said, "I wanna see if he gon' Big Red her ass out the goddamn window!"

Lyfe strolled over to Arri, his body radiating cool, calm, and collected. He looked her directly in the eyes and his smooth baritone voice said, "Arri, reschedule the meeting for Monday morning." He turned toward Payton and shot her a chilling ice grill. Afterward, he walked into his office and slammed the door behind him, leaving his wife center stage.

Payton pulled her shoulders back, draped her blue sable perfectly onto her shoulders, and checked her makeup in her compact mirror. Seeing that it revealed very little evidence of her almost being thrown out of a window, she tucked her clutch beneath her right arm and stood steady in her stilettos. Now she could address the motherfuckers that she felt staring and smirking at her; after all, she was still the top bitch. "I will fire every motherfuckin' body up in here," she held her left arm in the air, pointing her index finger toward the ceiling and looking wildly from her right to her left, "if you don't stop minding my goddamn business! You don't get paid to stand the fuck around!" She snapped her fingers as she headed toward the glass doors, which were etched with the company's name. "Get back to work!" she threw behind her as she entered the hall and stepped onto the elevator, disappearing behind the closing doors.

New York

Payton stepped over the cracks in the concrete and sauntered toward the black Lincoln Town Car, where the driver stood waiting for her with the door open. The heaviness at the bottom of her stomach let her know she'd entered the Wild Wild West, where anything fuckin' went. In twenty minutes flat Payton had gone from wanting Lyfe to stop being so ghetto—or machismo, or whatever the fuck this Compton niggah called it—to no longer giving a damn. It was clear that he couldn't stop beating his chest long enough to see that they were on the verge of having everything. So fuck it and fuck him. Fuck loving this motherfucker and fuck saving his ass. Both guns were drawn, and as far as Payton was concerned, let the casualties fall where they may.

She eased into the backseat and the driver closed the door behind her. She pressed a button to send up the soundproof partition and then turned to Quinton, who'd been waiting in the car. "I should spit in your fuckin' face!" ripped from her mouth.

"You should what?" Quinton said, taken aback and squinting his eyes. "What the hell are you talking about?" he said, filled with disgusted surprise as the driver knocked lightly on the thick glass separating them. Payton lowered the partition an inch and snapped, "What is it?"

"Where to?" the driver asked.

"The airport," Payton said sternly and sent the partition up again. She turned back to Quinton, yet before she could rip back into him her phone rang. She looked at the caller ID, saw it was her mother, and sent her straight to voice mail. When she called back again Payton turned off the phone.

She looked at Quinton, who was steadily blinking his eyes. "I thought we were going to stay out here until Robertson came," he said. "Why are we on our way to the airport? Wait a minute, what happened?"

" 'Fulfill his sexual fantasy,' " Payton said in her best impersonation of Quinton's voice. " 'He'll simmer down after that,' you said. Did that shit, and what did I get in return? Nothing. 'Fire Thomas and send Lyfe to New York for a month.' " She twisted her voice into an irritating and high-pitched whine. " 'You can handle your business better without him in California.' So I send him to New York, and not only does this motherfucker stay for damn near a month, he steps out of his zone and starts acting like he's numero uno. Mistakes one and two, courtesy of listening to your ass."

"You can relax with the insults."

"And you can relax with giving me advice, motherfucker!" she screamed in his face. "You can also relax sipping off my fuckin' money and do a damn job for once."

"I do my job—"

"Keep talking and in a minute you gon' relax your fuckin' ass, get up off of it, and walk back to California."

"Look." Quinton swallowed. "You're the one who keeps choosing to put up with Lyfe. I told you awhile ago that he didn't love you the way you needed to be loved. I told you that I would leave Dominique and drop any- and everything to be with you. I have never lied to you, but you continue to want to pacify his ass. You need to start appreciating those who appreciate and love you for you. Not some cocky and ungrateful-ass li'l boy, who thinks because his mama died with a needle in her arm that somebody owes him something. Fuck him. He wasn't the one who came into the company and tripled your millions. It was me. I have the college degree. I'm qualified. Lyfe is nothing. Now, that ought to tell you something."

Payton stroked Quinton's right cheek and cupped his chin. "Oh baby," she nibbled small pecks against his lips, "I swear you always know," she kissed him again, "the right moment to show how much of a hatin'-ass motherfucker you are." She looked him over, "Do you think I have the time to care about your jealous ass-pissing contests with my husband! I'ma tell you one . . . more . . . fuckin' . . . time, before I start looking at you sideways: play your designated position. Work that motherfucker, please. I need you on your game. I need you to be the man you were months ago, the man that I was undyingly attracted to. I need you confident and secure in who you are. I need you to be Quinton King, not Mr. I'm Folding."

Quinton swallowed and his eyes narrowed into Payton's. He couldn't figure out what it was about her that kept him wanting to never leave her side, "Listen," he said caringly, "why don't we both calm down, and you tell me what happened up there."

"What happened?" Payton said sounding as if she were on a crashing high. "I don't even know where to start. All I know is that I'm always trying to appease Lyfe. But nothing is ever good enough for him. Nothing. You really wanna know what happened?" She looked at Quinton with her eyes full. "What happened is that I went upstairs and realized that it's too hard loving this motherfucker." She turned her head away and wiped the tears sneaking from the corners of her eyes. She hated that this marriage hadn't turned out like she'd planned. Seemed her mother was right after all. Payton sniffed and checked her emotions. "So," she turned back to him, "I think we need to regroup."

"Sounds like we have a problem then?" Quinton said, as the driver pulled in front of the terminal.

"A big fuckin' problem." Payton popped two Extra Strength Tylenols into her mouth as she and Quinton stepped out of the car and headed into the airport.

To be . . .

New York

The day's sun set quickly and darkness crept over Lyfe, as he sat behind his desk with his office light off, his head held back, and worried eyes cast toward the ceiling. He hadn't felt like this since he was in prison and every day felt like combat. Sitting here it was clear that he was on the front lines once again, albeit this time in the boardroom instead of behind bars. There was no way he could continue to live this way. He needed to get out, to be out, to wave a white flag and hope for a peaceful journey to freedom.

But he knew Payton. And she wasn't the type to simply move aside and let him leave without a fight. She'd rather they both end up with nothing.

Yet, that was a chance he'd have to take because he was certain, beyond a shadow of a doubt, that the next time Payton hauled off like a grenade and went live in his face, he would have to kill her ass.

Lyfe rose from his desk and walked over to the window. He slid his hands into his pants pockets and his eyes traveled over the New York City skyline.

It was six o'clock in the evening, and he hoped that his staff was gone, because he couldn't bear to face them, especially Arri. He knew she'd be full of questions, but how could he explain to her that he was obligated to his wife—the very woman he told her last night that he "didn't come to New York to fuck around on"—had shown her ass and turned their marriage into some shit straight out of *Snapped*.

Lyfe wiped invisible sweat from his brow; this was too much to process. He grabbed his coat, walked out of his office, passed the cleaning crew, and left the building.

Thick clouds of the world's most expensive cigar smoke traveled through the air as Lyfe stepped into the exclusive Cigar Bar and Gentlemen's Lounge in the heart of Midtown, where an elite crowd of businessmen watched erotic dancers make love to steel poles and clap their asses onstage to the sounds of Keri Hilson's "Getcha Money Up." Lyfe stopped at the bar and placed an order for a glass of Louis XIII cognac and a premiere cigar from His Majesty's Reserve. He then took a seat in the last row of olive green recliners in the darkened corner of the room, sank into the deep and cushiony leather seat, and as a Brazilian dancer licked her nipples and pussy-popped onstage, Lyfe closed his eyes and drifted into his thoughts.

A few minutes later, "Is anyone sitting here?" forced Lyfe to open his eyes and look into the face of a white man with green eyes, who even in the dimmed yellow light glowed with the fakest goddamn tangerine tan he'd ever seen. Lyfe was instantly pissed. *Out of all the seats in the place, this Bruce Jenner motherfucker wants to sit next to me.* "Nah," Lyfe said, pointing to the recliner next to him, "help yourself."

"Here you are, Mr. Carrington," the waiter said, as he handed Lyfe a lit cigar and his drink.

Lyfe sipped and then placed his drink on the cherrywood end table. He took a long, hard toke from his cigar, closed his eyes again, and turned his thoughts to Payton. He hated that he had to manhandle her and treat her in such a fucked-up way, but she didn't give him much of a choice. Yeah, some of the shit she'd said stung, but putting his foot down was about more than a bruised ego. It was about laying down the laws and carving out the boundaries of his manhood, and showing her that there was just some shit he wasn't gon' take from no-fuckin'-body.

Lyfe opened his eyes and looked at the stage; one of the dancers was wrapping herself around the pole like a ribbon. Arri seeped into his thoughts, and Lyfe closed his eyes once more. He couldn't understand the unrelenting magnetism he felt when he was around her. Every time he saw her he found himself wanting to know what she dreamed of, what she thought about, what lay behind her beautiful chestnut eyes and cover-girl smile. And why there were times when she seemed so pressed and uneasy. He wanted to chill with her, laugh again, simply be in her company, and then after he'd done all of that, he wanted to bend her over and fuck her from the back until the walls cried out.

"I hope you don't mind me asking," the man sitting next to Lyfe said, barging into his thoughts. He pointed to Lyfe's cigar and said, "Behike?"

"What?" Lyfe said, put off, his hard dick suddenly deflating.

"Your cigar. Is it Behike?"

"Nah, man," Lyfe said curtly, "this is from a stock called His Majesty's."

"Ahhh, now that's a real moneyman's cigar," the guy joked, taking a pull from the cigar he was smoking.

Lyfe looked at him, and his eyes clearly told this mother-fucker to shut up, but the guy either didn't care or didn't pick up on the hint, as he continued on, "I'm a Padilla Dominus Churchill man, myself." The man took a pull from his cigar and released the smoke. "You ever try—"

"You know what," Lyfe said, "I don't mean to be rude, but I came here to clear my head and I'm just not in the mood—"

"Lyfe Carrington, is that you?" poured over Lyfe's shoulder before he could finish his sentence.

Goddamn. Lyfe looked up and saw two of his clients sitting at the table next to him, John Chin and Raymond Cunningham.

They walked over and Lyfe stood up and shook their hands, "How are you?" He smiled, praying that they would hurry and walk away.

"We're fine." Raymond gave Lyfe a sly smile. "Glad to see you're out and enjoying yourself."

"I'm trying." Lyfe gave a fake laugh.

"Well, this is the place to get into it," John said. "You know this place is a chain and has shares on the market. What do you think—a wise investment?"

"Hell no, would you tell 'im, Lyfe," Raymond said. "I keep telling him that the bottom will fall out of this place in five minutes."

"It's possible," Lyfe said, wishing they would all get the hell out of his face. "The market is funny right now."

"Not for Anderson Global it isn't, I have to tell you," John carried on. "Signing on with your company is the best financial decision we could've ever made."

"I knew you looked familiar," the guy who was sitting next to Lyfe said, as he stood up and nodded at the other men. "I'm Galvin Smith." He held his hand out and though Lyfe was still unable to place him he accepted Galvin's gesture. "I met you at a party you all had last year in Los Angeles."

"Oh, okay," Lyfe said, struggling to sound sincere. "How are you? What are you doing in New York?"

"I moved here a few months back."

"That's great." Lyfe forced himself to smile.

"Lyfe," John said, patting Lyfe on the back, "what are you doing when you leave here this evening? Let us take you out to dinner." He looked at Galvin. "You're welcome to join us."

"Oh noooo," Lyfe said, waving his hand beneath his chin. "Four men making dinner plans in the dark is a li'l—" Lyfe stopped himself mid-sentence, figuring the remark he was about to make about their dinner plans being suspect wouldn't be appropriate, so instead he said, "Listen, I appreciate the gesture, really I do. But actually I need to get back to the office." He handed his cigar to the passing waiter and said, "I need this wrapped to go."

"Are you sure, Lyfe?" Raymond said. "It's the least we can do for you all showing us such a great time in L.A."

"It was my pleasure, really," Lyfe said, as the waiter handed him his cigar in a gold cigar box, "but I have a big meeting on Monday I need to prepare for. Maybe next time."

"All right," John said, "if you insist. I guess you always being in the office is why everyone else is losing their shirt, but you all never have a losing quarter."

Galvin laughed. "It's because Anderson Global is the world's best-kept secret."

"That's what they say." Lyfe looked at his watch. "Listen gentlemen, have a good night."

"Nice seeing you again," Raymond said.

"Take care," John added.

"Yeah." Galvin nodded. "Hope to see you soon."

Lyfe was aggravated as hell; not an ounce of his stress had dissolved. He sat in his Escalade wondering what he needed to do and where he needed to go. He knew that he didn't want to go back to his hotel suite, because there was a chance he'd become enraged by his thoughts, catch a flight to California, and bust er'body's ass. Deciding against that, Lyfe considered the office, but he really didn't want to be there either. Then he thought that if he were at the office, at least he'd have something to do.

Hell with it.

"Late night?" the doorman said, tipping his hat and smiling as Lyfe entered into the lobby.

"Pretty much," Lyfe threw over his shoulder, and headed toward the elevator bay.

Once upstairs he walked inside, stood in the middle of the dark floor, and looked around. This was purgatory. No two ways about it, but he'd have to find a way to sort through it, otherwise, given the day he'd had, it was a clear indication that when all was said and done, he'd be headed for hell.

Lyfe hung up his coat and as he sat down at his desk his cell phone rang. He could tell by the ringtone that it wasn't Payton calling this time. He slipped the phone from his pocket and checked the caller ID: Quinton. "Yeah, this is Lyfe."

"Lyfe Carrington, wassup?" Quinton said, a little too god-damn jovial. The tone of his voice pissed Lyfe off.

"What is it?" Lyfe snapped.

"Damn," Quinton said, taken aback, "what the hell is wrong with you?"

"I'm just not in the mood for all of that smiling and shit you doing."

"How did you know I was smiling?"

" 'Cause I can hear it, motherfucker. Now, what is it? And by the way," Lyfe said, not coming up for air, "where the fuck you been all week?"

"I been working, I been here in Cali—oh wait, I did skip to Vegas for an overnight. Why?"

"Because all of your clients are calling here and every time I tried to reach you, you were nowhere to be found."

"What you want me to tell you, man? Hell, in between working and Vegas, I was bangin' my wife and had my side jawn sucking my dick. Don't be jealous 'cause you way out in New York hanging with your hands."

Although Lyfe was pissed, he chuckled a bit.

"So wassup with you?" Quinton asked, "You out in one of the greatest cities in the world, no wife, no crying-ass kids, and you sounding mad as hell? Why?"

Lyfe hesitated, "Payton . . . flew out here and showed her fuckin' ass."

"What? She flew to New York? When?"

"Today." Lyfe recapped for Quinton everything that went on, and then he said, "All behind an audit?"

"It's not your department," Quinton said seriously. "And maybe you need to listen to what she's saying. It is her company."

Lyfe was taken aback. "What the fuck are you saying to me? I'm heading an office and can't even look at the records and make sure they are in order? That sounds right to you?" Lyfe snapped, "What the fuck is really going on, Q? And don't give me no bullshit."

"I don't have no bullshit to give you. But you around here wondering why she's flipping, well it's because you're being insubordinate."

Lyfe laughed. "Have you lost your fucking mind? I'm her husband."

"And she hired somebody else to handle what you're trying to do. Who are you checking up on?"

"I don't know, you tell me."

"You're the one waging all of this shit. Leave it alone. Damn, why do you care so much? I told you a long time ago to use her ass for what she was worth and bounce. But naah, not you, you too upstanding for that shit."

"It's called morals, loving my wife, looking out for her company."

"Well, how much do you love her ass right now?"

Silence.

"Exactly my point."

"Listen," Lyfe said, "I got other shit to do," and he hung up, doing all he could to erase the conversation from his mind and get refocused. He turned on his computer and looked through the files Arri copied and scanned earlier this week. He remembered that he'd never given her the completed list of records that he needed, so he scribbled the remainder on a Post-it note and placed it on Arri's computer.

Once Lyfe was back at his desk, he looked around the room and realized that being here at ten o'clock at night was a bunch of unequivocal and ridiculous bullshit. There was no way that he wanted to be here, especially tonight, when he was stuck between wanting to fuck Arri and fuck *up* Payton.

Lyfe grabbed his coat and before the doorman could say a proper good night, he was gone.

Lyfe drove around for an hour before finding himself at Dextra's, with two orders of food packed to go, drinking his second Guinness stout, and listening to Wild Head sing the reggae version of the Persuaders' "Thin Line." He nodded his head, not only to the beat, but also to the lyrics. A million what-ifs raced through his thoughts as he wondered who and what was really in charge of tomorrow.

Lyfe felt his cell phone vibrate in his pocket as he took the last swig of his beer and then looked through the empty bottle. His mind told him fuck it. Simply fuck it. Fuck thinking, fuck rethinking, fuck figuring out the right timing, and the right things to say, how to begin, when to begin . . . fuck first impressions. Fuck it all. Life had too many rules, and at least for tonight, this Lyfe didn't wanna be bothered with structure. Because the truth of the matter was he didn't wanna be here either.

New York

Heavy drops of rain beat against the fire escape outside of Arri's open bedroom window, as she sat on the windowsill in hopes of cooling off from the stifling heat in her apartment. Dry and thick vapors of heat hissed from the radiators, leaving her with no choice but to seek refuge in the sky's dampness. Her eyes skipped from the neon red reflection of the adjacent bodega's awning to the people huddled beneath the bus stop, barely escaping the dollar vans and taxicabs splashing puddles on the curb.

Floetry's "Say Yes" was on rotation and played lightly in the background as Arri pressed her back into the window frame and enjoyed the rain washing over her. Her white silk negligee stuck to her breasts like glue and instantly became see-through once the water began to saturate it, clearly revealing her deep chocolate nipples.

Thank God for being ten flights up and shielded by her fire escape, otherwise she knew she'd be giving a peep show. And she damn sure didn't give that out for free. Arri closed her eyes, and as the wet breeze blew over her breasts and down her tight stomach, it made her think about soft and wet lips and a heated tongue licking her nipples and moving down the center of her body to her clit. Slowly she moved her hands between her legs, palmed her pussy and squeezed.

Shit.

This was the pits. She'd already seen two clients for the night, but that was about business—and right now she wanted pleasure. Besides, it wasn't enough to play with herself; she needed a strong back, defined chest, massive hands, and a hard pipe to do it, and Lyfe had just the equipment.

No matter how Arri tried to shake it, he turned her on every time she laid eyes on him. She knew that if Lyfe stayed in New York much longer she would need to look for another job. And it wasn't about her dire need to have her breasts in his mouth and her hips across his dick; that she could handle and put in perspective. But she hated the wondering about what had happened in his life, the places he'd been, who took care of him, and what made him upset or nervous when he fingered his beard, what his favorite things were to eat, who cooked for him, who ran his bathwater . . . After today she knew it damn sure wasn't his wife, so who was it?

Here I go again with this shit.

Arri reached for a Black & Mild cigar on her nightstand and lit it. After a few tokes she released soft clouds of smoke into the wet indigo sky.

She closed her eyes and hoped that she would be able to sleep, but the stifling heat had her suffering from insomnia. And it didn't help any that she was home alone. Khris and her son had taken Zion with them to New Jersey to spend the weekend with her mother, leaving Arri with no one to talk to, besides herself. And truthfully, talking to herself was rocking her nerves, because all herself preached about was needing to be touched, caressed, and fucked.

Twenty minutes into her rain bath, her eyes scanned the room and spotted a picture behind the leg of her highboy. Arri rose from the window and picked up the picture. Her lips gently pushed into a smile. It was a picture of her, Darlene, and Samara, all hugging and smiling, dressed for Easter in matching MGM jumpsuits. Arri cracked up laughing as tears snuck into her eyes. She returned to the windowsill and as splashes of rain speckled onto the Polaroid, the color started to run and Arri blew against it, hoping to dry the water quickly. She turned the picture away from the window and started laughing again.

"Arri and Samara," Arri could hear Darlene's voice ring in her memory, "we is so fly." They huddled before the bathroom mirror together, all squeezing their faces in. "You two look just like ya mama"—Darlene grinned—"which means y'all gon' have problems with niggahs. So let me tell you, don't let none of 'em use you." She scanned the reflection of her daughter's eyes. "I know y'all ain't grown yet, but you got a pussy, and as long as you got a pussy, men don't see no age. So, I'ma just lay shit out to you: niggahs ain't shit. Get you a man. A man who loves you, who wants to be around you, and not just from the first to the fifth of the month. And get you a man who goes to work at nine-fuckin'-o'clock. A man who, when he makes love to you it's slow and careful, not in an alleyway with broken glass beneath your feet, but in your bed. And if a man wants you he will come and get you. Don't you dare chase his ass . . ."

Arri's face was wet with tears, this was crazy shit, and as horny as she was she didn't need any memories messing up her dick desire. She wiped her face and could feel sleep pushing on her eyelids, so she rose from the windowsill, mashed the cigar in the ashtray, and as she lay down on the bed, she heard a hard pounding on her apartment door. Instantly she was pissed. "Goddamn." She sucked her teeth. She was not in the mood for unexpected visitors or motherfuckers knocking on the wrong door tonight. "You know what," she said as her negligee stuck like papier-mâché to her skin. "We gon' end this shit tonight.

Do not come here if you didn't call and if you have the wrong apartment start looking at the damn numbers before you knock! Now, why are you here!" She snatched the door open.

Arri's eyes filled with surprise and instinctively she took a step back. "What the—?" She arched her eyebrows in disbelief. "Are you serious?" She looked Lyfe up and down twice. "What are you doing here?" She stood blocking the entrance.

"You want me to leave?" he asked her, looking deep into her eyes.

Arri couldn't answer because she knew if she opened her mouth a lie was sure to slip out and there was no way in hell she wanted to turn him away. Instead her heart played the xylophone beneath her breast, her eyes slowly undressed him, and she repeated herself, "What are you doing here?" She crossed her hands over her breasts, remembering that she was damn near naked.

"Let me ask you again, do you want me to leave?" He looked her over, his eyes stopping at her crossed arms for a moment and then returning to her face.

She paused and looked him up and down again, more shock absorbed into her body. "This is a lot of nerve."

"It is," he agreed.

"Suppose my man was here?"

"Is he?"

"No," she said too quickly, hoping like hell she didn't make it obvious that she really didn't have a man.

Lyfe gave her a crooked grin, "Fuck 'im, then."

Whatever it was—arrogance, cockiness, or the coolest fuckin' swagger that she'd ever seen that oozed from this fine-ass man standing at her door with quiet insistence and persistence that she was going to step aside and let him in—it made Arri's pussy pump repeatedly and her nipples were so hard that they ached. "So," she said, collecting herself, "are you going to tell me

why you're here or should I assume that you stalk all of your secretaries?"

"You're more than a secretary," Lyfe said seriously. "Besides,
I don't stalk my secretaries, most of 'em are old, white, overtanned, and too damn skinny. Drink vegetable smoothies all
day, L.A. shit."

Arri fought with all she could not to laugh. "Umm-hmm."

"Besides, I came here to talk," he said. "You seem to be a
good listener."

"Run that past me again." She arched her eyebrows. "You
wanna talk? About what? Didn't you just tell me, last night, you
didn't come to New York to fuck around on your wife? And now
tonight you wanna talk?" She squinted.

"Yeah, I said that." He paused and reached for Arri's hand,
locking his fingers between hers. "And I'm sorry if I hurt your
feelings or embarrassed you when I said that. But try and understand that I had to back up for a minute. Shit was going way too
fast."

"And you don't think you being at my door is pushing shit
over the edge?" She let his hand go and crossed her arms over
her breasts again.

"Isn't that where you want it to go?" He ran his index finger
from the center of her lips down her neck. "Over the edge?"

Silence.

"Listen," Lyfe continued, "if you want me to bounce, then
I'm out—and like I said before, no foul and no harm. But honestly, I came tonight because I couldn't stop thinking about you.
I couldn't shake my desire to wanna look into your beautiful
face, pretty girl, and chill with you. I'm not saying you *should* let
me in, but I'm asking you to. Because tonight—if no other
night—I need you, and I don't give a damn about what looks
good, what's right, and what's politically correct. I'm here because I wanna be here. Now," he paused, "do you want me

here?"—he placed his index finger against her lips—"and tell me in one word."

"Yes." Arri knew she'd said it too hastily and too anxiously. She was not supposed to give in. But then again, what could be the harm? He wasn't her man, and the way her pussy tingled she convinced herself that he was here to serve only one purpose.

Arri took him by the hand and walked him into her apartment. As she turned to close the door, he pulled her to his chest and whispered against her lips, "I was at Dextra's and I hope you like curry chicken."

Arri couldn't resist his lips pressed against hers, so she slid her tongue into his mouth and kissed him. Moments later it clicked. "What?" she broke their kiss, "What did you say?"

His lips lingered against hers for a moment longer. "I wasn't sure what you'd like to eat." He turned toward the hallway and lifted a plastic bag with Thank You written on the front and filled with West Indian cuisine.

"Eat?" Arri swallowed and the weight of her hard nipples felt like rocks. "You came over here to eat?" she asked, surprised.

"And to talk." He gave her devilish grin. "Why, did you have something else in mind?"

Arri looked around her living room. She swallowed hard, her pussy was so wet he could swim in it, and here he wanted to dine? She had a good mind to ask him to leave. "Sure,"—she reached for her robe that lay across the couch—"let's eat."

"You don't have to put that on," Lyfe insisted as he pointed to Arri's robe.

"See, you playin'." Arri laughed, sliding her robe on and tying it tightly around her waist. She led him to the kitchen and as Arri placed the food on the table some of the gravy splashed on her chest and dribbled down her cleavage. "Oh . . . wow." She looked at Lyfe and smirked. "Can you reach for a paper towel?"

"Sure." He handed it to her.

"My hands are full," she thrusted her bosom toward his face, "can you get it for me?"

"See," he gently wiped the gravy from her bursting cleavage, "now *you* playin'."

Arri set the table with plates, food, and glasses of merlot.

They started to eat and Lyfe said, "The next time I come over—"

"Oh, you coming over again?"

Lyfe smiled, "And you gon' let me in too. Now listen, the next time I want you to cook for me."

"Hold it, you're inviting yourself over and I have to cook for you?" Arri took a bite of her chicken.

"What's the problem?"

"The nerve." She reached her fork into his plate for a taste of his stewed beef.

"What?"

Arri laughed. "You can't be cute and cocky."

"Would you have me any other way?"

"I didn't know I had you."

Before Lyfe could say anything his cell phone rang. He knew by the ring tone that it was Payton.

"You need to get that?"

"Nah," he said, sending Payton's call to voice mail. He looked back to Arri, who was eating more of his food. "And why are you all in my food?"

"Why," she stuck her index finger into the gravy on her plate and placed it to his lips. "You want me to give you something of mine to eat?"

"Don't ask me trick questions." He licked the gravy from her finger; his heated tongue sent chills through her hand.

While they ate they found themselves talking about everything under the sun, sharing funny memories and purposely leaving out the humorless ones. "Where does your sister live now?" Lyfe asked.

Arri walked over to the kitchen window and pointed between the black iron bars. "See that corner over there, that's her living room." She then pointed to the alleyway and continued, "And over there is where she sleeps."

"Damn . . . it's like that?" Lyfe said, flabbergasted.

Arri looked at Lyfe as if he had lost his mind. "She gets high and she damn sure can't live here. Hell, she used to sneak my mom's weed and shit and smoke it."

"Damn . . . so why did you stay here?"

"After all the bullshit, I guess this is home."

"I see," he nodded.

Arri didn't like where this was going. All this talk about her sister and her past was blowing the high she had from Lyfe's enchanting aura. . . .

She got up to clear the table, and then headed into the living room and turned on the TV. She called to Lyfe, "Are you coming?"

Lyfe stared at her; he knew she'd purposely changed the subject so he rolled with it. "Sure."

When he reached the living room Lyfe pointed to the TV. "Oh, hell yeah, *Star Trek* is on."

"Boy," she laughed, as they lay together on the couch, neither one of them thinking twice about the position they naturally assumed. Arri pushed her back to Lyfe's chest, "What you know about Darth Vader and Spock?"

Lyfe chuckled as he wrapped Arri in his arms. "First off, Darth Vader is from *Star Wars,* Willis, and Spock was a li'l Mexican named Gomez on *Star Trek.*"

Arri fell out laughing, his delicious cologne made love to her nose, "Yo' ass is silly. Now, you may have me on the Darth Vader, but Spock's last name Gomez? Please, he was a Jenkins."

"Pretty girl, you watch too many movies. Don't listen to Eddie Murphy, listen to me. Spock was Mexican and when immigration came looking for him he ran to space."

Arri laughed so hard she cried. "Please be quiet."

"Let me ask you a question." Lyfe stroked her hair. "You ever think about running away and never coming back?"

Arri turned in his arms to face him. "No," she said seriously. "If I ran away, then I'd be just like Darlene and Samara."

"Who was Darlene?"

"My mother, who left me and my sister here to fend for ourselves."

"How old were you?"

"Twelve."

"What?" Lyfe said, stunned. "Who did you live with? Who took care of you?"

"What do you mean? I took care of me. Don't worry, I was a good girl," she said sarcastically. "I went to school every day."

Lyfe sighed. "Damn . . . I wish I could have known you then, protected you."

"Don't," Arri said, as a memory of Ian once saying the same thing crept into her mind. "Don't make promises you can't keep."

"How do you know what I can't keep."

"Because I've heard that before."

"Not from me."

"Let's just chill," she said, "because by morning I'm sure you'll no longer be mad with your wife and you'll be out of here."

"I'm here because I want to be here."

"Then let's chill, please." She kissed him on the lips.

"You have a bad habit of running away from shit that you really need to deal with. But I'ma let you get that." He responded to her kisses. "Especially since I know you can't resist me."

"What?" Arri smirked.

"Who could resist me; after all, I'm fine as hell." He nibbled against her neck.

"You are really on your own sack right now."

"I'm just stating a fact. And you know it; look at me and tell me I'm not fine."

Arri drank in every ounce of him and just when she was about to tell him he was average-looking—nothing to write home about—the truth took over her mouth, and she said, "You're fine as hell . . . but you don't look better than me."

"Yeah, whatever," he joked, "you know you all up on me, girl."

"Oh, please, Mr. Yuppie Stalker, you broke your ass up in here, so don't get carried away." She waved her finger.

Lyfe kissed her earlobe and smacked her on the ass. "You wanted me to stalk you. And let me check you on this real quick: I am far from being yuppie or whatever other titles you keep tossing in my face."

"Oh please."

"Please, what? I'm serious."

"So you from the hood in California and somehow floated to the top. I get it, so spare me the 'I'm still down' shit. It's wearing thin." Arri knew what she'd said might've come off a little harsh—this was her boss after all—but after all this talk about Darlene, Samara, and thoughts of Ian, she wasn't in the best control of her emotions. The pain of being abandoned by everyone she'd loved was a festering wound deep down in her chest, so she continued.

"So while you were off living the high life with your trophy wife, do you know what I've been doing? I've learned that at the end of the day, no matter how hard I try, cry, or aim to please, nobody owes me a motherfuckin' thing. Period. Okay? So please stop pretending, because we both know that you being hood or knowing what struggling is doesn't go beyond the city you once lived in and you remembering how to speak slang."

Lyfe swallowed the digs she'd just carved into his chest. He cleared his throat and said, "Hear me on this, all of this fat ass," he smacked her ass, "got me a li'l open, but I ain't on it to the point of pretending. I came from nothing. Absolutely nothing. I don't even know if the house we lived in as kids was ours or an abandoned, city-condemned shack that my mother stumbled upon and had us all squat in."

"Lyfe—"

"I'm talking," he said sternly. "Now let me put you on to something you don't need to forget; I'm a grown-ass man and I don't have to impress you with bullshit, I know who I am and if you have a problem with it, then fuck it."

Arri sighed; it was not supposed to go south like this and she knew she needed to be cool and enjoy the warmth of lying in his arms. Especially since this was the tightest, yet the gentlest, she'd been held in years. His arms fit completely around her and she loved the way her head felt against his chest—beautifully protected, like she didn't have to worry about falling, or failing, or fucking up, because finally she'd found the man that her mother spoke to her about that Easter—one of the few days she'd ever seen Darlene sober—the very man her mother told her would come looking for her. She'd found him, ball and chained and someone else carrying his last name . . . but she'd found him.

And she knew by lying in his defined arms that she needed to just let the chips fall where they may. And she had to hurry and live this experience, before the fear of falling in love again snuck in and shut her emotions down, before that moment came when she would tell her heart to kiss her ass, and that being in the arms of this man—this married man, her married *boss*—was a bunch of dumb, ridiculous, and predictable shit.

"I'm sorry," spilled from her lips.

"Accepted," he said, kissing her on her forehead. "Now listen"—he pointed to the TV and restored the lighter tone of their conversation—"see the black chick on *Star Trek*?"

Arri turned back toward the TV. "Yeah," she said as a smile oozed through her voice. "What about her?"

"You know Spock was hittin' her off."

Arri playfully sucked her teeth. "He was not hittin' her off."

"Oh," Lyfe said taken aback, "he can hit off the green chicks from Saturn but he can't hit off the black one from Earth? Is that what you're saying?"

"It's a conspiracy, baby." Arri pushed her ass deeper into his shaft.

"Funny."

"And anyway, what does that have to do with anything?"

"Her last name was Jenkins."

Arri laughed so hard that water filled her mouth. "That is such bullshit."

Lyfe squeezed her tight and locked her in place by folding his fingers between hers.

Arri kissed the muscle closest to her lips. "I'm glad you're here." She traced the bulging vein that made a winding road down Lyfe's bicep.

"I'm glad to be here." He stroked her hair. "And given the fucked-up day that I had—"

"You wanna talk about that?"

"Nah, I don't wanna deal with that right now. Especially since I've tried all night to get peace and to silence my thoughts, and no matter how hard I tried, nothing worked, until I got here. After you stopped giving me the gas face, that is, like I was about to rob you and shit."

Arri smirked. "Hell, this is Brooklyn." She pulled Lyfe's arms even tighter around her, snuggled the deepest that she could into his chest. He stroked her hair and placed his left leg along the side of hers and they laid in silence until they drifted to sleep and the early morning sun lay a fan of golden rays over them.

California

The night lights of downtown Los Angeles sparkled overhead as Payton held a martini glass to her lips and lounged on her cliffside terrace. She wondered how it would feel to be by herself . . . forever. Would it be quiet and filled with deep, moving, and inspiring thoughts? Or would she yearn for more, desire love, and be bitten with the fear of dying alone?

She ran the tip of her index finger around the rim of her glass and wrestled against the pain taking up space in her throat. She fought like hell to hold back the tears sneaking out the corners of her eyes, so she quickly wiped them, careful not to smear her mascara. She swallowed what remained and internally lectured herself that crying was for the weak; she had too much to lose to be reduced to a bumbling fool. She hadn't made it this far by being emotionally exposed; she'd conquered it by ruling with an iron fist and taking no shorts.

Why the tears anyway? Certainly, I love Lyfe, but not enough to break. Not enough to put aside all I've built, all I've ever been. Payton's mother told her that love was for a feeble and easily influenced bitch, but that a smart bitch knew marriage was for advancement and privileges, status, and recognition. But Payton didn't listen, instead this time she married for love, good dick, and companionship.

Which was the real reason she didn't think twice about making Lyfe vice president. It certainly never occurred to her that he'd actually act like he *deserved* such a career path—working seven days a week, twelve-hour shifts, and warping before her eyes into the crème de la crème of businessmen. Why didn't he understand that that was not what she'd groomed him for. Hell, she could run her own fuckin' company. She'd only given him the position for the sake of looking up to par to the outside world, but within their bubble he was to be a doting husband, who was there to love her when she came home from a hard day at work, there to listen to her, understand her, and adore her—not to challenge the shots she called. He was supposed to be her man, at her beck and call, the one who loved her, flaws and all, and his opinion was supposed to remain buried underneath his admiration of her.

But it wasn't.

Lyfe was his own man, with his own hopes and dreams, and he wouldn't allow the job she'd given him to be for show. He had the audacity to want to work and the nerve to learn how to handle the investment banking machine better than anyone she knew. And once he got his confidence up, all of a sudden his thoughts became twisted and he started talking too fuckin' much, expecting *her* to cook for *him* and ruin her body by bearing his goddamn babies.

She didn't sign up for that shit.

Where was the appreciation? The sense of obligation? The gratitude?

Why was she sitting here, right now, as if she were desperate, clutching her cell phone in her palm, waiting, wondering, and burning up on the inside because he had yet to return any of her calls?

This was bullshit.

Where was this motherfucker, huh? And why was he so hard-pressed not to come the fuck home? He hated New York. Hated it. So why all of a sudden was he swingin' his balls and digging in her back that he was going to stay? And moreover, when did he decide that he was bold enough to ignore her phone calls?

"I don't believe this bullshit!" she bolted out, unable to keep it bottled in for a moment longer.

"What?" Dominique blinked. "Believe what bullshit? What are you talking about?" She placed her martini on the terra-cotta floor and looked at Payton, who sat across from her in the chaise lounge. "Have you been listening to a word that I've said?"

Payton focused in on Dominique; for the few moments that Payton was in deep thought, she'd forgotten that Dominique was there.

Payton batted her eyes and dipped the olive on the end of her stirrer into her drink. "What are you talking about, Dominique?" She ate the olive. "Of course I'm listening to you."

"Then tell me," Dominique practically pleaded, "what I should do?"

"About what?" Payton frowned, her tone making it quite evident that Dominique was working her nerves.

"About Quinton," Dominique quipped.

"What about him?"

"Okay, you're pissing me off. Here I am confiding in you and you're not even listening to me."

"Look," Payton leaned forward, "what do you want me to tell you? That it'll be okay? That love conquers all? Some Cinderella, princess and the frog bullshit?"

"I want the truth."

Payton quipped, "You know better than anyone that Quinton isn't shit. How many years have we been holding this conversation, huh? Do something else besides feel sorry for yourself."

"And what?" Dominique said, pissed, the scent of Payton's perfume burning her nose. "Be like you? It's not exactly any secret that your husband isn't feeling your ass either, my dear."

"It isn't my husband that you need to be concerned with. And furthermore, if it's no secret that my husband isn't," she made air quotes, "feeling me, then why are you sitting in my fuckin' face asking me for advice?"

Dominique hesitated, the truth of the matter was she had no explanation as to why she was here.

"How in the hell you ended up with a husband like Quinton," Payton continued, "I will never know. But I do know this, you better get your ass on board with every other bitch who's married into fame and fortune and accept Quinton's money in exchange for his short attention span and tolerance for your ass. Stop concentrating on the disdain and distaste in his eyes and go shopping, go hang out, have your ass a one-night stand, for crying out loud! Shit."

"Unlike you, I took my set of marriage vows seriously."

"Dominique," Payton said sweetly, "honey, maybe you should've been more like me, then you'd have it together. Otherwise you should've married Joe Blow the city bus driver if you wanted to demand fidelity. But when you marry seven figures and higher, there is some shit you just have to deal with, and your man possibly fuckin' somebody else is one of them. Don't be concerned with who he's doin', be concerned when he's mistreating you, ignoring your calls . . . or his ass falls in *love* with somebody else. *Then* all bets are off. Get a life of your own, outside of those damn Chihuahuas and those twins. Geezuz. You've had his sons, now move on to the next staying-rich trick: stash you some cash and relax. Let Quinton think it's all good, and then when you have enough money on the side, you can flex your tolerance level." She flicked her hand. "But until then," she laid back in the lounge, took her shades from her hair, and slid them on, "shut . . . the . . . fuck . . . up."

Dominique sat in shock. "I wish like hell you had stayed gone."

"I thought you were leaving."

"I am," Dominique threw over her shoulder as she stormed

to her candy-apple-red Mercedes minivan, parked in the drive-way.

Payton finished off her martini as she watched Dominique disappear into the distance.

A few minutes later, her cell phone rang. It was her mother. She stared at the caller ID and just as she decided to ignore the call, "Finally, she left," floated from behind Payton. "You need to tell Dominique that she has to call before she comes here," Quinton said, filling the doorway. "How long has she been gone?"

"She left a few minutes before you," Payton said without flinching.

"What did she want?" He paused. "Wait a minute, what do you mean, a few minutes before me?"

"Because you're leaving," Payton said, staring off into the distance. "Get your shit. New York was a bust and I've had enough."

"Payton—"

"Don't say good-bye." She waved him off. "Just let me hear your car leaving the garage." She closed her eyes, and lay back. "I'll call you when I'm in the mood."

California

Dominique sat with her heart racing in her chest and the seat's leather cushion sticking to her ass. She'd been sitting at Cocktails, a rooftop bar and lounge in downtown Los Angeles, for over an hour; nursing the heartache that sat between her breasts with shots of tequila chased with glasses of pinot grigio. The same ache that had convinced her that maybe Payton had a point.

So she went home, changed into a pair of hourglass fitting spandex pants, a cleavage-clinging corset, and spiked heels, and came here, hoping to clear her mind.

But nothing worked and the longer Dominique sat the more she thought about calling her driver to take her home; after all, her mind told her that this was pointless.

Dominique's eyes roamed the club and she spotted a tall and strapping brother, the color of midnight, with distinguished African tribal features, and a coal black goatee. He took a seat across from her at the bar and gave Dominique a soft wink. Though she tried to fight it she couldn't help but return his gesture with a smile. Dominique could tell that he was waiting for another clue that it would be okay for him to approach her, but she didn't give him one; instead, she diverted her eyes and looked away.

She placed her clutch beneath her arm and stood to leave.

"You would actually leave before I was able to buy you a drink?" Dominique turned toward the voice and it was the same man she'd noticed earlier, the only difference between now and then was that he was even prettier standing this close.

Dominique blushed and he continued, "At least one drink and then you leave." He looked her over and his eyes clearly told her that he thought she was beautiful.

His deep voice made her nipples hard. "Sure." She smiled. "Why not?" She sat back down. "I'll have a glass of pinot grigio."

Dominique watched him walk to the bar and wondered what it would be like to fuck someone besides Quinton and disregard her marriage. Would it feel sweet and nice, or wicked and high? Would she regret doing it? Would she enjoy the one-night stand hittin' her G-spot . . . or would she run out of the room, too consumed by guilt and confusion.

"Mind if I sit here?" he said as he placed her glass of wine and a frosty bottle of Heineken on the table, and pointed to the empty chair.

"Not at all." She smiled.

"What's your name, beautiful?"

She blushed. "Dominique."

"Sexy name," he said smoothly as they locked gazes, his voice deeper than any base drum. "I'm sure I'll enjoy screaming that later."

"Later?" Dominique looked taken aback.

"Oh my mistake," he said, "I guess I assumed that we would be together later."

The motherfucker was bold . . . sexy as hell . . . but bold as shit. "And your name is?" Dominique's nipples felt like rocks.

"Mandingo." He laughed and she imagined that he was telling the truth. "Nah," he continued, "it's Terrance."

Dominique looked him over, her eyes stopping at the imprint of the wedding band on his left index finger. She wondered if she should ask the obvious but then she quickly decided that she needed this moment to throw caution to the wind, to not be so goddamn careful, to for once not give a fuck . . . or to give a fuck to a man who wasn't her husband. She could feel her panties become moist as she tried desperately to keep a steady tone. His heated breath caused her pussy to pump twice, as he brushed his soft hand over hers. "Where's he at?" he pointed to her wedding band.

Dominique hesitated. "Who?"

"Your husband."

"Oh . . . umm, home . . . well, he's working."

"And you came here alone?"

"You ask an awful lot of questions." She chuckled nervously.

"How else am I going to find out what I want to know?"

She blushed. "You have an East Coast accent. Where are you from?"

"New York, but I'm at a business convention." He stroked her hair behind her ear.

"Really?" Dominique said, intrigued. "What kind of business?" she asked, catching sneak peeks of his chest hair through his slightly open Polo shirt.

"Investigative. What do you do?"

Dominique hesitated. "I used to sell real estate," she said excitedly.

"You should get back into it."

She chuckled. "Yeah sure, in between chasing my cheating-ass husband and four-year-old twins, I don't have time—" Dominique stopped midsentence. Already she'd been running her mouth too goddamn much. She looked into his eyes and for whatever reason she felt like her reveal hadn't turned him off. "So, there you have it," she said, pissed more with herself than with his inquisitiveness.

"Will this be your first affair?"

"What?" Dominique said, clearly caught off guard.

"Tonight, when I take you back to my hotel room with me, will it be your first affair. I swear, I would love to be your first."

Dominique took a moment and then she said quietly, "Yes."

"Well," he grabbed her hand, "you're overdue."

This was crazy; it was bad enough that she'd told too much of her business but now she was sitting here with a fine-ass stranger who'd just given her an open invitation to fuck. Her eyes roamed his body. She knew that she wanted him . . . she just didn't know if she needed to accept his invite. Being heartbroken didn't equal ho . . . or did it, at least for one night?

"Dominique," he took her hand, "throw caution on its ass." He kissed her palm; the tip of his tongue pressed against her skin. She wondered if he would lay it against her clit the same way if he were licking it.

Her pussy trembled. "I think I better get going." She stood to leave. "Thanks for the evening." She tucked her clutch beneath her arm. She walked a short distance away and turned around. "Aren't you supposed to be leading the way?"

Terrance smiled and he nodded his head. "After you, madam."

It was a one-night stand, no question about it. Dominique was fine with accepting their time together for what it was, because for right now her yearning to be touched outweighed regret. From the time they entered the doorway of his hotel suite, they were kissing, undressing, and tossing their clothes all over the room.

Dominique didn't want to give herself time to think, because too many thoughts would force her to question what she was really doing here and why she wasn't at home mothering her children and trying her hand at getting things back on track with her husband. Yet if she thought about that, really thought about that, then she would be pulling her hard nipple from between Terrance's lips, getting her things, and leaving. But that's not what she wanted to do. She wanted to fuck Terrance, bang the hell out of him, ride his dick, suck it, and cum all over it. And she wanted to pretend that Quinton was watching Terrance sink his thick and fat inches into her mouth, as Dominique slid to her knees.

Dominique imagined that if Quinton could see her licking the sticky head of Terrance's smoke-black dick and sucking each and every crevice of the fat mushroom tip, he would flip.

Terrance swerved his shaft against her mouth, as she moved her tongue like a hissing snake trying to catch its prey. Dominique loved the way he smacked her in the lips with his dick, forcing her to beg for more. "Come on, baby, let me suck it." She gripped it tightly between her cheeks. The heaviness of his member weighed sweetly on her tongue as his pelvis contracted and he laced her mouth with salty drippings.

Dominique looked into his eyes and swallowed, wildly licking the residue from her lips. Terrance lifted her onto the bed, parted her legs and went directly to sucking her clit. He nibbled just a bit; enough to make her pussy drip.

Dominique panted and within a few minutes her nut was butter between his lips. She raked her nails down the center of Terrance's back as she watched the way his black skin curled over her honey-glazed voluptuous body. The feeling he gave her was lovely and the thought of Quinton finding out where she was, forcing his way into this room, and witnessing what she was doing, made her cum more and harder than she ever had before in her life.

Terrance whipped Dominique around in the wheelbarrow position and fucked her from the back. Dominique loved the way his hips whipped her ass, as she screamed and called his name, "Terraaaaaaance!"

"What?" he held her ankles together. "You needed this dick.

Pussy all tight and shit. What? That ma'fucker ain't hittin' it? Well, don't worry, I'ma knock it down for him." He pounded into her ass.

Dominique heard what he'd said but the fact that she was cumming all over again made her mind spin and "Shhh . . ." was all she could manage to have fall from her lips, as blood rushed to her head.

He thrusted her with a hard hip, and Dominique could feel her pelvis tightening, as he pulled her onto her back and they fucked until the sun came up.

When Dominique arrived home, she prayed like hell that Quinton was there and for once they would argue about where she'd been all night. Her heels clicked loudly as she walked into their bedroom, where he opened his eyes and stared at her. "This how we droppin' it?" he asked her. Meeting her at the door.

"Droppin' what?" She attempted to pass him and he blocked her path.

"Why are you smelling like hotel soap?" He squinted his nose.

"I don't know what you're talking about." She fought like hell not to smile. She turned her back to him and as she attempted to pass him again he wrapped his arm around her neck and slammed her violently into the wall. "What the fuck you call yourself doin', Dominique, huh?"

She started to explain it to him in vivid detail, but the wave of fear that came over her wouldn't allow her to say much more in between her tears than, "I was out thinking and—"

He gripped her neck. "I haven't kicked your ass in a long time, but I will! Don't fuckin' play with me. You understand, you ain't been here all night and all of a sudden you walk in here smelling of hotel soap."

"Quinton—"

He gripped her chin roughly and spat, "Don't take your ass nowhere else without asking me, you understand? Because the next time I'ma whup yo' ass," he mushed her in the forehead, "and I mean that."

Her tears rolled over his fist.

"This is exactly why I don't touch your fat ass, because you are always doing some stupid shit." He released his grip on her chin. She could tell that this was about much more than her being out all night. He'd been pissed about whatever had happened to him last night and roughing her up was the easiest way to get it off his chest. "And don't ask me for no fuckin' money—"

"You know I need money for the boys this week, Quinton, and—"

"You should've thought about that on your way in here." He turned away and she noticed that he still wore the same clothes he had on yesterday. Now she knew for sure this had nothing to do with where she'd been.

"Where are you going?" she called behind him as he walked out of the room.

"I'm going out to think." She heard his car keys jingling in his hand and a few moments later the front door slammed.

New York

Lyfe sank deep into the cushions beneath him and pulled the soft blanket up to his chin. He couldn't help but smile as the scent of sausages, eggs, pancakes, and fresh-brewed coffee floated under his nose, and that's when it hit him: he wasn't in his hotel suite. Lyfe opened his eyes one at a time, and scanned his surroundings, from the massive black bookcase, filled with children's books and pictures of a little boy, to the black artwork that lined the cream-colored walls. There was no view of the New York City skyline, no wake-up call, and room service wasn't knocking on the door.

Instead, it was a view of a school, and a few people chilling on the block. The phone was there but it wasn't ringing; he was in a home, a real home, not a cold mansion on the cliffside of Holmby Hills, California. Not a five-star hotel suite, but a home where someone lived, loved, and had memories. And the food he smelled was home-cooked, something he hadn't had since he was sixteen and his brother failed at the attempt.

Lyfe pushed the cover back and sat up on the couch. He looked at his shirt, which lay on the side of the chair, and decided against putting it on right away. He slid his bare feet down the short hallway toward the kitchen and on his way he spotted a little boy's bedroom filled with toys and Spider-Man decorations everywhere: the walls, the bed, the curtains, the rug on the floor. He peeked in Arri's bedroom: a highboy, queen-size bed with a white leather, seven-foot-tall headboard, and all white linens—from the bed skirt to the comforter to the half-dozen pillows that decorated it. There was a leopard chaise and drapes hung to the floor and a petite chandelier hung from the ceiling.

Once Lyfe reached the kitchen, he stood in the doorway and leaned against the frame. He looked Arri over; she was now dressed in a mid-thigh, purple tie-dye dress that wrapped around her breasts like a tube top, and her cleavage poured out as if she had on a corset.

"Good morning." She smiled and handed Lyfe a cup of coffee with no sugar and a splash of cream.

"Good morning." He nodded, looking her over and accepting the coffee. "Guess I don't need to ask if you still respect me in the morning." He sipped his coffee.

"Guess not." Arri smiled as her eyes traced from the tattoo of a green-eyed panther on his left peck to the one that covered his right shoulder and stopped midway on his triceps.

"I'ma go and grab my gym bag out the truck," Lyfe said, calling for Arri's attention.

"Oh, okay." She blinked, returning her eyes to his face.

A few minutes later Lyfe returned and Arri motioned for him to sit at the table.

"So tell me,"—he smiled as she sat a full plate of sausages, eggs, and strawberry-topped pancakes on his plate—"who has a thing for Spider-Man?" he asked her as he began to eat.

"My man."

Lyfe practically spit out his food, "What?"

"My man, he's a collector," Arri said as she walked over to Lyfe with a fork in her hand. Boldly, she sat on Lyfe's dick, his morning hard-on felt like a massage against her ass. She stuck her fork into his plate and began to eat a piece of his sausage.

"Are you serious?" Lyfe asked.

"Umm-hmm." She nodded. "Now taste this." Arri placed a strawberry to his lips.

Lyfe took a bite. "So, what is he, pretending to be a kid?" he said sarcastically.

Arri smiled. "Pretty much." She wiped his lips with a napkin and fed him more of the strawberry.

"So how old is he?"

"You are nosy." She laughed. "But since you're dying to know, he's five."

"Five?"

"Yes, and his name is Zion."

"You have a son?" Lyfe asked.

"No, my nephew. My sister had a baby, she couldn't take care of him, so I'm raising him. Long story."

"Oh, wow, okay," Lyfe said as her luscious ass more than filled his lap. Lyfe placed his hands on her waist and ran them from her waist to her thighs. He lined kisses along the back of her neck and shoulder blades.

"I understand," he cupped her breasts and squeezed her nipples, "one of my sisters had the same type of shit going on." He slowly undid the tuck that held her dress together. "Found her with a needle in her arm. She died the same way my mother did. My brother has her kids."

"Really?" Arri said, surprised, as she locked her fingers between Lyfe's and together they ran their hands along the sides of her breasts and around to her nipples.

"Listen," Lyfe said, lifting Arri onto the table and knocking everything on it, including his unfinished food, to the tiles below, "I don't wanna talk about that shit no more." The dishes crashed and broke into a zillion pieces on the floor. "I'll replace 'em." He sat Arri on the edge of the table with her legs spread, facing him. He reached his hands beneath her dress, pulled her G-string off, and tossed it to the floor.

"Lyfe," she moaned as her pussy played double Dutch between her thighs. "Let's go in my bedroom."

"Nah," he said, as he slowly licked her clitoris ring, and then made his way over her jelly mountain. "We 'spose to eat at the table."

Instantly Lyfe knew she was worth the chance he was taking. She was the taste of heaven and her butterscotch was thick as he sucked the Jell-O—like firmness of her clit. "Damn, this pussy." He sucked her fat lips, doing all he could to fit them both into his mouth; and then sucking one lip at a time, while journeying two of his fingers into the land of never-ending wetness.

He opened her vulva and blew inside. "Such a pretty pussy," Lyfe moaned as he discovered what flavor pussy whipped came in.

Punanny like this was of another world, reincarnated from another time, a metaphoric high.

Shit. He smacked her on the ass and it jingled against his face.

"Lyfe . . . ummmm . . . baby." Arri placed her hands along the sides of his cheeks. Her hands moved with the movement of his mouth. "Damn."

He knew she was about to cum by the way she gripped the back of his neck, so he curled his tongue inside of her heated sex like a straw and sucked every ounce of liquid she had.

Lyfe stood up and unbuckled his pants revealing his beautiful prize. He kissed Arri on the lips, as her mouth dropped open. She grabbed his dick and stroked it.

Never in her life had she seen a dick this size. This was the dick that most women waited on a special dildo delivery to get, but she had it right here, and it was real, attached to a fine-ass man, who stood at the edge of her kitchen table holding her by her waist and preparing her pussy for the taste.

Arri could tell by the size that it would hurt going inside, but it was fine, she liked to play with pleasure and pain. Lyfe rubbed his dick in her wetness, and then he slowly entered her, both of them gasping, and pausing, and losing their train of thought as he ventured through her tightness and landed at her G-spot, where she began to scream, as he lifted her legs to his chest. "Damn, this shit is tight," he said as he cupped her breasts and bit into her skin.

This was crazy and they both liked—scratch that, they both loved being at the kitchen table, food splattered everywhere, and both of them calling out the other's name. This was sweetly insane, especially when Lyfe pulled Arri into the chair with him, where he curled her nipples into his mouth, and she rode his dick, as if she were a locomotive.

A few minutes into them making moaning music, Lyfe lifted Arri by the waist and held her for a brief moment aloft; he looked at the creamy evidence she'd left on his dick and said, "Look at that shit." He slid her back down on his lap and a few seconds later she turned around, placed her hands on the floor and threw her hips in a spinning dance move.

"Fuck!" Lyfe screamed, squeezing her ass cheeks. He slid his dick out, tossed her salad, and then he stood up and entered her again. He thrusted into her harder than he ever had or ever imagined that he could and her ass smacked his shaft, forcing the friction between them to scream out, until their levies broke and their rivers overflowed, hers sliding down her thighs and his all over her ass.

"Damn," he said as she turned around to face him and his dick immediately became hard again. "Now," he said, as she wrapped her legs around his waist, "we can go in your bedroom."

After making love all over the apartment until noon, they had one last stop: the shower. Lyfe watched the water cascade over Arri's hair, down her neck, and over her shoulders as she slid her kisses down the center of his chest, over his navel, and to his member. She slid all ten inches of him into her mouth with such precision and ease that Lyfe thought for sure he'd found her calling. Her mouth was like hot honey and her tongue talents superseded any others that he'd once called the best. The best was right here, a Brooklyn mami, with a New York state of mind, between his knees, blowing the strength out of him, and leaving him with no choice but to lean forward and place his hands through the shower's waterfall, and assume the Miranda rights position.

"This dick is sooo fuckin' big," she said as she licked, and then consumed his entire shaft in her mouth.

Lyfe looked down and watched Arri's mouth fuck his dick, as his blood rushed through his veins and cum trickled from the tip like an IV drip. "I'm 'bout to cum, shit," Lyfe moaned.

Arri grabbed his dick and just as it started to spray, she said, "Spin the silk right here, Daddy. Right here." She directed the tip of his dick to leave creamy strings around her nipples and between her cleavage.

"Look at that shit." Lyfe smiled and looked down as the shower ran over Arri's shoulders and washed his candy away.

Afterward, he lifted Arri by the waist, hoisted her in the corner of the shower and for the next hour they became a choir speaking some songs in tongues and others with the refrain, "Fuck me harder."

It took Lyfe two sunsets to remember just how much of a bitch reality was, especially when he wanted to bask in the illusion that nothing else existed except Arri and the bubble they were in, where they talked, laughed, made love, cooked, went bowling, made love, went to the movies, made love, went out to dinner, and made love. But then the Monday morning sun showed up, and Lyfe's cell phone continued to ring at a frenzied rate.

Lyfe stared at Payton's number on his caller ID, but he didn't answer; instead he clasped the phone in his palm and sent her to voice mail once again. He hated that no matter how hard he tried to fight against it, his mind had reset and he was back to being Lyfe Carrington, vice president of Anderson Global—the married vice president—who instead of going back and confronting his wife about what she'd done, went on an excursion and fucked his way through the aggravation, with his *secretary*, no less.

Now he was confused, because he didn't know what to call what he felt for Arri, but whatever it was he knew the shit was dangerous because it was too sweet and too deep to go away. Arri made him feel at home.

But coming home to her was not his life and she wasn't his wife. His wife was in California, blowing his cell phone up and filling his voice mail with ridiculous-ass messages.

There was no question that Lyfe had to leave here. There was no more forgetting about tomorrow. He could no longer be on the wings of a new pussy high; instead he needed to get back to dealing with how fucked-up things really were.

Arri kept her eyes closed and pretended to be asleep as her mind tossed and turned about how this weekend had been too good to remain true. This was the very shit she didn't want to happen. She wished Lyfe had never come over, or bigger than that, she wished that he had never come to New York. How was she going to go back to seeing him at work? What was she going to do with all of the laughs, memories, hopes, and wishes they shared? She wished she had slammed the door in his face instead of wasting days in the belly of an emotional setup, where now—at this very moment—her chest became full and she listened to Lyfe's footsteps ease out of the room to the front door, where the automatic locks clicked in place behind him.

California

The only light in her master suite streamed in from the night sky and shadowed off the cordless phone's number pad. Payton's four-inch python pumps kissed the blond carpet as she paced from the balcony to the bedroom door, back and forth. Her thoughts burned through her mind and lingered in her chest as she cradled the phone in one hand and gripped a double shot of Grey Goose vodka in the other.

It had been an entire weekend and she had yet to hear from this motherfucker, not a text, a voice mail message, a phone call . . . nothing. Absolutely nothing. She'd gone from being slightly on edge to full-fledged ballistic, leaving message after message, until she was in an unkempt tizzy.

Payton stumbled just a bit, one too many vodka shots disrupting her balance. She dialed Lyfe's number once again and a few seconds later she was directed by his voice mail to leave a message.

She thought about hanging up, but then a voice in her head told her to try this one last time, and to be nice and soft, perhaps it would get his attention and he would call her back. Payton swallowed an ounce of her drunken pride, "Lyfe," she said into his voice mail, "this is Payton, we need to talk."

She waited five minutes and after getting no response she tried again . . . and again . . . and then she screamed into his voice mail, "I will not be ignored!" She hung up and quickly called back, "We just really need to talk."

She waited an hour and no response. She picked up the phone and this time instead of it ringing she was sent immediately to his voice mail, and just as a ball of flames filled her mouth and she was bent to spit fire out, the robotic voice of his message system said, "You cannot leave a message because this user's voice mail box is full."

"What the fuck!" she screamed at the top of her lungs, tossing her phone across the room. This had taken her completely out of her zone and she needed to find a way to bring this motherfucker to his knees. After all, she was in charge, and she didn't sweat, or carry around unneeded stress, and the fact that she was standing here going through changes when she was the puppeteer was unacceptable. She handled the strings and Anderson Global was her fuckin' company.

Payton looked at the clock; it was eight a.m. in New York. She sniffed and wiped her face. "Okay, motherfucker," she said, and walked over and picked up her phone off the floor, "you wanna play hardball." She reared her shoulders back and dialed a number. "Well let's get ready to rumble."

New York

"Good morning," Lyfe nodded as he stepped onto the elevator and stood behind two armed security guards, with the words Big Brother's Watching Inc. painted in neon yellow letters on the back of their navy blue uniform shirts. Lyfe sipped his coffee, careful not to splash it on the lapel of his Jack Spade trench coat, as thoughts of Arri and what he would say to her this morning pushed to the forefront of his mind.

He wished a thousand times that shit between them could be different. Maybe if he didn't have so much rocking his brain with Payton acting insane, or if he weren't confused about what he was going to do and where his marriage was headed—perhaps if those things didn't take precedence he could fuck Arri and keep it in perspective. But he couldn't.

"Fuck it." Lyfe shook his thoughts away. His morning was already off to a late start and he didn't need to continue beating himself up over some bullshit he couldn't control. "Excuse me," he said to the security guards, as he attempted to pass them.

Instead of responding they exited the elevator as well, walking the same beaten path as Lyfe, and once they arrived at Anderson Global's glass doors, they pushed them open and Lyfe's eyes scanned over them. "Excuse me," Lyfe said, walking in front of the guards, "may I help you?" He stopped them in the foyer.

"We're here to provide backup," one of the guards said.

"For what?" Lyfe frowned.

"Back here, guys," said an unknown guard with a Big Brother's Watching Inc. uniform on. He stood in the doorway of the partition that separated the employees from the foyer and the main receptionist area, causing Lyfe to spin around quickly and notice a sea of boxes, and an uproar that brewed behind him. "What . . . the . . . fuck . . ."—he turned around and walked in where his employees were—"is going on here!" There were four armed security guards standing in the center of the floor, watching his employees pack all of their things in cardboard boxes. Most of the employees were visibly pissed; there were some crying, and others outright cursing the guards.

"Oh here he is!" one of the accountants said, and pointed to Lyfe. "It's good to know that you think this is an occasion to drink goddamn coffee and shit."

Lyfe looked confused, and turned toward Arri, who was also packing her things. He walked over to her and said, "What's going on?"

"Your wife called this morning and fired the entire office. The guards were here waiting for us when we came in and they instructed us to get our shit and get out."

"What?" Lyfe blinked. "Wait a minute." He pulled out his cell phone, dialed Payton's number, and his call went directly to her voice mail. "Shit!"

"Mr. Carrington," poured tearfully from behind him. He turned around and it was his mail clerk, Terell. "I got, I got," he stuttered, "I ga-ga-ga-got six-six-six-kids and a set of ghetto twins on the way. And I ja-ja-ja-just got straight with child support—"

"Six!" Anna, one of the secretaries from accounting screamed, storming across the room. "Motherfucker, you told me that you had only two children when you moved in with me. And who the hell are those twins by? And when the hell you start stuttering?"

"He said ghetto twins, honey. That means two pregnant mamas," Khris said. "I told y'all last week at the copy machine that he was on the creep with Donna."

The floor became silent for a brief moment and suddenly Anna charged toward Donna, but was halted by one of the guards. "You messing with my man, trick! You silly bitch, I'ma kick yo' ass!"

"You won't be doing shit to me!" Donna started screaming, and then turned toward Terell. "I can't believe you're doing this, Terell! You told me my baby was the only one!"

"You just been creeping your ass all through the office, huh?" Anna spat, reaching over the guard's shoulder for Terell. "It's okay, 'cause I'ma bust yo' ass up. Fucked-up, no credit, having no money, moochin' ass, dick like a nine-year-old-li'l-boy-ma'fucker! I tell you what, you better get some of these fuckin' boxes and one of these guards to come move your ass from my crib, 'cause it's about to be a deadly-ass situation, motherfucker."

"Oh my Jesus," Mare-Hellen said. "Well, I'll just have to clutch my pearls, an office full of freaks living in sin. That's why the wrath is upon us. All y'all going to hell."

"And where you going, Mare-Hellen?" Khris spat, " 'cause word is, he was tappin' your wrinkled-ass pussy too!"

"That was before I was saved. And my pussy ain't wrinkled. Don't make me lose my religion"—she took her tambourine from her box and shook it—" 'cause I will."

"Whatever." Khris waved her off. "I don't have the time to deal with this bullshit. We don't have a job." She turned to Lyfe, who was steadily dialing Payton's number, only to receive her voice mail.

"Mr. Carrington," Khris said, "with all due respect, you should've thrown her ass out the goddamn window if this shit was going to happen."

"We need our jobs," one of the accountants said, "and in this economy, where are we going to find another one?"

Lyfe looked into Arri's eyes and said, "I'ma take care of this."

"You talking to me?" She paused. "Hmph." She started packing her things again; a picture of Zion being the last thing she tossed into her box.

"Wait a minute," Lyfe said tight-lipped. "What the fuck does that mean?"

She ignored him and he said, "Can I see you in my office for a minute?"

"Hell, yes, you can," Khris interrupted, and Arri gave her the evil eye. "Take your ass in there." Khris curled her lips, "And get our goddamn jobs back."

"No." Arri said, looking at Lyfe and then to Khris. "Fuck it."

"Arri," Lyfe called.

"It's cool," she said to him. "You don't owe me shit, not even a good-bye."

"Can you give me five minutes?" he pleaded.

"I can," Terell said. "What you need, somebody to book you a flight to the main office? What? Somebody to drive you?"

Lyfe stared at Arri for a moment longer than he should've, then turned to everyone and said, "Leave your boxes on your desk and go home. I will take care of this."

"Somebody better take care of this," Mare-Hellen said, as everyone started to walk out single file, "or this motherfucker will be going up in flames!"

California

Payton sat behind her mahogany desk, tapping the center of her Chanel-covered lips with the rim of her half-empty wineglass. She crossed her right thigh over the left one, and swung the tip of her money-green ostrich stiletto beneath her desk. She batted her extended lashes while looking intently at Quinton, wondering what the fuck had possessed him to barge into her office and slam the door.

Payton watched beads of sweat curl into the anxious creases running across Quinton's forehead, as she pointed to the door and said, "You wanna try that motherfucker again? And knock this time."

"Listen," he said sternly, "not now."

"So what, are you planning to come back in a few days? Because you will be stepping back into the hallway and exercising some respect when you come into my domain. I haven't forgotten that I'm still pissed with you."

"Would you listen? Damn." He sighed. "Be pissed later when you want some dick."

"Awwl, that was cute, Quinton, you're trying to put me in my place again." She sipped her wine. "I like that." She sipped again and then pointed her drink toward him, causing some of the white wine to slosh around the sides of the glass, "but don't push me. Now, what do you want?"

"We have a problem here." He pointed to one of the files on her desk. "Six months ago, one hundred people liquidated." He pointed to another file, "And last month a thousand people liquidated. And you're so busy playing games with this motherfuckin' Lyfe, that all your money's running out the door."

"Quinton," she frowned at the sweat rolling along the side of his face, "would you do something about that?" She handed him a Kleenex. "And stop being so damn nervous, jumpy, and concerned when it comes to my husband. I'm fucking you. And quite well, might I add, so you need to stop running around here like some li'l baby-dick niggah scared of getting flushed out by a grown man's hard-on. Geezuz, it's so unattractive. And as far as *my* money, and people liquidating, we've seen this before and with time it resolved itself."

"Resolved itself? How?"

"Quinton, we're not Fanny Mae, this is doable." She refreshed her drink.

"Are you turning some profit to pay these motherfuckers?" Quinton looked confused. "Did I miss the memo on people having faith in the economy? Motherfuckin' Bear Stearns is crumbling again and ING . . . don't even get me started. And I know your ass ain't waiting on no government bailout money. 'Cause if the white boys are getting denied, our black asses are headed back to sharecroppin'. And as far as your husband, who I can't believe you're still claiming, I don't give a rat's pussy about his ass—"

"Oh, Quinton, that was gross." She handed him another Kleenex.

"You get my goddamn point!" He snatched it from her hand and wiped the sweat from his brow. "He's around here sticking his nose in everybody else's department. I told you, we should've given his ass a grant to play with for repeat offenders or some other bullshit. Why is he so hell-bent on knowing the ins and outs of the accounting department? What the fuck is his ass hiding?"

Payton didn't answer; instead she sipped her drink.

"You don't have to say anything," Quinton carried on, "because I know you get my point. Which is exactly why when you fired the whole crew in New York, you should've put that motherfucker on the soup line with their asses!"

"You may have a point, Quinton. But what I don't understand is why the hell are you so hyped about the shit?"

"Because you're not handling his ass. He's handling you."

Payton paused. *Was it that obvious?*

"Everybody's liquidating!" Quinton snapped. "And you're off in La-La Land trying to appease this ex-felon."

"Don't call names, Quinton, because your ass is from Oakland. I wouldn't be surprised if you were once throwing up gang signs."

"All I'm saying," Quinton stressed, "is that you need to do something about him."

"And what do you suggest?" Payton batted her eyes.

"Kill his ass," he said coldly.

Payton nodded. "Wow, Quinton,"—she sipped more of her wine—"I say if you got the balls, swing 'em."

Silence.

"That's what I thought," Payton carried on. "So if you're done, what you can do is take your mad ass back to your office," she pointed toward the door, "and locate a reputable employment agency to assist with staffing in New York."

"That won't be needed," Lyfe said, opening the door and stepping across the threshold.

A smile bloomed on Payton's face and her eyes lit up. "Checkmate." She grinned, while nodding at Lyfe. "Mr. Carrington." She clapped her hands together. "Welcome home."

Quinton did his best to hide his pissed-off surprise. "Lyfe, wassup?"

"You got it," Lyfe said to Quinton but never taking his eyes from Payton. "I need to speak to my wife. Alone."

"No problem." Quinton shot Payton a loaded eye before turning on his heels. "Later, Lyfe."

"Yeah," Lyfe paused, "later." He closed and locked the door behind Quinton and spat at Payton, "You can't answer the fuckin' phone now?" He sat in one of the twin, black leather wing chairs facing Payton's desk. "What the fuck is your problem?"

Payton's eyes danced in delight as she sipped her wine. Her nipples hardened at the sight of her fine-ass husband and cream thickened between her thighs as she watched him struggle like hell to remain cool, but she could tell by the veins jumping on the side of his forehead that he was due to explode at any moment. "Mr. Carrington," Payton said smoothly, "I see you've finally found your way home."

"Why haven't you been answering the phone?" Lyfe said abruptly.

"Did you call me?" She looked at her cell phone, which sat on the edge of her desk. "Hmmm, seems you did."

Lyfe stroked his beard. "What the fuck is on your mind that you would fire an office full of goddamn people? Those people have families, lives, children, and other shit they have to take care of!"

"Did you go to New York and become a community activist or some shit? Or do you still have some community service to complete, because I know," she said calmly, "that you didn't walk your ass up in here, being a one-man union, rallying for some other motherfuckers that I don't give a damn about. Because seriously," she held her hand up and fanned her fingers, "they can all suck my dick—"

"What the—"

"I'm talking," she spat, yet never raising her voice, only inching her eyebrows upward. "And don't interrupt me again. Now, either you're getting high, you have lost your damn mind, or you simply have me fucked up." She wagged her index finger, and then pointed to her chest. "I reign supreme in this motherfucker. This is my queendom, and I'm not going to remind you again," she stabbed her finger into her desk, "because the next time I'ma fire yo' ass, homie. So the way I see it," she rose from her desk and walked over to Lyfe, "you owe me an apology." She ran the tip of her index finger around his collar, and along the side of his face.

Lyfe loosened his tie and stared long and hard at Payton. His eyes could never deny how beautiful she was: butter-smooth skin, legs that went on forever, and an ass that popped out perfectly. He looked her over and said, "I'm not sucking your dick." He stood up, never unlocking eyes with her. "So, you're right, fuck it."

"Then why are you here?" She stood before him and removed her silk blouse from the waist of her skirt and unbuttoned it. "Because it seems to me that if you want your office back, then you need to show me how bad you want it." She placed her hands on her hips and arched her back, her nude bra completely revealing her full caramel breasts and peaked nipples. "Because I'm not playing with your ass. And I know,"—she slid back on her desk and her skirt inched up her toned thighs—"that you didn't think you were going to come up in here and flex on me again. Is that it? Did you really think that I was such a weak bitch that you could control me?" She laughed. "Oh hell no. Let me explain this to you." Payton opened her legs wide and between her sheer black thigh-highs was a fat and dripping-wet shaved middle. "You owe this pussy." She patted her hands against it. "And I'm sick of you thinking you can walk around here as if you've done something for me, when the truth of the matter is, this pussy saved your life."

"You're reaching."

"*This pussy*," she stressed, "made you what you are today, and I don't think that you quite understand that." She squinted. "This hot pink flesh," she opened the lips and ran her fingers between, "got you out of a fuckin' UPS truck, stuck in a federal felons' program, and gave you a life that slingin' rocks on the corner would've never afforded you." She stirred in her juices.

"I gotta go." Lyfe stood up, yet his hard dick let Payton know that he didn't really want to leave.

She arched her brow. "Yo' ass will stand there and fuckin' listen." She paused. "Because the truth of the matter is, you didn't start hangin' with the big boys until you kissed this creamy punanny." She slipped her fingers into her slit, and pulled them out to roll the wetness over her lips. "You know how to run this investment banking machine because of this pussy." She palmed her middle. "And you have the audacity to tell me you're not going to suck my dick? You have the balls to disrespect it, Mr. Compton? When underneath that tailor-made Versace suit, those crocs, and blingin'-ass platinum and diamond cuff links, and even that well-groomed box beard, is a broke-ass, rap-sheet-havin', South Central motherfucker. Now, the way I see it, you can appease this pussy—aka, suck my dick—or you can leave, run back to New York, and tell the field hands that they are no longer needed. Oh, and make sure you tell that bitch—you know, that pretty-ass secretary of yours—that she's the first one who must go—"

"Secretary—?"

"Don't," Payton waved her finger, "don't try and lie to me, because I saw how she looked at you and I am far from stupid. Besides, I know your sex habits and you can't go two fuckin' days without jerkin' off. And you think I'ma believe that you haven't tapped nothing and you've been gone for over a month? I'm not that naïve, just keep the li'l tramp in her place."

"What are you talking about?" Lyfe frowned.

"You know what I'm talking about. Did you really think that out of all of my employees out there, not even one of them was loyal to me? Please. I've heard the whispers, and I don't know if you've fucked her or are getting ready to, but don't let some outside, broke-down pussy mess up what you got over here, Tiger

Woods." She rubbed her finger in a circular motion over her clit, "Now, how are we going to handle this?" She looked down at his hard dick. "Are we going to keep playing chess or you got other ideas?"

Lyfe stood silently for a moment and then he stepped away. Payton watched him walk toward the door and then to her surprise he rushed back toward her, snatched her from her desk and onto the zebra print couch. "Why is everything always a fuckin' game with you?" He hoisted her black mid-thigh skirt around her waist and their bodies danced in a forceful erotic rhythm. To anyone walking in they would've looked to be wrapped in a physical fight. They weren't . . . but then again, they were.

There was nothing passionate about their relationship—their marriage was about lust, mind games, challenges, and power moves. All of which resulted in an animalistic attraction to each other. And if they could control their hard-ons and G-spot tantrums that came from pushing and thrashing against each other's buttons, if they could sit back and be quiet for a second, they would see that all they had between them was a beautiful piece of nothing.

Lyfe bit Payton on her ass cheeks and then rammed into her wet slit. Instantly her pussy walls felt as if they were sweating buckets of water and dripping all over his dick.

Payton turned her head to the right and looked at Lyfe out the corner of her eye. "That's all you got?"—her ass jiggled against his shaft—"New York must not mean shit to you."

Lyfe eased his dick from Payton's heated pussy, ran it between her ass, and sank it into her third middle. He gripped Payton by the back of her neck, yanking her head back, and said, "Is that it, is that the spot?" He whipped the inside of her ass with his dick.

Payton struggled to answer as moans bullied her tongue to create grunts and groans, but within a few minutes she collected herself. "You ain't," she fought off another moan, "doing shit. I said hit it!" She bucked her ass like a horse gone wild. "What the fuck is the holdup? Or are you slippin'!"

He pounded her in rapid succession and Payton quickly spat, "Now you wastin' my goddamn time!"

Payton placed four of her fingers into her pussy and toyed with it. Her mouth hung open and Lyfe's strokes crashed into her ass and he bit her on the side of her neck. "Now tell me again," he rammed her, making her skin thud against his, "is this the spot!"

She couldn't answer, she was speechless.

"Fuckin' freak!" Lyfe carried on, "All you think about is dick!"

"That's your payment to this pussy—" Payton stopped herself midsentence as her head turned wildly. She felt herself on the verge of floating into the Twilight Zone as hums oozed from her mouth.

"You didn't answer my question." Lyfe's dick beat into her ass.

"Oh," she fought off screaming, "are you still fucking me? I thought you'd stopped."

"Ai'ight." Lyfe whipped her around to face him and as her head lay on the couch her legs spread completely open. Lyfe slid back into her ass and her muscles clamped around his dick, causing him to remember, if only for the moment, why he had yet to let her go. "Now let's try this again, look in my face," he stroked, "and tell me if this is the spot."

Payton thrashed about and did all she could not to tell him that this was the best dick session they'd ever had, the only thing missing were the nipple clamps and noose, or any other thing that would simultaneously bring intense pain and extreme pleasure. Lyfe pinched her nipples. "Answer me."

Payton pounded her fist into his back, "Yes!" She could no longer hold it in. "That's it!" She creamed all over his dick.

Lyfe smiled and said, "Now ride it." He pulled her onto his lap, yet she fought against it and instead she crawled to the top of the couch and sat on his face. "Suck it."

Lyfe looked at her heated and melting pussy and he wanted to tell her, "Hell no!" but his tongue inched out of his mouth and before he could control it, his tongue was running wet waves over her bullet-size clit. She jiggled her ass over his face and he gripped her ass cheeks, sucking in between her vulva until it dripped over his lips. Afterward, Payton slid from his face to his thighs, taking a squat position on his dick. The sound of their skin popped against each other like rubber bands. Payton pinched her clit as she bounced like a squatted duck against his thighs; the motions caused her juice to thicken and ease from the inside, forcing a scream to soar from both of their mouths.

Lyfe's warmth ran between her thighs and instantly the guilt of being manhandled by her dug into his chest.

A few moments later, after they'd collected their breaths, Payton said, "Now your mission has been accomplished."

After a quick shower in Payton's private bathroom, Lyfe stepped out of her office with his suit meticulously draped over his delicious body. He watched her pour two glasses of wine and say, "Let's have a toast."

Lyfe hesitated and his gaze lingered on Payton longer than he expected.

She pointed the glass toward him and her eyes clearly asked why he was taking so long. "We're at least civilized?" Payton asked.

"We can be." He accepted the champagne, "What are we toasting to?"

She kissed him on the lips lightly. "To you remembering what you need to do to earn your keep." She clinked his glass. "So let's recap and go over the rules of our mutual understanding: as long as you look pretty," she stroked his chin, "fuck me like you did today, do what I tell you to, and don't ignore my calls anymore, then we're fine."

"So that's what this is all about," he said, as if it had all finally clicked, "me ignoring you all weekend." He smirked and the corner of his top lip curled. "Ahh, so we're throwing these kinds of fits? But see, what you don't seem to understand is that you chose the wrong ghetto-ass-Compton-motherfucker if you expect me to fold, concede, or surrender to whatever kinda fuckin' war you're trying to wage with me. He was on the other corner, the one you passed to get to me."

"Really?" Payton questioned.

"Pretty much," Lyfe said confidently. "And what you need to understand is that the very thing that makes me different, the very thing that keeps your panties wet," he spoke against her lips and his minty breath covered them like a kiss, "is that underneath this Versace suit—as you so eloquently put it—and these platinum cuff links, and this well-groomed box beard is a man who doesn't have shit to lose."

"You would lose this money and I would see to that."

"How?" Lyfe pressed. "Impress me, please. You're going to do what? Create a prenup? What? Because from what I remember when we got married all we signed was a marriage license. So, like I said, I wouldn't lose shit; as a matter of fact I would walk away with half of yo' shit. So, let's recap and reiterate the rules of Lyfe's understanding. As long as you behave"—he kissed her on the forehead—"and be a good little lady who stays in her place," he sat his empty glass on the end of her desk, "you have nothing to worry about." He paused and when Payton said nothing in return he winked his eye. "Cross check."

Payton stared at Lyfe and for the first time, she actually thought that she just might need to kill him. She lifted her glass as if she were toasting to him again. "Have a safe flight," she said.

"Yeah, I'll do that." Lyfe turned toward the door and walked out of her office.

New York

Dull yellow streams of light from the fading streetlamps and the sounds of cars splashing through the rain set the stage for A Smooth Operator's fantasy. It had been one too many nights since Arri had taken her cyber stroll, and just when she thought that maybe she would attempt to tuck this shit away for good, her nine-to-five blew up in her face, reminding her once more that this right here—standing before a strange man with his dick in his hand, awaiting her erotic performance—was all she had to fall back on.

Maybe that was fine, because as sure as there was a spring breeze men would always want pussy, whether it was flesh to flesh or innovative masturbation via the computer screen. Perhaps her thoughts of stopping and becoming an average and everyday woman were ludicrous, and maybe she needed to learn to be appreciative. Shit, there was obviously no need to stop—at least no time soon—besides, she'd learned a long time ago to work with what she had. So here she was again, handling her business: her client said that his fantasy was to fuck a street-walking bimbo, and for a fee she agreed.

Arri placed the Webcam toward the open window and facing the street, to give the illusion that she was a prostitute pounding the pavement, and as if it were planned, a trucker's horn blew loudly outside of her bedroom window. She stopped pacing and turned to face the computer screen. She could see her client's eyes absorbing the view of her black lace bra, black fishnet thigh-highs, six-inch Cinderella platform heels, and red hot pants that were cut so high up her ass that at a quick glance they resembled bikini panties.

The sunny blond wig she profiled in swayed over her shoulders as she placed her hands on her hips, popped chewing gum on the side of her cheek, and said to her client, "Wassup, Daddy?" She blinked her extremely long, fake, curly blue eyelashes. "What you out here for tonight?" She smacked her lips and popped her gum once more.

"I'm just driving around," he said, sounding like a tired old truck driver.

Arri licked her lips. "A handsome and big-dick daddy like you, out here all alone?" She squeezed her breasts and blew him a kiss. "So tell Mama what you need so you don't have to be lonely." She palmed her pussy and then stuck her index finger suggestively in her mouth.

"Why don't you show me what you got for me?"

Arri turned her ass toward the camera, stuck it out as far as she could and slowly bent over, gradually peeling her shorts over her ass, stopping midway down her cheeks and shaking her ass in a stripper's frenzy. Afterward she dropped her shorts to the floor.

Arri slapped both of her ass cheeks and the sound sizzled around the room. "Is that what you wanted to see, Daddy?"

"More," he commanded while squeezing the head of his dick. Arri complied, gripped both sides of her behind and allowed him to see all that glistened in between. "Fuck," he moaned in delight. "I want you to ride me"—he paused—"and reverse the cowgirl so I can watch that ass swallow my dick."

Arri eased onto her inflatable dong seat; which at first glance resembled a plastic blowup seat, but it was far from that: there was a nine-inch rabbit dildo, and a clit tickler that felt ice cold to the touch. Arri turned her face away from the camera and worked the stage like she was on Broadway. It was pretty easy to do, especially since this was Arri's favorite toy, one that always allowed her to get lost in the chills it sent up her spine and through her fingertips. "Oh . . . ummm . . . Daddy . . . ummm," she squealed, "this dick is so big."

"You like that shit?" he grunted. "That's how I fuck my bimbo bitches!"

"However you like it, papí."

"I wish I could fuck you all night long."

Arri could tell by the sound of his voice that he was due to cum, so she rode the dildo stool until the bottom started to rock and as her ass knocked against the seat the client screamed, "Doooooooon't stop I'm cummmmm . . . ming!"

Once the client gave another hard grunt, Arri knew he was done. She turned around and noticed how exhausted he looked. His dick dripped and ran over his knuckles.

Arri's lips turned into a frown as his mouth hung open and he started to snore. She checked her account and then shut the computer down.

After she showered she went to Zion's room and peeked in on him. "I'm not sleep," he said as she turned to walk out.

Arri laughed. "And why not?"

"Because . . ."—he paused—"I was thinking that maybe . . . I should ummm . . . sleep with you tonight."

"Oh really?"

"Yes, really." He grabbed his blanket and Spider-Man toy. "Let's go, 'cause I'm tired."

Arri watched him as he walked out of his room and she said, "Just for tonight."

Arri lay down and Zion snuggled beside her, his body heat felt like soothing butter as he wiggled under her arm. "Auntie, do you ever think my mommy will get better?"

Arri paused, the question completely catching her off guard. "I hope so."

"I don't," he said matter-of-factly, "because if she does then you might send me back to live with her and I don't ever want to go back to live with her again. Do you know she slept on the street and in dirty houses with wood on the windows? I was so scared, Auntie."

"I don't want you to be scared, so you stop worrying about that. I love you and you can live with me forever if you want to."

"Yay!" Zion pressed his mouth into Arri's cheek, and blew hard against it; the slobber from his lips provided an extra-wet coating.

Arri cracked up laughing. "I'ma get you." She tickled him.

"Okay, okay." Zion laughed so hard that tears filled his eyes. He hugged Arri tight and said, "I love you."

"I love you too." She squeezed him.

"Auntie," Zion called her as her eyes started to drift toward sleep. He pointed toward the single stream of light easing in from the streetlamp, "Why does that stool have a big ole pee-pee?"

Arri's eyes popped open wide. "Oh my God!" She rushed from the bed to deflate the seat and place it back into its case.

"I've never seen anything like that before," Zion said, impressed.

Six a.m., and Arri's eyes peeled open at the all too often pounding on her apartment door. She sighed and decided that this time she was going to use her peephole. Her mind was already made up that whoever it was would be left standing there. Slowly she crept to the door, stood on her tippy toes, looked out the peephole, and her eyes took a tiny glimpse of Lyfe with his hands fumbling around his beard. *Worried again.* She hated that she was never blinded of his beauty. He raised his fist, preparing to pound again, but she opened the door before it landed.

Her eyes ran over him as she noticed he had on the same suit he wore yesterday. She could see her reflection, as she stood before him in a black satin negligee, dancing in his gaze.

"I hope you don't make this a habit," she said.

Lyfe hesitated. "My apologies for coming by here so early—"

"What is it?"

"I won't take up too much of your time."

"You already have."

"I just want you to know that everything worked out with the office. You and everyone else can come back this morning."

"Listen,"—Arri hesitated as her presence hugged the doorway—"I'm not . . ." she swallowed, "I won't be returning."

"What?" Lyfe said, caught completely off guard. "What do you mean?"

"I'm done. I already have another job."

"You already have another job?" he said, taken aback. "Since when?"

"That's really none of your business."

Lyfe gave a disbelieving chuckle. "I understand that you're upset with me. I get that."

"You don't know me well enough to get shit. Fuck you."

"We can arrange that."

"Leave!" Arri attempted to close the door and Lyfe slid his foot in between.

"Come on, Arri, I'm sorry about the other night, and yeah, the way I left here was wrong . . . and I'm really, really sorry about that. But for you not to come back to work . . . ?"

"I'm done," she said, tight-lipped.

"Ai'ight." Lyfe stepped back. "Well, I guess I'll see you tomorrow, then."

"What do you think, this is a joke? I'm finished."

"Nah, it's not a joke, but until you accept my apology I'll be here, every day, at six o'clock in the morning. And you know I'm persistent. Hell, I might start showing up here at lunchtime too, wanting to eat and shit."

Arri could feel her lips untwisting and laughter filling her chest, which pissed her off even more.

"Don't make me start camping outside your door."

"Auntie," Zion said, tugging on the back of her nightie, "who is that?" He stuck his face into the crack of the door and looked up at Lyfe. "I'm Zion," he said. "Who are you?"

Lyfe squatted to his knees. "Oh, you're the man who lives here?" He winked at Arri, and then looked back to Zion. "I'm Lyfe—"

"And he was just leaving," Arri said.

Lyfe ignored her. "You like Spider-Man, don't you?"

Zion's eyes lit up. "I love Spider-Man! You like Spider-Man?"

"He's cool," Lyfe said, "but you know who my favorite is?"

"Who?" Zion asked excitedly.

"Iron Man."

"I love Iron Man too!" Zion looked Lyfe up and down. "Do you know Iron Man? You kinda big like him."

Lyfe gave Arri a sly smile. "Am I big like Iron Man?"

Bigger, Arri thought and then twisted her lips. "Look, we have to get ready for our day."

"All right." Lyfe looked down at Zion and gave him a pound. He looked back to Arri and said, "Every day."

"He seems nice, Auntie," Zion said as Arri held his hand and locked the front door. "Is he a superhero?"

"Zion," she sighed as they entered the bathroom and she turned the shower on for him, "take a shower so you can get ready for school."

"Okay," Zion said, as he removed his pajamas and started

singing what he could remember of the Spider-Man theme song. "Spider-Man / oh Spider-Man / on the ground or in the air . . ."

Arri couldn't help but smile at how cute he sounded. She leaned against the bathroom sink, and though her intentions were to listen to her nephew sing and rave to him about how much he deserved a Grammy award, her mind took the wrong turn and traveled the path to where thoughts of Lyfe were stored. She gripped the edge of the pedestal sink as her nipples tingled and her thighs felt weak. She could feel Lyfe sliding his tongue down the center of her belly and just as his tongue curled around her clit, she jumped and realized that her phone was ringing.

"Spider-Man/oh Spider-Man . . ." lingered behind her as she walked out of the bathroom and grabbed the cordless phone. "Hello?"

"Gurl!" It was Khris. "Mr. Carrington just called here and said we can report back to work this morning."

"Really?" Arri said, unimpressed.

"And let me tell you," Khris carried on, seemingly oblivious to Arri's tone, "I had to catch myself when that smooth-ass mofo called me on the phone. I almost offered him my services."

"What services?" Arri asked, confused.

"Fellatio, cunnilingus . . ."

"Oh . . . my . . . God, you are going too damn far."

"What-the-fuck-ever," Khris continued, "we all have our fantasies. But anyway, I hope you're getting dressed, because we're going to be on time today, no more of that running late shit."

Arri sighed. "I'm not going back."

"What?" Khris screamed. "You're not *what*?"

"I'm not going back."

"Did the recession memo miss yo' ass? Open the door," Khris

snapped, "so I can slap you. Have you lost your goddamn mind? Yo' ass know you be trippin'."

Arri paused. She knew what she was about to confess to Khris would catch her off guard, but hell, she needed to confide in someone. "Khris, this weekend when you took Zion with you and Tyree . . ."

"Yeah . . . and what? You got another job and didn't tell me—?"

"Would you listen?"

"I would listen if you were making some goddamn sense."

Arri sucked her teeth. "Listen, Lyfe—"

"Lyfe?" Khris questioned in disbelief. "You on a first-name basis with the overseer?"

"Well, he came over here to my apartment—"

"Oh hell no. Did you fuck him?"

"No, yes . . . well, it was more to it than just fucking."

"Your nasty ass was gon' keep that a secret. Does he have a big dick?"

"Yes—"

"And you couldn't send him across the hall? Gurl, I know he put it down. Chile, that's the kind of man I would just let slap me all in the eyes with the dick. Every time I saw him I would be wagging my tongue, going yum-yum-yum."

"Just let me know when you come up for air."

"Don't get an attitude with me—you just better be ready for Erica Kane, for when that bitch flies through here and wanna kick yo' ass. Don't worry, we'll jump her ass, though."

"Anyway—"

"Wait a minute—ding-ding-ding—something just came to me. You've been fucking this mofo and we still got fired? What, you ain't suck his dick—?"

"You are sick."

"Oh no, honey, you better jaw-break the shit outta that motherfucker. And anyway, when the hell you get the nerve to be screwing your goddamn boss? You just a typical li'l slutty-ass secretary, huh—"

"Khris—"

"Oh wait, are you the reason why that bitch came in there and almost got tossed out the fuckin' window? We all got fired 'cause he was off fuckin' yo' ass? Oh hell no, you owe me."

"Oh my God—"

"But that's some fierce shit, though, girl, that mofo was gon' splatter his own wife all over the goddamn street for your pussy! Scandalous. I love it! You think you can fuck our way to a raise?"

"You know what, when you're done holding this one-sided conversation, call me back. Because I'm trying to be serious with you and you're ranting and raving about him being fine and having a big dick."

"You're trying to hold a serious conversation with me?" Khris said. "Really? Well let me ask you this—do you have another job lined up to take the place of this one?"

"Not exactly."

"Not exactly." Khris paused. "Translation, hell nawl. So answer me this, do you still have rent to pay and a child who needs health benefits?"

"Yes."

"Hmmm, okay, and you're quitting your job because you fucked your boss?"

"Well—"

"Translation—hell yes. And you expect me to think you're trying to hold a serious conversation? Which part of that sounds serious to you, 'cause all that shit sounds silly as hell. Or maybe it's just me."

"I didn't ask you to pass judgment."

"I'm not, I'm just keeping it real with you. I love you like a sister, which is why I have to tell you that you're sounding re-tar-ded," she said, enunciating every syllable, "cra-ay-zee. Stoop-id . . . as hell to me. You fucked Lyfe and now you're upset enough to quit your job? Huh? What part of the game is that? That's why men always beat us at shit; we get too emotional. Listen, you don't quit your job behind dick. You go to work and act like nothing ever happened. Give his ass the cold shoulder, but you go to work—every day. Now put your goddamn clothes on, so when we take the boys across the street, we'll be on time for the train."

Arri twisted her lips and released a deep breath out the side of her mouth; she hated that Khris was right. The mere thought that she would leave her job and not have another at least in the works was crazy. A Smooth Operator was okay, but she wasn't living the high life or no shit like that. "You're right." She sighed.

"I know, girl, but that's why I'm here to get in that ass when you say some shit that makes no goddamn sense. Now hurry up so we'll have enough time for you to tell me how big his dick was. Geezuz!" Khris shouted as she hung up.

Arri held the phone to her chin as she looked at herself in her vanity's mirror. "You slippin'." She shook her head. "Just handle your business. That's it. Do your job. Don't say any extra shit, and keep the thoughts of wanting to slip beneath his desk and suck his dick out of your head."

Arri stepped away from the mirror and commenced to getting her and Zion dressed for the day. She purposely lagged behind, though, because she didn't want to have to deal with Khris and her multitude of questions.

By the time Arri arrived at the office, things were pretty much back to normal. The office chatter was afloat, Terell was delivering mail, and Lyfe was standing in his doorway watching her make her way to her cubicle. She shot him a loaded eye that clearly said, "Unless it pertains to business, don't say shit to me."

He gave her a crooked grin, and she did her best not to roll her eyes and instead simply took her seat.

New York

An early morning crowd moved swiftly through Central Park, as Lyfe sat on a cement bench next to a resting jogger. He tapped his fingers on his Styrofoam coffee cup as he struggled like hell to focus in on the financial section of the *New York Times*. But he couldn't; especially since his quick and unplanned walk through the park confirmed that two men were following him. And though he only knew one of them—Galvin, the overtanned motherfucker he'd met at the cigar bar—he now knew that both of them, beyond a shadow of a doubt, were cops.

Fuck.

Lyfe rattled his paper. He did his best to present as cool, calm, and collected, but inside he was nervous as hell. He tried to think of all the crimes he'd committed—before he turned his life around—and hadn't answered to. He wondered if they were following him because of some warrant he forgot he had, or some trumped-up charge the Feds were infamous for creating.

Shit.

Lyfe narrowed in on the financial section of the paper, yet before he could get to the third sentence, his eyes wandered to where Galvin stood by a rickety breakfast truck, dunking his glazed doughnut into his steamy cup of coffee. Galvin smiled at Lyfe and gave him a thumbs-up.

Let me get my ass out of here.

Lyfe closed his paper and tucked it under his arm.

"Lyfe," Galvin called out to him as he stood to leave. Galvin held up his index finger—an indication that he wanted Lyfe to wait for a moment—but before Lyfe could protest or simply walk away, Galvin was already before him, wearing a tan trench coat with a Burberry lining. Standing next to Galvin was a tall, dark black man with a neatly cropped haircut. "Lyfe," Galvin said, slapping him on the back, "how the hell are ya?" He smiled and pointed to the man next to him. "This is Keenan."

Keenan held his hand out and Lyfe accepted his gesture as he looked him over suspiciously. "Nice to meet you," Keenan said, a little too damn chipper.

"Yeah," Galvin said, smiling, "seems we keep meeting a lot, you know." He pulled a pack of Newports from his inner coat pocket and pointed them toward Lyfe. "Smoke?"

"Nah," Lyfe said, "but help yourself."

"That's right, rich man's stock only," Galvin said. "Well, a son of a bitch like me can only smoke eight-hundred-dollar cigars during income tax time, 'cause every other time, I'm a living-from-Friday-to-Friday kinda man, ya'know?" Galvin held his cigarette loosely between his lips and flicked his Bic until he caught a steady flame. He puffed the butt until the tip of the cigarette became a crackling light. Afterward he took a strong pull and released an O of smoke from his thin cherry lips.

Lyfe could no longer fake a smile or pretend that he felt comfortable standing here. "Listen, Galvin, Keenan," he nodded at them respectively, "I need to get to the office. Take care."

"Certainly, Lyfe, a hardworking man like you, surely we understand," Galvin said, "but before you go," he placed his hand on Lyfe's forearm and instantly Lyfe's bicep tightened and he shot Galvin such a fierce look that Galvin threw up his hands in defeat. "Pardon me," he said as his cigarette dangled from between his lips. "No harm intended. I just wanna ask you something."

"Peep this," Lyfe snapped. "Don't ask me shit." He looked Galvin dead in the eyes and then moved on to ice-grill Keenan. "As a matter of fact, why don't you tell me something. Tell me why you keep fuckin' following me? You got something you wanna say to me?"

Galvin took a pull and let out the smoke. "We don't mean to make you paranoid, Lyfe."

"Certainly isn't our style," Keenan said as he sipped his coffee.

Lyfe snorted. "How about this: if you got something you wanna tell me or some bullshit you wanna charge me with, then you need to bring it. Otherwise," he looked them over and said slowly, "step . . . the . . . fuck . . . off. Now, excuse me."

The entire day had flown by and Lyfe hadn't been able to get anything done. He knew something was plain and simply fuckin' wrong, he just didn't know what it was. He'd been unable to think straight all day and between thoughts of Galvin, Keenan, and the unpunished crimes he'd committed, he found his eyes lingering, undressing, and attempting to relieve stress by getting lost in flashbacks of making love to Arri.

All week she hadn't said more than hello, how many copies, and good night to him. And before he could even think to ask her to stay late, or attempt to hold a conversation with her, she was gone. He thought about showing up at her place, but quickly decided that the thief in the night bullshit had grown stale. And since he was a grown man and had been for many years, he didn't have time to be chasing her. He'd already sent her flowers every morning and she had yet to say, "Thank you, I appreciate the gesture," nothing, so to hell with it. He was at a loss on what he needed to do, so he hunched his shoulders, stroked his box beard, and figured, *fuck it*.

Lyfe rose from his seat and paced his office; he held his ringing cell phone in the palm of his hand. It was Payton. He sent her to voice mail. He had too much on his mind to be entertaining her melodramatic, controlling-ass bullshit. He looked out the window and onto the street, seeing nothing that impressed him; his eyes roamed to the clock: four p.m.

Fuck. He grabbed his coat and walked out of his office. "I'll be back," he threw over his shoulder to Arri. He wasn't sure if she'd caught what he said or not, because she didn't once turn away from her computer.

Jonathan Butler's guitar filled the Shark Bar as Lyfe sat on the bar stool, sipping a glass of Hennessy and drifting deep into his thoughts. He looked into his drink and saw a snippet of Payton, a flashback of Arri, and a snapshot of the blue Caprice Classic that he had spotted in his rearview mirror as he drove over here. He closed his eyes and tried his best to make sense of all of this.

"You're under arrest," drifted sternly into his ears and caused him to jump. He quickly turned around and noticed a few men gathered at a table laughing and joking with one another. "This is too much," Lyfe said to himself as he knocked off the rest of his drink and left.

The late winter wind whipped across Lyfe's face as he entered the all-glass-enclosed lobby of his office building.

"Evening, Mr. Carrington," the doorman said, and tipped his hat. "Another late night?"

"Pretty much." Lyfe stepped onto the elevator. "Pretty much."

As Lyfe approached the double glass doors of Anderson Global, he could see Arri's curved back while she leaned into her computer. She held a pencil in her hand, tapping it against the side of her forehead.

"Arri?" He looked at her, surprised. "You're still here?" he said as the doors swung closed behind him. "Why are you here so late?"

"I have some work to finish up for accounting," she said, her voice clearly on edge.

"Accounting?"

"They asked me if I would mind compiling this report for them, since Donna is on maternity leave. Besides, I could use the overtime."

"Yeah, but it's after eight, you can finish that up tomorrow. I'm sure Zion's waiting on you."

"I have a sitter and I can lock up too, if that's what you're getting at."

"I know you can lock up, I'm just saying—"

"You don't need to say any more," she snapped so hard and curt that Lyfe instantly took a step back.

He placed his hand on the sides of her rolling desk chair, and turned her toward him. "Let me know when you're done having a fit, throwing a tantrum, or whatever you call it, so that I can hold a conversation with you." He bent over and looked her directly in the eyes. "Ai'ight?"

"I don't have fits and I'm not throwing a tantrum. I'm doing my job."

"So then, let's get to the point. How long are you going to be upset with me?"

"Upset with you?" She batted her eyes. "About what?"

Lyfe chuckled. "Oh, so, is this the name of the game? Act as if the weekend we spent together didn't exist."

"Oh," she said as if she were thinking, "we did spend a weekend together. Wasn't that the one where you left and never said shit to me?"

"It wasn't that easy for me to leave."

"You could've said good-bye, take care, something; instead you treated me like you left money on the nightstand."

"That wasn't my intention."

"Look, we settled our curiosity by fucking last weekend. Cool, we can move on. I'ma do me and you do your Mrs."

"It's more complicated than that, Arri."

"I don't see how, when I just made it quite simple. What we had no longer exists." She blew into the palm of her hand. "Poof, gone. Okay? No guilt, no hurt, and no misunderstandings."

"So you're not falling for me?" He pressed his forehead against hers. "That's what you're telling me?"

Silence. She wanted to belt out, "No," but even the thought of such a lie burned her mouth.

"I fucked up," Lyfe continued, "and I know that I'm married, I know. But it's complicated."

"I'm not into being a complication, so let's just simply walk away."

"But I'm too selfish of a motherfucker to do that. And I'm relentless as hell."

"Well, that's on you"—she dusted her hands together—"because I'm done."

"So, what you're telling me is that if I'm standing here telling you that no matter what I do or how hard I try to fight, I can't help but fall for you—that means nothing to you?"

Silence.

"Answer me, and if you say it doesn't, then I promise you I'll never bring the shit up again."

The only sounds that could be heard were the echoes of the copy machine's motors burning. "Tell me." He brushed her lips with his own. "Tell me something, because I wanna get back to laughing with you." He kissed her again. "I wanna make you smile again." He sucked her bottom lip. "When all is said and done . . ." he slipped his tongue into her mouth, "I wanna make love to you again."

Arri hated that she was responding to his kisses. This was not the way she planned her response or had rehearsed it in her head. She was supposed to tell him to get the fuck out her face, stand on her heels, and leave him festering in his spot. But she didn't and she couldn't; instead, she allowed him to lift her from the seat as she wrapped her legs around his waist and be carried to his office; where he pressed her back into the floor-to-ceiling window, with the evening skyline of the city resting behind her.

"I don't know" were the only words she was able to formulate, as she watched him unbutton her blouse and line kisses over her shoulder. "I just . . ." she said, stopping for a moment to moan as he planted wet and sloppy kisses on her nipples. She wanted to stop his hands from roaming her body but she couldn't get her mouth to stop moaning as she melted into his tongue kissing her breasts. "Lyfe . . . I can't." She watched the tip of his tongue flick against both of her nipples and then bite them slightly, making her mouth hang open and her pussy cream in preparation of his tongue, his dick, or both.

"Shhh . . ." he said as he slid to his knees, and opened the eyes of her pussy. "Look at this pretty pussy." He slid his tongue over her clit. "I want you to watch me make this pussy melt."

"Mmm, Lyfe . . ." she moaned, watching him suck, nibble, pull, and pop her cherry in his mouth. She could feel her pearl turning to Jell-O as he twirled it between his lips and then sucked it as if he were trying to get to the center of hard candy. Never had she felt or ever dreamed that her sex would be eaten with such intensity. Hell, maybe he needed to fuck up again, if this is what came along with his apologies.

Her eyes drifted closed. The electrified licks to her clit forced her to dream of marriage, kids, him sucking her body into a double nut over and over again.

"As wet as this pussy is, you gon' tell me you're not falling for me. Who the hell gon' believe that?"

Lyfe licked, as Arri gripped his shoulders and his tongue moved deeper and deeper through her creamy trenches. She reached for his beard and pulled his face up to her own, greeting his lips with a silky kiss.

Lyfe picked Arri up and carried her to his desk, where he

lifted her onto it, knocking everything on it—stacks of unreturned phone messages, files, Payton's picture, and the wooden plaque engraved with his name—to the floor. Her skirt rose over her ass and their fingers entangled as they both pulled her panties off and he tossed them to the floor. Hurriedly she unbuckled his pants and revealed his hardness.

"I'll never hurt you again." He opened her legs like scissors and brushed the head of his dick against her wetness. Slowly he pushed into her warm flesh, while taking his hands and caressing her breasts; he loved the feel of her nipples between his fingers.

His meat was hot, and hard, and heavy as Arri squeezed her velvet walls.

"I'm sorry, baby." Lyfe moved his body like a monstrous chocolate wave as he soared into her. "You forgive me?"

Silence.

"Did you hear me? I said I was sorry."

More silence.

"Oh, you're not answering me." He held her legs straight up in the air.

"Yes . . . oh God," she screamed as he rocked in and out of her.

"Not God, baby; He didn't apologize, I did."

"Wait," she gasped, and her mouth flew open with every word. "Wait, maybe . . ." Arri moaned, "maybe we should—"

"Should what?" Lyfe stroked. " 'Cause you know I'm not stopping."

"But the office door is wide open."

"I don't give a fuck." He threw her a hard hip and she started to scream again. "Make 'em lose their fuckin' minds!"

Arri paused, his mind-blowing strokes were on a mission to enter her stomach, her chest heaved up and down as she screamed out, "Lyfe!"

"That's right, tell 'em what the fuck my name is, I don't give a damn." He flipped her over, her ass faced his shaft, and his pipe dripped with heavy cream. He bent his head down and started eating her pussy again. He sucked her damp and luscious lips, licking between her ass cheeks, and then back to her clit, where his tongue served it with zillions of chills. It was all Arri could do to stay balanced on all fours and not tip over the side of the desk.

"Lyfe," she moaned, "fuck."

He slowed his licking down and began sucking her pussy slowly. "The left side," she instructed, as he began to lick the left side with all that he had. It was as if his tongue was a dick, soaring through her wet pussy with chilling meticulousness. "Lyfe!!!!!!" she screamed, biting the side of her right fist.

Lyfe flipped Arri back over and he could tell by the look on her face that her mind was in a different place. He kissed her titties roughly as they bounced in his face. "I asked you a question." He smacked her on the ass. "Do you forgive me?"

"Lyfe—"

"What?" He pounded her with his dick.

Doing all she could not to scream, Arri said, "I can't . . ."

"Oh you can't?" He pounded her pussy harder than ever before, the swift motions of his hips were sounding like a wet towel soaring through the air. Arri knew when they were done it would be impossible to walk.

Lyfe pounded her over and over again, driving his point from her throbbing middle to the pit of her stomach. "Can't isn't an option."

He soared in and out of her until all she had left was the truth. "I forgive you."

Lyfe let out a sigh of relief, as he held on to Arri and she held on to him and they exchanged orgasms.

Arri stroked Lyfe down the center of his chest and said, "Lyfe—"

"Shh . . ." He kissed her on the forehead. "All I need you to do is trust me."

Arri hesitated; she thought of a thousand responses that she could give him, things she could say, but looking into his eyes, she could see the same look he must have had on the block, before the boardrooms and business suits. She saw a certain level of confidence with only a slight tinge of fear.

"Why should I trust you?" She looked him clearly in the eyes.

"Because I need you to. And I don't have no long explanation, no speeches, nothing elequent to say other than I've never felt like this. Ever."

"But in the end, what does that mean?"

"Just roll with me, Arri." He paused, "Just roll with me."

New York

"**R**un away with me," Lyfe whispered in Arri's ear, as she turned over in bed and looked into his face. She stretched and then wrapped her arms around his neck.

"What are you talking about, run away where? There's no *where* to go. Besides, I have to take Zion to school and go to work. We can run away tomorrow, it's Saturday."

"Zion should go to school." Lyfe kissed Arri on the neck and pulled her on top of him, "But you can take today off." He placed his hands on her hips.

"I don't have any time to use like that. Zion has asthma and I was out a lot when he was sick—"

"It's okay." He smiled.

"I don't know if I should call out—"

"You wanna call out? Call out to me. I'm the boss."

Arri paused; he *was* the boss.

"Plus I wanna take you somewhere," Lyfe continued.

Arri smiled, "Where?"

"When's the last time you've been out of New York?"

"The last time I was in New Jersey." She laughed.

"No, silly," he kissed her, "I mean when's the last time you've been in the midst of the sea, on an island. Just gone somewhere and chilled. It's a whole world out there—"

"And what, you wanna give it to me?"

"Yeah . . . I do."

"All right." Arri turned around and slid down Lyfe's chest in a sixty-nine position. "Right after this."

He opened her pussy lips and licked in between. "Yeah, you're right, right after this."

"Where are you taking me?" Arri smiled as Lyfe turned left into a small airport. "You know I have to come back home and get my baby, right?" she joked. "Khris only agreed to keep him overnight."

"I know." Lyfe laughed as he parked the car and then walked around to open her door. "We'll be back by tomorrow afternoon." He took Arri by the hand and led her to the small plane he'd chartered to take them on a mini excursion.

"I want you to do something for me." Lyfe looked into Arri's eyes.

"What's that?" She twisted her lips.

"It's legal." He laughed.

"It better be." She giggled, feeling like a sixteen-year-old schoolgirl who'd just cut class to be with her boyfriend.

Arri wanted desperately to forget Lyfe's circumstances; but as she looked around at the private jet, the runway, the packed Louis Vuitton luggage he surprised her with, she remembered that he had a wife and that technically this was all her shit. "Are you sure that we should . . . be . . . you know, here like this?"

"Listen to me, for once. For this one time if at no other time, I want you to chill with me. Simply chill. Nothing else exists except for this moment and the time we have ahead of us on our trip. I want you to see what it is to get out of your circumstances, to not be drowned out and beat up by life and shit that just doesn't seem to stop. I just want you to enjoy me . . , and enjoy this. Don't worry about nothing else. Tomorrow when we return to Earth," he gave her a sexy wink, "we'll think about it then."

Arri pressed her forehead against Lyfe's. "You scare me."

"That's because you fell in love with me. And your problem is you don't remember when."

"You are so fuckin' cocky," she said as they boarded the plane.

"You know it's true." He laughed.

"Are you trying to tell me something?" Arri said.

"Nah," he said seriously, "I'm not trying to tell you, 'cause I've already said it."

Arri didn't respond or press Lyfe any further. Instead she lay back and as her mind tried not to make sense of what she was feeling inside, her eyes roamed around the navy blue carpeted plane, with a beige leather couch instead of row seats. She sat beside Lyfe and buckled herself in; she didn't know where they were going and at this moment she didn't care. She placed her head on his shoulder, closed her eyes, and ten minutes later they'd taken off for the Cayman Islands.

When Arri awoke, they were landing on a private estate with an airplane hangar, a tennis court, private white-sand beach, surrounded by the clearest and the prettiest turquoise water she'd ever seen, and in the center of it all was a two-story Queen Anne beach house. Leading from the private road to the front door were two adjacent rows of palm trees. Ceiling fans lined the first- and second-story open porches, and along the sides of the house white sands led to a waving sea. Arri had never seen anything this beautiful. "This is . . ." she looked around, "breathtaking."

"And for the next two days, it's all ours." Lyfe held Arri by the hand as they exited the plane.

"Is this your first time here?" she asked him, continuing to take in the sights.

"No," he said, kissing her on the forehead. "I came here once before when I was doing some illegal shit I shouldn't have been doing, and I needed to come to a place where there was no extradition, and this was it."

"What were you doing . . . that you shouldn't have been doing?" Arri slid her shoes off and walked barefoot through the sand.

Lyfe laughed. "What, you wearing a wire or some shit?" He playfully patted down her breasts.

"If you wanted to feel my nipples, all you had to do was ask."

"I gotta ask now?"

Arri kissed Lyfe softly on the lips, "No, you don't have to ask at all."

"I didn't think so." He responded to her kisses.

"So are you going to tell me?"

"No."

"What, you have some open warrants or something?" She laughed. "Don't let me find out there's a bounty on your head."

"And what you gon' do?"

"Get my baby," she looked him in the eyes, "and come here to be with you."

"That's what I thought."

"You have a habit of riding your own sack. You know that, right?"

"Nah, I thought that was your habit."

"Anyway," Arri laughed, "this is such a beautiful place." Arri looked around at the grounds and the staff buzzing about.

"Yes, it is," Lyfe agreed. "Why don't you go in the house and get changed. I'm sure the chef has prepared a wonderful dinner."

Over dinner Arri and Lyfe talked about everything under the sun. They laughed, joked, and after they finished eating they resumed their tour of the grounds, settling at the infinity pool.

Music pumped through the underwater speakers as Lyfe waded in the water between Arri's legs and she sat along the edge of the pool. "What did he do?"

Arri was obviously taken aback. "Who are you talking about?" She tried to force herself to smile but couldn't.

"You know what I'm talking about"—he draped his arms over her thighs—"I'm talking about how scared you are to let yourself go with me."

"I'm having an affair with you, isn't that enough letting go?"

"Is it? Or do you want more?"

"What do you want?"

"I want it all. I told you that I was selfish as hell. But it seems to me that you hold most of my cards, but I have very few of yours, so let me ask you again, what did he do?"

Arri hesitated, confessions were not her thing. Being here, like this with Lyfe, had already taken her out of her emotional comfort zone and now he expected her to take everything she'd ever been through, fought through, conquered, loved, and lost; open the wounds and lay them out before him. He expected her to trust him enough to share things she'd never even told Khris . . . Ian . . . She wasn't sure she could do that. Yet something in her heart and the look in his eyes assured her that it would be okay to confide in him. So . . . she chanced it.

"His name was Ian and I met him when I was nineteen, and we were supposed to get married." Arri closed her eyes and recounted for Lyfe her relationship with Ian from the beginning to his death at the end. "So I don't fuck with love too tough." She chuckled a bit. "Because it's always some bullshit."

"You don't think it's bullshit. You just scared as hell."

"And how do you know that?"

He began kissing her stomach and untying the sides of her bikini panties. "I can feel it, and I can see it. But I'ma do all I can to show you that it's okay to be yourself with me. Because from what I see and from where I'm standing this is where I'm supposed to be," he whispered as he French kissed the center of her breasts to her navel, untying her bikini bra, and slowly pulling it off.

She watched him suckle her breasts as she opened her legs wide and he slid his fingers into her middle. He massaged her clit and she raised up just enough so that he was able to slip her bottoms off.

Though his eyes were looking up at her, he slid his tongue into her throbbing pussy; her clit instantly became jelly between his lips.

"You love eatin' pussy, don't you?" she moaned.

"I love eatin' *your* pussy," he corrected her.

"Do you believe in love at first sight?"

"Now I do," he said as he sucked the pinkness of her hot flesh. She lay back and ran her hands across her breasts and squeezed her nipples. "You just gotta let it go, baby. Just go with the flow. Stop holding everything in." Lyfe continued his licking session between her legs. "Just like you need to let this nut go." He ran two fingers along the sides of her sugar walls as he slowly licked her silkiness, pulling the lips covering her vulva between his teeth. They were sweet yet salty as his tongue took a generous bath in her cum. She had the prettiest pussy he'd ever seen and he didn't want to stop kissing it. "I ain't never"—he licked, his fingers twirling inside her—"leaving you. Tell me you know that."

She placed her hands on his head. "I know that." She squealed.

"This pussy so fuckin' sweet." He slipped his fingers out, sucked the cream off, stuck them back in, and resumed to eating her again.

"Uhmmm . . . damn, Lyfe baby, that feel so fuckin' good." Her eyes rolled to the top of her head. "You suckin' the hell outta my clit . . . lick the right side"—her legs shivered against the sides of his head like an erotic butterfly—"damn . . . baby . . . move your fingers faster . . . yes . . . yes . . . that's it . . . Oh

God!" This had to be paradise. Or better yet, the best fuckin' high in the world . . . the euphoria of this motherfucker would put the sweestest crack trip to sleep.

Arri's head turned from side to side—she couldn't think of what to call Lyfe, there were no adjectives left—yet as she watched his head move up and down and his tongue hiss out of his mouth, it clicked; she now knew what to call him. It was simple: he was the best.

Arri pressed her nails into his shoulders and belted his name, "Lyfe—oh God Lyfe—wait, baby." She started to get fidgety as her cum slid from between her thighs and into his mouth, his tongue continuing to move as if it were battery operated. "Lyfe, stop, baby please, wait—I need a moment."

"Hell, no, I'm not stopping." He could feel her pussy dripping honey on his tongue, "That's it, baby. Drip." He sucked her pussy between his lips. "Drip."

"Uhmmm," she moaned, her head threatening to explode, "I want some dick!"

"You sure? What, you want some dick?"

"Yes, baby."

"Say please." He continued to nibble on her clit.

"Please," she said as he continued to lick her pussy, making her mind, her soul, and every other part that she claimed as her own take flight and float above her body. "Baby, pleazzzzzzzze!!!!!!!" she screamed.

Arri could hear the staff on the other side of the estate buzzing with their duties and she knew they could probably hear her scream, but she didn't care. Lyfe climbed out of the pool, stepped out of his trunks, and lay on top of her. He kissed her from the top of her head straight down the center of her body, kissed her clit and back up again.

Lyfe spread her legs and sucked her chin as he slowly slid into her. His dick was so thick and so long that he prepared himself for her to scream as she did the first time he pushed it all in.

Arri's mouth flew open as she pressed her nails into his back, and just when she thought it was due to end and he was completely inside of her, there was more dick to contend with.

Lyfe could tell Arri was struggling to keep it together. "Focus on me, 'cause I'm not pulling out."

"It feels so good, but it's sooo big, Daddy."

"But you knew that." He stroked. "And you gon' take this dick and get used to it."

"Oh God, I'ma scream!"

"Stop screaming." He gripped her ass cheek. "You'll scare the staff, then they gon' come over here and I'm not gon' stop. They'll be watching me fuck you."

Her stomach heaved up and down, and her breathing felt stifled. "Oh baby . . . my baby . . . Lyfe . . . Sweet Jesus . . ."

Lyfe threw her legs to one side of his shoulders and began pounding into her. "Sweet-ass fuckin' pussy." He held his head down and sucked her breasts.

Afterward he turned her over and placed her on top of him. Arri leaned forward and placed her arms around his neck. She kissed him all over his face, his neck, sucked his nipples, and eased down his chest, where she arrived at his cream-covered lollipop, slowly working it into her mouth. He was so endowed that Arri couldn't even count the inches; it had to defy the laws of arithmetic—there were no measurements for it. Yet somehow she was able to deep-throat him and bless him with the head job a man like this deserved. She licked and sucked his rigid walls, as if he were all she ever wanted. "Fuck!" Lyfe said as he felt his nut rush to the tip.

Wanting him inside of her, Arri slipped him from her wet mouth and climbed back on top. She gasped as his dick reentered her.

"Steady baby . . ." Lyfe moaned as he placed his hands on her hips, controlling her movements. "That's it, that's how you ride Daddy's dick." He thrust her back and forth . . . forth and back . . . over and over again. The music of their skin clapping, slapping, and loving each other soared into the air, as footsteps tipping across the lawn could be heard behind her. Lyfe opened his eyes and saw the maid tipping away.

Arri arched her back, "I'm cumming, baby."

Lyfe couldn't respond because he was exploding inside of her, and finally, for the first time since he'd been a grown-ass man, he felt like this is exactly where he wanted to be. Like everything he'd ever done, everything in life was for this one particular moment, where he could look into the face of the one person he felt would love him and never ever ask for anything in return.

He pulled her to his chest and knew he would never let her go. "I will never let anyone hurt you ever again," he said as they exchanged explosions.

Arri knew when she awoke the next morning that she was in another world, far away from New York, far away from Brooklyn, and all of the other demons that she so desperately wanted out of her life. The only thing missing was Zion.

She turned over and kissed Lyfe in the center of his chest. "Wake up, sleepyhead." She playfully bit him on the side of his neck.

"You know that kinda shit," he said as Arri's cell phone rang, "makes my dick hard, right?" He rolled on top of her and she opened her legs to allow him in. Her phone stopped ringing and then it immediately started ringing again.

"Maybe you ought to get that," Lyfe said, reaching for Arri's phone and handing it to her.

"Yeah." She sat up as he rolled off of her. She looked at the caller ID. "It's Khris." Her heart started to beat quickly. "Is everything okay?" she said when she picked up the phone.

"Arri," Khris said, clearly upset, "I think you should come home."

Arri did her best to remain calm. "Where's Zion?"

"He's fine, he's in the other room with Tyree."

"Then what's wrong, Khris?"

"Your sister, Arri." Khris paused and Arri could hear the tears in her throat. "She's gone."

Arri's heart dropped to her feet, "What do you mean she's gone?"

"She died. She was found dead across the street in the alley. Drug overdose."

Arri dropped the phone to her lap and shock consumed her body. Tears streamed down her face as Khris's voice echoed from the phone. A million thoughts raced through Arri's mind about how she would never again see her sister. She would never be able to dream with her, cry with, and beg her to please get it together. It was not only over, she was now officially alone.

"What happened?" Lyfe asked her, as he held her in his arms.

"My sister died," she cried. "I need to go home."

"Of course," Lyfe said, kissing her on the forehead. "Let's go home."

New York

After the cremation and the spreading of Samara's ashes in the river, Lyfe spent three days with Arri and Zion, forgetting once again that this was not his everyday life. Because the harsh reality was: no matter how much he didn't want to face it, he had a company, a wife, and other shit to do; which was why he told Arri that he had work to finish up and needed to get back to his hotel suite.

The night was extremely quiet as Lyfe pulled into the hotel's parking garage and closed the door to his Escalade. His hard-bottoms clicked along the concrete as he thought about Arri and hoped like hell he didn't make her promises that life or unforeseen circumstances would force him not to keep. He knew she would never forgive him if he fucked this up, and he wasn't willing to take that chance.

He walked through the dimly lit rows of cars and thought he heard footsteps behind him, yet when he turned around there was nothing. *I'm losing my fuckin' mind.* He shook his head and continued swiftly on his way, only to be distracted by the sound of footsteps behind him again. Slowly he turned around and a stray cat hopped out of a garbage can.

Fuck it. I'm done thinking about this shit.

"Mr. Carrington," the doorman tipped his hat as Lyfe entered the side entrance. "No valet parking this evening?" He looked surprised.

"My mind is in a million places all at once, Lawrence. Hadn't even thought about it," he tossed over his shoulder as he walked onto the elevator.

Lyfe stepped into his hotel suite, and though everything appeared to be in place he could tell by the foreign scent that lingered in the air someone had been here. He looked around his suite, checked his important papers and his computer, which was still intact.

I'm changing suites in the morning.

He looked at the clock and though he tried to fight it, he wanted to call and hear her voice one more time for the night. He searched his pocket for his cell phone and came up empty.

Shit. He grabbed his keys. *It must be in the car.*

Lyfe headed back to the lobby and as he exited the side door, he felt a tap on his shoulder. "Lyfe Carrington."

Fuck. The last time someone called his name like that he was being sentenced to prison. He turned around and Galvin and Keenan were standing there. A smile ran across Galvin's face. "We need to speak to you, Lyfe."

"Now," Keenan emphasized.

"Speak to me about what?" Lyfe snapped.

Galvin and Keenan flicked their billfolds open and revealed their respective federal agent badges. "A few things, but we can start with one in particular—"

"How about we don't start with shit." Lyfe smirked. "Now back . . . the hell up, because I won't be answering a damn thing. If you're reading me my rights and I need to get my attorney, then let's handle our business."

"Attorney?" Galvin frowned, and pulled a cigarette from his pocket. "You're not being charged with anything."

"Then what the fuck," Lyfe paused, doing his best to shield his thundering heart from his voice, "do you want?"

Galvin flicked his Bic and lit his cigarette. "We just wanna ask you some questions."

"About what?" Lyfe said, clearly aggravated.

"About how well you know your wife."

California

I *never thought I'd have to kill him.* Payton sat in the center of her crisp white camelback sofa and sipped a glass of chardonnay. Her eyes skipped around her evening cliffside view of the Hollywood Hills, as the flicker from her candelabra gave life to the glowing reflection of her face in the adjacent glass wall.

She studied the low-hanging clouds hovering around the mountains as she pressed the wineglass to her lips and left a kiss behind on the rim. Thoughts of how hours had faded to days and days had faded to over a week of her not hearing from Lyfe, ran through her mind . . . and that's when it clicked that once again she'd been reduced to stalking his voice mail.

Payton thought about ripping through the New York office again, but quickly changed her mind when she remembered that embarrassing Lyfe and demanding his attention was too much of a wild card to play. So she lay her head back on the sofa, looked toward the vaulted ceiling, and mulled over a plan of how to get this ungrateful motherfucker back under control.

The sounds of Sade's "Soldier of Love" played softly in the background as Payton sipped her wine and hummed the chorus: "Too late for love to come turn it all around . . ." And just as she got into the edginess of the beat and could hear the drums speaking to her, the doorbell rang, causing her to jump and splash some of her wine over the sides of the glass and onto her fingers.

"I'm not expecting anyone, Gretchen," Payton said to her maid, who'd walked from the kitchen and into the foyer to answer the door. "Send them home!"

"And leave without my goddamn money," poured from behind Payton. "I don't think so."

Payton sucked in a quick and nervous breath as she turned around to face her mother, Dianna, who was handing an apologetic-looking Gretchen her silver mink stole and her white quilted leather Chanel shoulder bag. Payton looked her fifty-six-year-old mother over: from her salt-and-pepper, short, cropped, one-sided bob, honey-colored skin, to her perfect posture and wonderful hourglass shape. Payton forced herself to smile as she remembered what the calendar date was.

"Payday." Dianna grimaced, lighting her long, thin, chocolate-brown cigarette. She stuck the platinum holder of her cigarette butt between her lips and took a hard pull. The smoke snaked from her mouth as she looked at Payton. "Is this how they're greeting their mothers in Holmby Hills now? On their asses?" Dianna spat, and before she could go on, Payton looked at Gretchen and said, "You may leave for the evening; my mother and I need to sort through a few things."

"Yes, ma'am," Gretchen said as she put Dianna's things in the hall closet. A few moments later she was dressed to leave. "Good night, Mrs. Carrington."

"Good night," Payton said, as Gretchen closed the door behind her.

"I asked you," Dianna stressed, "if sittin' on their asses is how they're greeting their mamas out here."

Payton fought back a stressful sigh as she rose from the couch and walked over to greet her mother. She kissed her on both cheeks.

"Much better," Dianna said as she sat in the white leather armchair facing the sofa and continued, "For a moment I thought I needed to remind you which side your bread was buttered on."

"Really?" Payton retook her seat and arched her brow. "Seems your bread is buttered over here."

"Hmmm,"—Dianna took a pull of her cigarette and then hissed a string of smoke into the air—"it's starting to occur to me that every time I'm away from you too long, you lose fuckin' control," she said evenly, never raising her voice. "I was in Morocco, laying some groundwork, and already you're forcing me to put you in your place. Your sister doesn't even act this unappreciative when she sees me—"

"She doesn't even claim you and she doesn't claim me either, not as her sister. And I don't give a fuck."

"When's the last time you've seen her?"

"A while ago and I hope she doesn't bring her pathetic ass back here. I really can't stand her."

Diana cackled. "I swear I really drove home the bitch in you when you were a child."

"Mother, please." Payton rolled her eyes.

"Are you getting nasty again?" Diana asked. "Why must I check the shit out of you every time I see you? I'm not the goddamn one, okay? Now, you seem to think that I'm playing with your ungrateful ass. So, let me have you understand," she eased up in her chair and spoke with her lips stiff, "I don't play with my money and my men, in that order. You know when the first of the month is. This shit isn't new to you."

"I have other things on my mind."

"Like what?"

"Like my marriage—"

"Marriage?" Dianna gave a sinister chuckle. "I know you're not counting that ghetto-ass project you picked up off the street."

"Don't speak about my husband like that!"

"Fuck his ass!" Dianna spat coldly. "You think I give a fuck about that black bitch? The best thing about him is he's black as smoke and fine as hell . . . oh, and he probably has a dick like a Clydesdale, but other than that, he's the same kind of shit as your damn daddy. Period." She leaned back in the chair. "So like I said, Deneen, don't fuck with my money." She held her hand out.

Payton reached for her purse, scribbled on a check, and handed it to her mother. "Are you leaving now?"

"Hell no, rude ass." She looked Payton over. "Looks as if you gained a little weight." She took a long toke. "And I hope like hell you are not pregnant, because that corner-store hoodlum you're running around with is not the one to be ruining your body for."

"I'm not pregnant," Payton snapped.

Dianna looked Payton up and down. "You better watch your goddamn tone." She took a pull and blew out the smoke. "Every time it's my payday I'm noticing that you get flip, fly, and fucked-up at the mouth. But trust me, I will check you so fuckin' hard you won't know what to do, and you better know it."

"Is all of this necessary?"

"You started it so I'ma finish it; because unlike everyone else around here you're trying to impress, I know exactly who you are and exactly where you're from, and it's not Hollywood, California, it's N'Orleans." She put on an enhanced Southern accent. "So I suggest that you knock that high sadity bullshit down, 'cause underneath that four-thousand-dollar Dolce and Gabbana lounge outfit you have on and all of that bling-bling that's blinding me, is a geechie-ass li'l bitch from the bayou." Dianna waved her finger. "So don't push me and I won't need to go there."

Payton hated that her relationship with her mother was more of a business arrangement than anything else; as far as Dianna was concerned, everything was business: money, marriage, children, fucking. Nothing was for free, not love, not lust, not even a blow job. It all had a price, and the only ones who didn't charge a man for shit were stupid bitches who didn't understand the true power of a killer pussy.

"Now let's get down to business." Dianna mashed her cigarette in the ashtray. "When are we blowing this motherfucker?"

"I can't leave now!" Payton blinked in disbelief. "I'm established." She paused. "And I have *enough* money."

"Established?" Dianna waved her hand dismissively. "Your late husband, Carlton Anderson of Anderson Global, was established. *You* are an opportunist, and if you keep hanging around this motherfucker you're going to have problems. *Now* is the time to leave."

"No it's not."

"Too much time in one place makes no sense," Dianna attempted to convince Payton.

"I *said* now is not the time."

Dianna reared back in her chair and her eyes combed Payton from head to toe and back again, "This motherfuckin' Lyfe." Dianna sighed. "Is that the real reason why it's not time? It's not time because you slipped up and married for a fucked-up reason."

"I . . . love . . ." Payton said slowly, "my . . . husband."

Dianna rose from her chair and walked over to Payton. She reared her left hand back and slapped Payton so hard that her neck whipped to the left and seemed to get stuck there. Dianna roughly cupped Payton's chin. "We don't do love, we do business. So you better," she spoke slowly, "get this shit straight. This is a job and we don't fall in love. And especially not with no bastard that doesn't have shit besides a big dick to offer. You think that motherfucker gives a damn about you? Answer me!" she screamed at the top of her lungs in Payton's face.

Dianna assisted Payton's head in shaking no. "Exactly," Dianna said callously. "He's off rendezvousing with that cheap-ass secretary bitch, and you know it."

"How do you know that?"

"I know everything. Just like I know that Anderson Global is not your fuckin' family business. Sign that shit over to Carlton's kids. Carlton's been dead, and we've already cleaned this place out. Mission accomplished, there isn't much left in this motherfucker. What are you holding on to, air? Now, unless you want me to blow that two-bit nothing you married's brains out, li'l girl, you'll be ready to leave this motherfucker thirty days from now. Otherwise," she positioned her hand like a gun, "click, click. And trust me, just like I laid your damn daddy out, I will not think twice. And you know my motto: Go hard or go to hell. Now, don't fuck with me."

Payton scanned her mother's eyes and knew she meant every word she said.

"Now, if you want that bitch to live, you'll get off your ass and get on your grind." Dianna released Payton's chin from her grip, retrieved her things from the hall closet, and slammed the door behind her as she left.

Tears rolled over Payton's cheeks as she sat still on the couch. She heard her mother's car race out of the driveway and her thoughts burned through her mind. She rose from the couch and grabbed the phone off the receiver. Her fingers punched hard against the dial pad. She listened to the phone ring. "Quinton, I need you to get over here now!" and she hung up.

New York

The devil was a funny motherfucker; he had to be. Otherwise, Lyfe wouldn't be able to make sense of how he sat in a secluded booth in the hotel's sports bar, looking two federal agents in the face, as they gave him blow-by-blow reasons of why they believed Anderson Global, once one of America's finest institutions, had become one big money-laundering scheme.

Lyfe eased up in his seat and leaned toward the agents. "Have you lost your mind? My wife's company—"

"Her late husband's company—" Galvin interrupted.

"Whatever," Lyfe said, fighting like hell to be something he wasn't: calm. "Anderson Global is a legitimate investment banking corporation that has been in business since 1968—"

"And 2006," Galvin said, "was the last time the investment arm of Anderson Global was legitimate. The mortgage arm—"

"Legit," Keenan said.

"The credit card arm—"

"Legit—"

"But the investment banking arm—"

"Is bullshit," Galvin lit a cigarette, "and that's why we're here. Because we know that you, under the three strikes law, can't take the chance of going back to prison—"

"Like I said before, are you charging me with something?" Lyfe stroked his box beard.

"Not if you help us." Galvin arched his brow intensely.

"And if I don't?" Lyfe arched his brow with the same level of intensity.

"Then you get fucked with no Vaseline, like the rest of 'em," Galvin said. "What do I care? Because, from where I'm sitting," he let out a long string of cigarette smoke, "your ass is as guilty as the rest of 'em. And as soon as you try and climb out the cesspool, the district attorney is going to make sure you're covered with so much shit, you won't know what you've gotten into."

"Then by all means," Lyfe picked up his glass of Hennessy and sipped, "let's get it on."

"Do tell me, Mr. Carrington," Keenan said, sounding as if he were a prosecuting attorney cross-examining Lyfe, "what are your credentials?"

Lyfe hesitated.

"Please inform the court: what exactly entitles you to run a multimillion-dollar investment company, beside how much your fine-ass wife appreciates your pipe."

The vein in Lyfe's neck tightened as he pointed his finger in Galvin's face. "You don't know shit about what I do with my wife."

"Hmmm." Keenan bobbled his head slightly from side to side. "I move to strike, but we all know," Keenan continued his act, "that your degree in the ins and outs of California prisons, or your Crip set, not even your criminal background, makes you fit for such a position. So, let's see, what could it be: your charm," he held his hands out as if he were counting on his fingers, "your wit, or could it possibly be," Keenan tapped his index finger against his temple, "that you have simply upgraded your crimes from the streets to the boardroom? And that you lured rich people to come into your wife's company to invest their money, and then you passed them on to your coconspirator— excuse me, your chief investment officer, Quinton King. Mr.

King then sheltered the money in various offshore accounts, most of them with your name on them.

"Would you please explain to the jury how such a sophisticated operation came to be? Are you an innocent bystander or simply an opportunistic criminal?"

Lyfe didn't flinch. "Well, if all of that is true, then why are we sitting here sipping cocktails? It sounds like you need to be charging me, 'cause as of right now, I'm not assisting you with shit."

"Testing the three strikes law is up to you." Galvin mashed his cigarette in the ashtray.

"I'll take my chances."

"Pretty much slim to none," Keenan interjected.

"I've always been the underdog, so I pretty much like those odds," Lyfe retorted, "especially since you would have to prove me guilty and you don't have shit besides some bogus-ass theory that you made up on your way over here."

"Really?" Keenan reached into the inside pocket of his trench coat, pulled out a business envelope, and opened it. "Let's see what we have here: On March 3, 2006, two days after your wedding, you moved four million dollars into a Swiss account, and then you took half out and invested in foreign bonds."

"What?" Lyfe said with a dash of too much surprise, as a vision of Payton danced before his eyes, *Honey,* she'd said a few days after they were married, *sign this.*

"What is it?"

"A joint offshore investment account. An insider tip told me that this is one to invest in . . ."

Lyfe blinked, and warred with his eyes to hide his immeasurable level of surprise. "It's not illegal to invest, it's not even illegal to have Swiss accounts."

"True," Keenan said, moving on to another banking statement. "But it is illegal to take investors' money and use it as your own. Now, let's see what else we have here. On July 23, 2006, you moved a whopping twenty million dollars into Monte Carlo, another offshore account." He handed Lyfe the bank statements, looked into his eyes, and said, "Yes, Your Honor, we have a verdict—we the jury find the defendant guilty of fraud, money laundering, and theft." He pounded his fist on the table. "You're sentenced to life in prison."

Lyfe hoped like hell that the rapid speed of his heart didn't show on his face. He took another swig of his Hennessy and said, "Bullshit. All of it, well-prepared bullshit. I never laundered any money. So, do what it is you came to do."

"Fine," Galvin snapped, "I don't give a fuck if you make Pookie the punk suck your dick or you become somebody's bitch in prison, but it would seem to me that you would want to get out while you can."

"I haven't done anything," Lyfe insisted, his voice becoming slightly elevated.

"Well," Keenan shrugged his shoulders, "you'll fit in perfectly when you go back to prison, because they're all pretty much singing the same tune."

"I don't believe this," Lyfe said, more to himself than to them.

Keenan snapped his fingers. "Oh, wait, here's some more well-prepared bullshit." He slid Lyfe a list of offshore banks. "More accounts in your name. Again, Your Honor, we the jury find the defendant—"

"What do you want from me?" Lyfe snapped.

"Help us," Galvin said.

"How am I supposed to do that?"

"It's easy," Keenan leaned in, "twenty million dollars in cash will do the trick."

"What the hell are you talking about?" Lyfe frowned.

"You know exactly what we're talking about," Galvin said, tight-lipped. "And in exchange we won't turn in the evidence we have on you to our superiors. We'll simply turn in what we have on your wife. So, we suppress the evidence and you walk away, start a new life, and tell everybody left here to kiss your ass. Besides, it's your wife who'll give us the headlines. You're small fuckin' fish, and we go after sharks—anything smaller than that, we let the trigger-happy police handle those shits. We want headlines, a front-page bust, so, consider this your plea bargain—no jail time, and not only do we all walk away rich, it gets us the decorated career we're looking for."

Lyfe chuckled in disbelief. "You're trying to muscle me?" he said, taken aback. "Crooked fuckin' pigs."

"Call it what you will, but from where I'm sitting you don't have a choice. You can play hero, roll the dice on three strikes, or you sacrifice your wife and we all walk away wealthy."

Lyfe sat silent for a moment. Too many thoughts were going through his head to decide what was the most pressing issue he had to deal with. Yeah, Payton had been a bitch during their marriage, but she didn't deserve this. But what if the paperwork that they gave him was legit? Then what? Is this why Payton was so resistant to the audit? There was no way in hell he could go back to prison, especially for something he didn't do. He looked at their gleaming silver FBI badges and shook his head. "I need some time," Lyfe said, knocking off the rest of his drink. "How can I reach you?

"Don't worry," Keenan said as he and Galvin rose from their seats, "we know how to reach you."

New York

Lyfe had been sitting in his office from the time he left the FBI agents last night until five a.m. this morning, poring over the financial reports, records, and computerized files, and nothing made any sense. There were accounts showing gains when even the dumbest motherfucker knew that the stock market was on its ass. This was insane. He slammed his fist onto the desk and shook his head.

It was a front. All of it, a disaster, the next piece of shit that was sure to send him to prison for the rest of his fuckin' life.

Lyfe could feel his heart inching its way from his chest and into his throat. He couldn't understand why he hadn't seen this coming. Why did he expect that this shit was fuckin' legit, when the financial world was falling down all around him. This is why Payton wanted him in New York; this is what she didn't want him to know . . . that she was robbing every-fuckin'-body who could see straight blind.

"What the fuck!" Lyfe screamed at the top of his lungs and pushed everything off his desk. His nameplate made a thud as it hit the tile below and the papers scattered violently about the room. Tears filled his eyes, but Lyfe was determined not to cry . . . he couldn't cry . . . because that shit was for the weak at heart. And that's not what he was.

He sat staring at the computer, the financial account fading to black on his computer screen. He wondered if moving the twenty million dollars was the right thing to do . . . when all of the information he had was based on an assumption. He wasn't able to prove if there were really offshore accounts in his name. Could he tell if money had been moved from Anderson Global accounts? Yes. Did the amounts moved match the bank statement copies the FBI gave him? Yes. But did he have absolute proof that Payton was doing him in? No.

And suppose it wasn't Payton. Hell, maybe it was Quinton. Shit, after all, it was his department that made the hard sales and invested the money. All of the higher-ups in the company knew that Payton's power was more for show and for when she felt like flexing it, but other than that, she was just there.

He had to speak to Payton; they needed to push aside their marital discrepancies and discuss what was really going on. The only problem was explaining to Arri that he was going to California to see his wife.

New York

Arri could tell by the way Lyfe was fucking her that something had happened between the time he left her last night and when he showed up at her door this morning. Given the way he'd abandoned all finesse and was instead stroking her hard and rough and the usual soft and sensual sucks to her nipples were borderline abusive, something was troubling his thoughts. Her breasts had always been his favorite to toy with, yet he was mistreating them and making her nipples sore.

She opened her eyes and watched his shaft make heavy metal drumbeats as it slammed against her pussy lips. It wasn't that the sex wasn't good, it was, and Arri had already cum twice; it's just that with each nut he gave her, he became rougher and more on edge. She knew he hadn't cum yet, and maybe that was part of his frustration, but she also knew she couldn't take much more of this rough-ass lovemaking.

Lyfe flipped Arri over on her stomach at rocket speed and gripped her by the back of her neck. Now she was sure beyond a shadow of a doubt that his mind had fled the scene.

"Lyfe!" she screamed his name as his hips soared against her ass.

He didn't answer; instead he took her hands that gripped the sheets, pulled them behind her back, held her wrists together, and forced the wheels on the corners of the bed to sing.

Arri turned her head to the right and looked at Lyfe; every vein in his arm and hand was highlighted and bulging through his skin. He bit into his bottom lip as he rode her ass like a Roman chariot, forcing her a few seconds later to cum solo again.

This was the first time they'd made love without him saying a single word, only grunting, groaning, and roughhousing her in all sorts of positions. He pulled her to the edge of the bed, where he twirled her around in a wheelbarrow position. Instantly every ounce of blood in Arri's body rushed to her head and her hair covered her face. She loved the high of being fucked upside down, but she knew that his dick was too big for their daily sessions to ever be this intense.

He slapped her hard on her ass and then he pounded into her in a rapid succession, before putting her back on the bed, placing her backward across his middle, and watching her ass leave behind erotic lotion all over his dick. Lyfe gripped her by the sides of her hips and plopped her up and down on his cock until she'd released her overflowing dam and he'd finally rained like a tsunami all over her ass.

Arri eased off Lyfe and sat alongside him, her knees pulled to her breasts, as Lyfe folded his arms behind his back and stared at the ceiling. "Did you enjoy that?" she asked.

"Enjoy what?"

"What the hell we just did?"

"What are you saying?" He frowned and turned toward her. "We make love damn near every night and now there's a problem?" he snapped, sitting up with his back against the headboard. "Whatever argument you're looking for tonight ain't the night for it. Check me tomorrow, but see tonight, it ain't going down."

Arri drew in a deep breath. "What," she paused, "is wrong with you?" She placed her finger against the center of his lips, "And don't give me no bullshit."

"It's nothing."

"Oh, here we go with the nothing-is-wrong-with-you shit; it's obvious that something has you fucked up."

Lyfe sighed and pulled Arri on top of him. He stared at her and he said, "Anything you have to tell me, that I need to know, tell me now."

Arri was caught completely off guard.

"Why are you saying that? What is that about?"

"Everybody," Lyfe's eyes seemed to drift into space, "has been lying to me. Nothing is real . . . Nothing. So if it's anything, I need you to tell me."

Arri's heart beat fast as she wondered if he knew about A Smooth Operator, and if he did, how? She knew she needed to tell him, but how exactly do you explain that you've been fucking men via the Internet to pay your rent? She swallowed. "I do have something to tell you."

Lyfe's hands dropped from Arri's waist.

"What is it?"

She could hear the hesitancy in Lyfe's voice. "Listen," Arri felt her heart build resistance, "I've been raising myself since I could remember, so I've had to do what I had to do."

"And what was that?" he said coldly, as if he was preparing for the worse.

"I was a stripper, but when my nephew came, I couldn't keep that up, so I had to take care of him another way."

"And how did you do that?"

"I started working at Anderson Global in the day, and at night I set up an erotic site." She swallowed the hard lump in her throat.

"What were you doing on the site?"

"What do you think? Fulfilling men's fantasies. Fucking them via the Internet. So what,"—she pushed back the tears rocking her eyes—"now you know. And I will not"—she pointed into his face—"apologize for taking care of my business." She stared at him, and when he didn't say anything, unwanted tears filled her eyes and she said, "It's cool, that's why I don't fuck with love."

"Too late." Lyfe placed his hands back around Arri's waist. "You're already in love."

"I can get over it."

"Really?" he asked. "Well, I can't. Listen, you can tell me anything, because believe me, I have done some shit that makes me not able to ever judge anybody. I know what it is to have to survive. But let me ask you this, were you *only* doing this over the computer, and not in person?"

"I wasn't a whore."

"I didn't say that you were."

"And I'm not apologizing for it—"

"So what are you saying, you're still doing it?"

Silence.

"I need you to stop."

"Why?" she snapped.

"Because, I'm not comfortable with that shit."

"I have to pay my bills."

"I'ma pay 'em!"

"So, you gon' pay me to be your whore. Is that what you're saying? No thanks, I can take care of myself."

"You gettin' on my damn nerves with this defensive shit. I didn't fall in love with a whore. And all I'm saying is that you don't have to do that computer shit anymore—"

"And why is that?"

"Because it's other shit that we need to deal with."

"Like what?"

"Like how everything around me is just falling apart?"

"Tell me." She cupped his face.

He massaged her waist. "I need to leave."

"Leave?" That wasn't the response she expected.

"I'm coming back." He grabbed her wrists and she immediately snatched her hands back.

"Where are you going?" she asked in more of a panic than she intended.

"To California, only for a few days."

"Business?" Her heart thundered in her chest.

"You could say that." He stroked his box beard.

"Don't play semantics with me."

"Listen," he sighed, "I need to go and see Payton."

"Your wife?" She swallowed hard as if she'd forgotten that he had one. She hopped off the bed and wrapped her terry cloth robe around her.

"Yes."

Arri wanted to flip, but why? Weren't moments like this all a part of fucking somebody else's husband? "It's cool," she said, her mind telling her to break off their relationship but her heart telling her to chill.

"I'm coming back, Arri, and I'll only be gone for a few days, a week at the most."

"It's okay," she said, doing her best to keep visions of him fucking Payton from taking over her eyesight.

"I'm not going out there to play perfect husband," he said.

"And you're not going to get divorced either, so let's stop this conversation while we're ahead," she said as her stomach started to feel queasy. "Otherwise, you might come back, and I'll be gone." She walked swiftly to the bathroom to shower.

"Arri." Lyfe knocked on the door as she turned on the shower. "Let me come in. Arri." He pushed against the door and walked in. He watched the water cascade over her perfect body.

"I love you," he said to her, as he slid into the shower behind her, "and I need you to trust me." He took the washcloth from her hands and began rubbing it over her back. "Just trust me, Arri, please. I need to know that you believe me when I tell you I love you." He turned her around and looked at her deeply, and she could tell there was more to his leaving than he was saying. "I need to come back with you still here."

Arri knew she was treading into territories her heart didn't need to be in. She needed to let it go, let this go, let him go, but she couldn't, especially when she knew she would be right here waiting for him, and his dinner would be ready, his bath would be drawn, and her pussy would be wet, just the way he liked it. "I'll be here," she said as they started to kiss and make love under the shower all over again.

California

Payton had planned death many times, written many eulogies, and said many, many words of reflection, but never in all of the ten years that she'd been a black widow—only taking small sips of time between each marriage to snare her next prey—had she ever envisioned herself attending her own burial.

Yet, here she was. At the gates of hell: naked, scorching hot, drowning in buckets of sweat, seeing only black with snapshots of fire in the distance. A place where she didn't have reservations for another fifty, sixty years, yet she'd arrived early, clearly unexpected, and on the verge of bustin' this motherfucker wide open.

And she was certain this was death . . . it had to be . . . otherwise how could she explain sitting here like a zombie, frozen in time, replaying the exact moment when twenty million dollars went missing from her account; and even worse, she had no idea who'd moved it, given that they signed in under her name and used her password. She knew damn well that she didn't do it. She wondered if it was Quinton, but if she wasn't mistaken, at the time of the transaction he was here, eating her pussy . . . or so she thought.

To think that when she married Lyfe she considered herself retired, but now that most of her money had done a magic trick and disappeared. Her personal and business accounts had a dollar and fifty cents between them.

She'd arrived in hell early, and she had yet to truly enjoy the fruits of her labor. Her first couple of husbands were target practice—small-business owners with only a few millions—case studies until she mastered the ins and outs of what killed quickly and couldn't be detected. After two bouts of target practice she'd been ready for upgrading: a fifty-year-old multimillionaire French politician, Jacques Pierre, with no heirs, who thought her brown, sexy skin was exotic and he had to have it.

So she married him. Over a span of three years she traveled the world with him and chose her next prey, Carlton Anderson, CEO and owner of Anderson Global. She'd picked the day she needed Jacques dead, because she'd heard rumors that Carlton was courting another woman, and Payton's mother insisted that she hurry and get to him before she missed the mark. So instead of killing Jacques with a poison that worked slowly she got straight to the point and strangled him.

He loved to be tied up, whipped, and walked around in a collar. He loved to suck on the heels of her shoes and he would cum from her walking on his chest in five-inch stilettos. But most of all, what he loved more than anything was having a noose around his neck and her choking him until he was unconscious.

So she granted him his last wish and when she was sure he was dead, she kissed him on the forehead and called the police frantically. She told them what had happened and they quickly covered up the murder; there was no way France wanted to be embarrassed by a freaky politician, so they closed the case, citing the cause of death as heart failure.

Shortly after Jacques's murder she was back on the grind: Los Angeles, California. She'd had stellar plastic surgery and chose the name Payton.

Payton was sophisticated, and intelligent, and it didn't take her long to become reacquainted with Carlton. She attended Anderson Global's annual New Year's Eve event, and six months after their initial meeting, they were married.

Payton introduced him to the wonderful sex life of erotic asphyxiation and when it came time for him to depart the earth, it was easy to strangle him and get away with it as a sad case of wild sex gone wrong.

Shortly after this is when the fuck-up, the trip-up, and the slow ride to hell began—she met Lyfe and took a chance. She couldn't help it—the first time she saw him she knew what all the girls in high school raved about; she knew what it was to have the giggles for no reason, to have untamed butterflies float in your belly. She knew what it was to have a man because you had to have him—not because you had to have his bank account.

But it was all a mistake.

She should've seen Lyfe and not seen him at the same time. She should've kept her appointment with the plastic surgeon and gone on to become Chelsea Davis, instead of Mrs. Lyfe Carrington; there was no purpose to it, no reason. It was stupid, and now here she sat completely out of control.

"We're going to fix this." Quinton squatted before Payton, as she sat on the edge of her bed, the single stream of moonlight bathing her back as it inched its way into her master suite.

"How?" she said, holding her cigarette between her fingertips, the burning tip slowly making its way to become one with the butt.

"Because we may not know where the money is at this very moment, but Lyfe's ass hasn't gone any fuckin' place!" He stood up and began pacing before her.

"We don't know if Lyfe is behind it." Her cigarette ashes flaked to the floor.

"Who else would do some shit like that to you? Huh?"

"You have access to that account too, Quinton."

"I wouldn't do anything like that to you, and besides, you know where I was."

"There's been more than one transaction. One last night and one today, Quinton. More than twenty million moved from the company's account." She started to tell him about the money missing from her personal account and about the money she'd been washing in Lyfe's name, but she quickly changed her mind. "I need to know where my goddamn money is!"

"Well, then you need to look at Lyfe."

"He's never gone into the accounts. I never gave him access; he would have to have hacked . . ." She paused "No, he wouldn't do that to me."

"I don't put a damn thing past that niggah," Quinton spat. "When's the last time you heard from Lyfe? Has he come back home to see you, to make love to you? Hell, after all, you are his wife. Has he been consulting you about anything? No, he's been over in New York, pumping his chest and shit. He was never doing an audit; he was trying to figure out ways to swindle you out of your money." Quinton wiped sweat from his brow with the back of his hand. "And now he's sitting back, laughing and shit, plotting and planning to run off with that whore he's fucking— on top of your money—while we sit here, too scared to make a move. You need to pump a bullet in his chest, that's what you need to do."

Payton looked at Quinton and without blinking she said, "Why don't you do it?"

Quinton hesitated and Payton knew instantly that he was a weak link. The weakest link that she'd ever come across in her years of grifting. It was beyond her how she'd involved this motherfucker in helping her pilfer a damn thing.

It was a joke, really, a test of his weak rubber-band will, a last-ditch effort to see if she should spare his life.

Sweat lined Quinton's brow and he said, "I think he would get the message a lot clearer if you were to do it."

He was such a queen.

"I know what'll make you feel better." He smiled at her and began to kiss her along the side of her neck. Payton wasn't in the mood, really, but she needed something to help her release her stress, so she lay back and allowed Quinton to undress her.

Payton hated how the clock steadily ticked and invaded her ears as she rode Quinton's dick. Thoughts of how Lyfe had made a total fool out of her ramped through her mind. She'd risked everything to remain in California with him, and what did he do for her in return? Nothing, zilch. But then again, scratch that, because he did give her one thing: he gave her his ass to kiss.

She hated to admit it, but maybe Quinton and her mother were right: the nerve of this motherfucker to really think that he had a right to not only run the East Coast branch of her company, but that he didn't have to speak to her in the process. She'd had enough.

Payton slid two of her fingers between Quinton's lips and squeezed her velvety walls around the head of his dick. She knew by the way his eyes rolled to the top of his head that he was off in another world.

"Fuck!" he screamed, as she continued to ride him. "Break the head!" he hollered out. "Break that motherfucker off!" he howled, as he came like a thunderstorm inside her.

Payton kissed him and Quinton rolled on top of Payton, and as he slid down her belly, he whispered, "I would kill for you, baby."

Hours later and between the blinding rays of the West Coast sun, Payton lay in her king-size bed and the smell of cigar smoke slithered beneath her bedroom door. She blinked and sniffed, and sniffed and blinked, and then she inadvertently did it again. Her heart ran a marathon in its chamber. She eased a deep sigh out the side of her mouth and shook her head. She didn't smell anything . . . at least she prayed like hell she didn't . . . because that would mean Lyfe was somewhere in the house, while Quinton lay in her bed.

Shit.

She sat up and looked toward the door; it was cracked but the only thing she could see was the gold corner of her Picasso painting.

Untangling the sheets from between her thighs she eased to the edge of the bed. Quinton grabbed her hand. "Where are you going?" His eyes peeled open. "Come back to bed."

She snatched away. "I think Lyfe is here."

"What?" Quinton immediately sat up at military attention. "I knew we should've run away while he was in New York. Fuck," he said, tight-lipped.

Payton's eyes scanned the room. Why was Lyfe here? Why? When he hadn't been back to California in months? When she hadn't even heard from him? And why would he show up after millions of dollars had been moved from her accounts. Unless he was behind everything.

"I gotta get the fuck outta here," Quinton said nervously, as sweat formed on his brow.

Payton wrinkled her nose, "Would you," she said calmly, "shut . . . the . . . fuck . . . up? Is that possible? If Lyfe had seen you, do you think you would be waking up, huh?"

"That's not the point."

"It is very much the point." She rose from the bed. "And the truth of the matter is we don't know if he's here or not." Payton slid her feet into her mink-covered stiletto slippers, tied her silk robe around her waist, and walked toward the door. She looked back at Quinton. "Lock it," she said as she closed the door behind her and proceeded down the corridor, following the smell of cigar smoke.

Once she reached Lyfe's home office she pushed the door in slightly, causing the hinges to creak. As the door slowly became ajar, she could clearly see sitting on Lyfe's desk a glass ashtray holding a burning Cuban cigar, and rising from it was a ghostly screen of silver smoke.

Payton's heart dropped to the bottom of her feet and she started to panic. Her chest heaved and she did her best to calm herself down. *Think . . . think . . . think . . . Where the fuck is he?* She looked around his office in fast-forward motion, but there was nothing . . . not a footprint, not even a piece of paper out of place. Her eyes continued to scan the room.

The safe.

She walked swiftly to her office, checked the safe beneath her desk, and it was empty. All of her papers, all offshore account information—gone. He'd been here and he'd fucked her in the process. Quinton was right. This motherfuckin' Lyfe was robbing her blind—and judging by the evidence he left, he wanted her to know it without question.

Payton backed out of her office until the back of her head hit what felt like a brick wall. "Ahh!" She jumped and turned around, only to look into Gretchen's face.

"Mrs. Carrington," Gretchen said apologetically, "I'm so sorry. I was just coming to clean your office."

"Was he here?" Payton asked in a panic. "Is he here?"

"Who, ma'am?"

"Lyfe!" Payton screamed, "Mr. Carrington!"

Gretchen jumped. "No, ma'am, the team and I have cleaned the whole house, except in here, and I haven't seen him."

Payton thought about leveling Gretchen's ass, but quickly decided that she had bigger fish to contend with. "Just watch where you're going," she barked, and swiftly walked toward her master suite.

She turned the locked knob and snapped, "Open the door!"

Quinton quickly unlocked it and she walked in, her face revealing clear disbelief of what had taken place. "He was here," she said in a soft whisper, more to herself than to Quinton. "And you were right. He was behind everything."

"Where is he now?"

"You think I fuckin' know?" She stabbed her index finger into her chest, as her voice trembled.

"That motherfucker," Quinton said, pissed.

"I have to go, Quinton, so I need you to get out!" She pointed toward the door.

A smile ran across Quinton's face. "Where are you going?"

"New York. Now leave. Go home to your wife. I'm sure she'll be relieved."

"She's gone. She took the twins and left me, but don't worry, I'll be there, waiting for you to come back, and then finally we'll be able to blow this motherfucker!"

"Yes, we will," Payton said, as her thoughts drifted out of the room. "We certainly will."

California

Lyfe watched the air traffic controller swing his arms like flags, one over the other, as he waved the orange caution lights and led the red-eye flight out of the City of Angels. Lyfe did all he could to stop the merry-go-round of thoughts, mixed emotions, and sinking feelings of betrayal from crawling up his spine, but no matter what he did, he couldn't shake them.

Payton
Quinton
Fucking each other . . .
I would kill for you . . .
Anything for you . . .
Offshore accounts . . .
Stocks . . .
Bonds . . .
Setup . . .
Three strikes . . .
You're out . . .
Prison . . .
Dirty pigs wanting their share . . .

"Fuck!" Lyfe screamed as he pounded into the arm of the chair.

"Is everything okay?" the stewardess asked as the plane began to taxi.

Lyfe blinked. "Yes," he said, hesitating, "Yes, everything's okay."

The stewardess shot him a fake smile and patted him on the shoulder. "Well, get ready for the ride. The pilot said there may be some turbulence tonight."

"Yeah." Lyfe nodded as he popped open his briefcase filled with bank statements that he'd collected from the safe in Payton's home office. "I'm sure there will be."

Lyfe reclined his seat and thought about the conversation he had only hours ago with the overseas bank. Each account number that he'd gotten from Payton's safe had matched up with what the FBI said, with money totaling into the hundreds of millions. There seemed to be a history of money being deposited every few months and then mysteriously leaving, depleting most of the accounts to zero, and then the cycle would start all over again.

This was crazy. Insane. He couldn't believe that here he'd come to talk to Payton, holding on to his last bit of trust and belief that either this shit was a dream or the FBI was wrong. But as he stood there in his house, watched his wife in bed with his friend, he knew that nothing in his life for the last few years had been as it seemed.

Lyfe watched them make love for as long as he could stand it before he slowly backed away from the bedroom door. For a moment the sight and reality of what was really happening to him made him forget his way around their mansion. He couldn't remember if he needed to go up or down the stairs to get out of there, and then he stood still for a moment and reminded himself that he was there on a mission, to clear his name and get this shit straight. He couldn't be concerned with who Payton fucked; he had enough to worry about with her trying to set his ass up.

Lyfe reclined in his seat and as the plane rocked through some turbulence he closed his eyes and prepared for a long flight.

Six and a half hours later, Lyfe caught glimmering glances of Keenan and Galvin's ridiculous-ass silver tie clips. They were sitting at the gate, sipping black cups of coffee and leafing through the morning's paper. Although they didn't look up, as Lyfe walked past he knew it was only a matter of moments before they were behind him and buzzing in his ear on whether or not he'd made a decision.

Lyfe walked into the small airport café, and sat near the picture window, where the outgoing planes were the raging view. He placed his briefcase next to him in his chair and a few moments later the waitress came over and he placed an order: "Coffee. No sugar."

"I'll have a cup as well." Keenan smiled, taking a seat.

"And I'll take another," Galvin snorted, at the waitress, as he took his seat. "Especially since I don't know how my morning will be."

"We didn't know if you needed a ride home from the airport or not, Lyfe." Keenan smiled as the waitress set their coffee on the table and walked away. "So we took the liberty of showing up. You know," Keenan said, "just in case."

Lyfe felt like putting holes in the walls with his fists, but fought like hell to hide it and seem as if he was in control. "Appreciate the gesture," Lyfe said as he pressed his coffee cup to his lips.

"So what's the jury going to find?" Keenan asked.

Lyfe looked at Keenan and then at Galvin. "That I'm innocent."

"My boy." Galvin smiled.

"I'm your boy now?" Lyfe's vein started thumping.

"You know I didn't mean it like that." He turned to Keenan, "You talk to him, 'cause I just got pissed off."

"Oh wow," Lyfe said condescendingly, "I didn't mean to do that. Certainly isn't my style."

"I tell you what better be your style,"—Keenan leaned into the table—"twenty million dollars in cash. No slick shit. Don't try and put no trace on the money or no other crazy shit, because believe me, we will turn your ass in, and you'll be exchanging your name for a row of goddamn numbers. You know I don't give a fuck. Instructions," he tapped the envelope, "on how the money needs to be delivered. Don't fuck up or it will be a problem."

Keenan and Galvin rose from their seats and Lyfe watched them walk out of the café. A few moments later he left, and hailed a cab to the office.

When Lyfe walked into his office at Anderson Global he could feel anger creeping up his back. "Motherfuck!" he said, flopping down in his chair, his heart racing out of control. "What the fuck am I supposed to do now?"

He held his head down and a few moments later he shook his feelings of uncertainty off, and made up his mind that he knew exactly what to do, especially since he had everything to lose.

This chick . . .

New York

"Auntie," Zion tugged on Arri's arm as they walked across the street from his school, "there goes Iron Man." He pointed to Lyfe sitting on the small brick stoop in front of their building.

As if remote-controlled by his presence, Arri's pussy creamed and her nipples hardened. She watched Lyfe slowly puff on his Cuban cigar, and the memory of his tongue holding the same exact grip on her clit caused her brow to sweat. She fanned her face, and Khris, who was walking with her, said tight-lipped, "Is this creative overtime?"

"Would you be quiet?" Arri whispered. "You know he can hear you."

"Yeah, he does hear every damn thing, doesn't he?" Khris shot a phony smile at Lyfe. "Mr. Carrington," she said, "funny seeing you here."

"Wassup, Khris," Lyfe said. "And by the way, Lyfe is fine."

"Hell yes, he is," she snarled. "Zion, Tyree, come on upstairs with me."

Once the door closed behind Khris and the boys, Arri walked up the three short stairs to where Lyfe sat. "I thought you were going to be in California for a few days," she snapped with a little more edge than she intended.

Lyfe looked taken aback. "What's that about?"

"What?"

"The attitude."

"I don't have an attitude. I'm very clear on how I feel."

"And how is that?"

"I'm done." Arri turned away from him, and walked into the building.

He followed her into the elevator. "What the hell is this?"

Silence.

"I asked you a question," he said as they stepped off the elevator. "What the fuck is your problem?" He slammed the door as they walked into the apartment.

"Don't slam my goddamn door!" she screamed.

"Then answer my damn question!"

"You wanna know what the fuck my problem is?" Arri waved her arms frantically in the air. The ache in her head caused pain-filled tears to well in her eyes. And though they danced in her throat, the fact that they threatened to spill out fucked with her even more. She wasn't ready to be this vulnerable, but there was only so much she could take. Her words warred with her tears as she spoke. "You really think you can go out to California, fuck your wife, and I'm supposed to what, sit here and be okay with that? Hell no. I'm done with that bullshit."

"I haven't fucked anybody but you. And before you go accusing me, why don't you ask me?"

"You don't have to explain shit to me—"

"Arri—"

"Yes, Arri changed her fuckin' mind. I'm not about to be some weak-ass mistress on the side. I feel cheap as shit. How did you really think I felt with you being gone? Happy? No. I'm done."

"And when did you decide this?"

"The day that Ian was killed right there in my fuckin' doorway is when I decided that I couldn't and I wouldn't do bullshit anymore!"

Lyfe could tell Arri was hurting; hell, he was hurting too. He grabbed her by the hand and pulled her to his chest. He pressed his forehead against hers and said, "You know what," he backed her into the corner of the room, "you wanna do this, let's fuckin' do this. 'Cause this don't have shit to do with Payton, or any other bullshit; this has to do with you loving me and not being able to tell me. So say it."

"What are you talking about?"

"Tell me you love me, so we can get past this argument you're making up, because you know damn well in your heart of hearts that I'm not making love to nobody but you. Now tell me and don't give me no politically correct, homegirl fuckin' answer. And don't tell me shit about my circumstances and I don't wanna hear that you're scared, because I can see that. What I wanna hear is that you love me. In three words."

Arri looked into Lyfe's face and she realized that being in his arms went beyond feeling safe and secure. It was like . . . like . . . loving Superman. It was magnetic. Fire. Passion. Finding forever, all in one man. Tears streamed down her face. "I love you," she practically whispered, "but I can't do this with you."

Lyfe stood up straight and said, "So this is it? That's what you're saying?"

When Arri didn't respond Lyfe turned toward the door. Arri could tell in his steps that he was waiting or hoping that she would say something. And she could also tell that if she said nothing that this would be the last time she'd ever see him.

"But I'm scared . . ." Arri said softly. "I'm scared as hell to love you as hard as I do. And I don't understand it . . . and I don't know what to do with it."

Lyfe stopped in his tracks and turned back toward Arri. "It's simple, just give it to me, please. Because, right now, at this time in my life, when everything I thought was real has turned out not to be, I need you to love me. I need you like air. I want you to have my babies."

"I wanna have your babies," she confided, "and I want your last name, I wanna be . . ."

"Say it."

"I wanna be your wife."

"And you will be, but I gotta ask you something first."

"What?"

"I need you to run away with me. Not like before, where we came back in a day. I mean for good. Just you, me, and Zion."

"Lyfe," Arri hesitated, "why are we running away?"

"Because I can't stay here."

"Why not?"

"Because Anderson Global is a cover for a money-laundering scheme."

"Say that again."

"Payton and Quinton King have been stealing money from the company and setting me up in the process."

Arri gasped. "Are you serious?"

"As hell, and I'm not going back to prison."

"But you didn't do anything."

"Arri, listen to me. Everybody in this motherfucker is crooked. Everybody. Nobody has been honest with me—but you. And the goddamn FBI is involved in this shit."

"FBI?"

"Yes, and even they're crooked as fuck."

"What do you mean they're crooked?"

"They're the ones that gave me all the damn information and bank account numbers. That's the real reason I went to California—to try and get some answers."

"And what did you come back with?"

"That my wife is fucking Quinton and planning to screw me in the process."

"And what about the FBI?"

"In exchange for not turning me in—and only focusing their

case on Payton, regardless of the fact that they know I'm innocent, they want twenty million dollars in cash."

Arri's heart dropped in her chest. "Twenty million . . . Oh
my God, what are you going to do?"

"I'ma give it to 'em."

Arri stared into deep thought and then she said, "Well, if
Payton and Quinton are stealing all of the money, where are you
going to get that kind of money from?"

"I'ma steal it back."

"Steal it back? And how is that?"

"Don't worry about that."

"I have to."

"Would you let me handle this?"

"How are you going to handle it?"

Lyfe drew in a breath. "I need you to sit down and let me tell
you about a few things that I used to do."

New York

The only light in the room came from the crackling end of Payton's cigarette. She took hard and long tokes as she sat in Lyfe's hotel suite, waiting—the last two days—for him. She'd come dressed for the occasion: coal black and fitted Vera Wang strapless dress, four-inch sling-back stilettos, and a midnight black .9 millimeter.

She patted the gun against the center of her Chanel-covered lips and wondered about the exact date when she'd been replaced. It was obvious that she'd withered to nothing. That she'd lost. But so be it. If he'd chosen some broke, pathetic bitch over her, then fine. But one thing was for certain: there was no way in hell he would take care of that whore with Payton's money. She'd kill his ass first, and that wasn't about bruised love, jealousy, or any other heart-pacifying bullshit—that was about business.

It was obvious that Lyfe was a bad investment. But that was fine, she could take being loved and left on the chin. But the one thing that rocked her mind and ached her spine was this ungrateful motherfucker stealing from her. How could he have no regard for her after she'd saved his life? He wasn't shit, had never been shit, and would never be shit. He may have been hood but he was a white-collar fuckin' thief, and given the way he snuck in and out the house, leaving behind cigar smoke and wet tire tracks, she knew without a doubt that this niggah was up to his old tricks again.

Payton checked her magazine clip.

Get ready . . .

The clock steadily ticked and before she knew it an hour had gone by and then two . . . and three . . . And at the exact moment when she thought she would have to prowl the city to find his ass, the doorknob twisted.

She knocked the safety off the gun.

Get set . . .

The door pushed open.

Go . . . !

"I wouldn't make any sudden moves if I were you." She looked Lyfe over as he stepped into the center of the room and dropped the briefcase he carried in his hand to the floor, causing it to pop open and papers to scatter everywhere. She could see him staring at her through the dark in utter surprise. "Don't look at me like you're stupefied or some shit." Payton blinked. "You had to know I was coming, goddammit. You knew when you stole all my fuckin' money that you'd declared war. So man up, soldier, walk in here with the same heavy-ass balls you had when you ripped me the fuck off."

Lyfe looked down at the gun. "What . . . the . . ."

"Oh please, cut the bullshit." Payton sucked her teeth. "We're not on TV, now sit the fuck down." She pointed at the chair sitting on the opposite side of the desk where she sat. "Right there."

Lyfe hesitated and she repeated herself, arching her eyebrows with every word. "Sit . . . the fuck . . . down. And a bitch ain't playing." She pointed back to the chair.

Lyfe didn't know what to think, but he knew he needed to remain calm. "What's this about?"

Payton laughed. "Are you fucking kidding me?" She smiled sinisterly. "Are you serious? What's this about? You need to freshen up on your acting skills, because they're a little rough around the edges. You know what this is about."

"Nah," he eased into the seat, "I don't."

"Well let me refresh your memory. You snuck into my house. The same house that when I took you off the streets I let you stunt in. Then you stole all of my banking information, hacked my accounts, and now all of my money's gone. Sound familiar?"

"Nah." Lyfe did his best not to sound nervous, but sweat had gathered in the palms of his hands. "I don't know what the fuck you're talking about." He looked perplexed.

"I swear to God, you better not deny another fuckin' thing or you'll die sooner than expected." She massaged her temple. "Now, my advice to you is to turn on your computer," she pointed to his laptop, "and transfer my fuckin' money back where it belongs. You understand? Get on that computer, and on the count of ten you better be done." She cocked the gun. "One."

Lyfe stroked his beard. "Payton—"

"Nine." She pointed the gun directly at his forehead. "Didn't I tell you to cut that goddamn computer on? Are you testing me? Is this what new pussy does, cause you to turn into some disrespectful, play-too-much li'l bitch? Is that it? You think I care anymore about who you want to be with? You don't have to want me, but one thing you're not going to do is elevate that broke-down bitch off of my money. Fuck that."

"It's not like that, Payton."

"Not like what?" She blinked. "Did I dream you playing house with this bitch—"

"She's not a bitch!"

"And you taking up for her? I oughta shoot you for the motherfuckin' audacity—" Payton's heels tapped against the floor as she walked around the desk and kneeled before Lyfe. "I'm not the bitch you need to play and I would think that you would know that." She shook her head. "And after all I've done for you, this is how you repay me?"

"I didn't do anything to you, Payton."

"Oh, you did a lot to me—and you know what's funny? I was more of a widow being married to you than I was to Carlton, and I killed him. Now," she stood up, "give me my fuckin' money back!"

Lyfe felt as if a thousand pricks of jagged glass stabbed their way through him. "You did what?"

"Don't act stupid, you know I can't stand subpar."

"Payton," Lyfe shook his head, "I swear to God, I don't know what the fuck you're talking about. I don't. All I know is that Anderson Global has gone from being an upstanding corporation to some money-washing bullshit. Now you run up in here," he stared her down, "all willy-nilly and shit on me, and where you leave your boy? Is he still in your bed?"

"So you admit it, you were in the house? So I know for a fact you stole my shit."

"You better check Quinton, 'cause I don't have a damn thing."

"I checked the safe, you took all of my banking information."

"I didn't take shit."

"You're willing to die behind a lie?"

"Fuck it, you're going to kill me anyway. Ain't that right, didn't you just admit that you killed your last husband? And for what, money?" He looked into her eyes. "The only irony here is that you're going to kill me and I don't have a dear fuckin' dime."

"You have the money you stole from me."

"What did I just tell you?" Lyfe stood up and looked down at Payton. "Why would I steal from you? Huh? What purpose would that serve? I wanted to love you, to be committed to you, but you acted as if you owned me."

"I did own you! But you wouldn't go with the fuckin' flow!"

"What flow? Two sets of books? Stealing? Your turning this company into a front? Hell no, I was in prison twice—two strikes—and then I'm down for life. You think I made a change to go back to prison? What the fuck! I ain't have no problem driving for UPS!" he screamed. "I'm not risking my freedom for greed! Fuck that."

"Niggah, please. Are you done?" She looked at him as if he'd gone crazy. "Really, are you? 'Cause that little criminal-turned-civilian speech just worked my fuckin' nerves. What you are is a hacker. Now, er'body else might think you went to jail for drugs, stealing cars, or whatever other typical li'l Compton shit they do, but I know better. You were too busy on your foster mother— or whatever the fuck you had—computer stealing money directly from rich motherfuckers' accounts, setting up your own transactions. Trust me, there's not much difference between you and me, which is why we're husband and wife, so don't try and act as if you're so upstanding, because I ain't buying it. Now, like I said, get me my fuckin' money back and not a penny less. Otherwise, it's gon' be some slow singing and flower bringing." She nodded her head for emphasis. "Just so you know."

"I don't believe this!" he said, more to himself than to Payton. "Here you accusing me of some bullshit I know nothing about! Got the FBI muscling me and shit—"

"FBI?" Payton said, taken aback.

"Yeah." Lyfe walked over to the window and pulled the drapes back and pointed out the window at the Caprice Classic. "The F.B. fuckin' I! They follow me all day and all fuckin' night. And you wanna know why? Because you set me the fuck up, put some bullshit in my name."

"How do you know that!"

"The FBI fuckin' told me, who else. You, oh and your boy. Quinton laying up in bed, laughing and shit. Plotting to do me in. And here you are accusing me of stealing your money? You can't be serious. Who you better check is Quinton."

Payton blinked. "Quinton? Don't put that shit on Quinton. He wouldn't have the balls to do no shit like that."

Lyfe snorted. "Yeah, and that's just what he wants you to think. And all while he's robbing your ass blind. What did he do, convince you it had to be me, tell you you needed to fly to New York and take care of me? Where is he, Payton? Because if you think he's waiting on you to come back to California, you better think again."

"You're bluffing, trying to twist shit."

"Are you listening to yourself? Quinton moved all of your fuckin' money into his accounts. That's what I was coming back to California to tell you, but instead of being able to hold a conversation with you, you were too busy sucking the devil's dick."

"Yeah, and you got mad and went into my accounts."

"Nah, I didn't go into your accounts, but I hacked the shit out of Quinton's."

"And why would you do that?"

"Because when I did the audit, guess what I came up with, some online transactions to an unknown account. Dig a little deeper and guess whose name is on it? Quinton's. Not only did he steal from you, he was sloppy in doing the shit."

"You're lying."

"Fuck it, then."

Lyfe picked the papers up off the floor and quickly returned to his seat. "Look at the dates," he stabbed his finger at the bank statement, "look at the fuckin' dates. Two days after we got married, money in, and three days later money out. And where did it go? Quinton's account. Same thing here . . ." he pointed to another month, "and here—"

"But all you're showing me is money from the company's accounts. I had other accounts . . . in your name . . . where is that fuckin' money, 'cause it's gone."

"Accounts in my name?" Lyfe swallowed. "You were trying to set me up for washing money?" He clinched his jaw, "I can't believe you would do some shit like that to me," and rose from his seat.

"Sit your ass down!"

"No, fuck that! If you gon' shoot me, shoot me. Fuck it. Go

hard or go to hell. You only married me to set my ass up and be your fuckin' fall guy—"

"I loved you!"

"You didn't love shit! You were so busy trying to own me and make me into what you wanted me to be that you missed Quinton pulling the okey-doke on you. All while I'm out here busting my ass and this motherfucker's making a fool of you. He's probably somewhere laughing at your ass right now, hoping you killed me, all while he packs his shit and leaves you high and dry. And how are you going to get away this time? Huh? Investors are liquidating like fuckin' crazy, the economy is fucked, and people are going to want their money. And what are you going to give them?

"Are you going to tell them that the statements you've been sending out are all phony? That the losses you may have reported on some of their statements are nowhere near what they've really lost? Huh? What are you going to tell the FCC? That they have the wrong person? What are you going to get, plastic surgery? You won't have any money for that, because you'll be broke—courtesy of Quinton King."

Payton's whole body stung as Lyfe's words rang true in her mind. She felt dizzy, as if she was going to fall. She braced herself by holding on to the sides of the desk. She looked Lyfe dead in the eyes and backed out of the suite, leaving him standing there.

New York

It was a minute-by-minute struggle for Lyfe to keep it all together, knowing that once this transaction was made he would be gone. And he wanted nothing more than to pick up his shit and run, especially since he'd hacked all of the accounts and transferred the money into Arri's name.

But he couldn't flinch now; he had more to lose now than he'd ever had. Besides, there was no way in hell that he was going to surrender or shake hands with defeat. He was in too deep and he knew that if he slipped, even for a moment, that it would be the death of him.

Lyfe lit a cigar and laid his head back and smoke floated out the crack in his driver's-side window. He watched Keenan and Galvin pull behind him in their Caprice Classic.

Fuck.

He hated doing this shit, but he had no other choice, especially since time was of the essence—yet it seemed that each passing minute was taking forever to get here.

He looked in his rearview mirror and Keenan flashed the car's headlights. Lyfe hopped out of his car and walked to the trunk, where he had a duffel bag filled with twenty million in cash.

Lyfe looked Keenan over, as he approached the car. He wanted nothing more than to whup his fuckin' ass. Hands-down.

"See what washing money can do for you." Keenan smiled, while Galvin stood back and watched.

"Look," Lyfe snapped, "I ain't washed shit. So let's just get that straight." He handed him the duffel bag and said, "It's all there."

Keenan unzipped the bag and smiled at Lyfe. "Trust if it's not all here, we certaintly know where to find you. Nice doing business with you."

"Anderson Global," Galvin smiled, "the world's best-kept secret."

Once Lyfe was certain they were gone, he drove to the small airport on the outskirts of the city to meet Arri.

She stood outside of the hangar, waiting for him, with a sleepy Zion holding on to her leg. Lyfe walked over to her and kissed her on the lips. "One more stop and then this is over."

California

Nina Simone's "Summertime" spun into the California night and played wickedly as a backdrop for Payton's thoughts as she raced up the winding coastal roads of Los Angeles. Everything had gone wrong. Everything. It was all fucked—had all blown up—and nothing was as it should've been. She'd made three deadly mistakes since she'd been in California and became Payton: trusting a longtime lover a little too long, mistrusting his ass a little too late, and marrying for love. All of which she would soon resolve.

She didn't deserve this—to be in this type of pain—not when she'd been born the puppeteer. She had the world dancing on her strings and suddenly and without warning the strings were wrapped around her neck. Nevertheless, the choke hold would begin to end today, because there was no way in hell she would be etched into the stone of history lynched like this.

The cigarette she smoked dangled between her fingers, and the ashes blew into the wind as she whipped around a sharp curve, doing her best to outrun the haunting thoughts stampeding through her mind. She could still hear the echo of Lyfe's words.

She should've listened to her mother, who told her when Carlton died to steal the profits and bail, that she didn't know shit about investment banking, that it wasn't her domain, or her training. She was raised to work with the deadly power of her pussy, not run a corporation. She was supposed to be the one who upheld the family dynasty.

After Carlton died, her life was planned. She was lined up to move on to the next wealthy motherfucker—even her next name had been chosen: Chelsea Davis. The new identifications were together, the passports created, and the plastic surgery appointment for a face-lift and a breast augmentation had already been scheduled.

But what did she do instead?

She stayed.

Fell in love.

Married Lyfe.

Became high off a new supply of power and prestige, when she should've stuck to her generational business; rich black widows, who got in and got out inauspiciously. Instead she became a power fiend who savored the flavor of being in charge.

She didn't sign up to make real financial decisions for clients; she didn't give a fuck about them. That's why she had a board of directors and top-notch employees. They'd been running the motherfucker; even when Carlton was starting to succumb to heart trouble—courtesy of slowly fed poison—the staff steered the ship, which is why she trusted Quinton. He was a devoted, respectful, and longtime trusted employee who she never dreamed of ever having to fire. And along with bonuses she gave him pussy as a reward for being such a good boy.

Dianna must've seen all of this coming, which is why she held her hand out for money, because the heat of sticking around this motherfucker was worthy of at least a few hundred grand a month.

Payton flicked the cigarette she smoked from her silver bullet convertible Ferrari over the edge of the open road. She positioned her Moschino bug-eyed goggles on her face just right, tossed the ends of her Chanel scarf behind her shoulders, gripped the steering wheel with both hands as tight as she could, and pressed the gas to the floor until all she could see was lightning whips of road and rock.

Her brakes screeched and her car jerked once she reached Quinton's driveway. It was a good thing that he lived on a secluded hill, where there were no neighbors for at least three miles; otherwise she was sure that someone would hear her heart racing in her chest.

Seeing only Quinton's car in the driveway, she knew that Dominique hadn't run her dumb ass back home . . . at least not yet. Payton hung her purse over her shoulder, grabbed her black studded flogger from the front seat, and exited the car. She peeked at her reflection in the glass and ran her hands along the sides of her black patent-leather trench coat. Her six-inch pencil heels made her ass sit up as she popped her glistening lips together, sauntered toward the front door, and pressed the bell. For a moment she smiled; despite the betrayal, she had to admit that for once—outside of how well she thought Quinton worked within the company . . . oh, and how good of a stroke he landed against her G-spot—she was impressed with the weight of Quinton's balls. He'd actually had the nerve to steal from her, and moreover, he actually thought that he would get away with it . . . and live.

Payton chuckled a bit, and before she knew it she was belting out hardy resonances of laughter. The nerve of this white-collar, Yale-educated, preppy motherfucker; and here er'body, including her mama, swore that her Compton thug would rob her ass blind.

Payton heard Quinton approach the door. She leaned against the door frame, and once Quinton filled the doorway she looked him over in his jeans, Ralph Lauren suit jacket, and Polo shirt. It was obvious he was on his way out, at least until she rang his bell.

"Going somewhere?" Payton gave him a crooked grin as she

untied the belt of her trench coat, revealing her in a cupless, glow-in-the-dark latex suit, with a slit that ran from her wet and warm pussy lips to her luscious ass. The same suit she'd worn when she'd first took Quinton's fucked-up advice of what to do about Lyfe. As a matter of fact, Quinton had been the one to pick out the suit and insist that she wear it to get the ball rolling.

And she did . . . and yet here is where it ended.

Payton enjoyed the feeling of déjà vu. She was certain that this would place Quinton in the very position he wanted Lyfe in: on his back. She flicked the end of her flogger into her right hand.

Quinton licked his lips and smiled. "Damn." He inadvertently grabbed his crotch and squeezed it. "I didn't expect to see you, baby, especially wearing our special suit." He grabbed her right nipple.

"Were you getting ready to leave?" She pointed over her shoulder. "I realize that I came without calling."

Quinton hesitated. "Hell no, I don't want you to leave. I'ma single man now and you can stay as long as you want to." He kissed her on the lips and grabbed her nipple again.

Payton purred just a little as her pussy creamed. The thought of getting her rocks off and playing God to this bastard all at the same time drove her wild. "Have you already gone to New York and taken care of Lyfe?" he questioned, helping her to remove her coat as she walked into his foyer.

"I took care of him." She nodded as she looked around and saw three suitcases lined near the front door. "What's with the luggage? Were you planning to go somewhere without me?" She chuckled. "You wouldn't leave without saying good-bye, would you, Quinton?"

"No, baby." He nibbled her neck and then took her by the hand, leading her to the bedroom. "I wouldn't never do no shit like that. Those are things Dominique left behind. Besides, aren't we supposed to run away together?"

Payton didn't respond; instead she followed Quinton and as he led the way she did her best to hide that she was disgusted with the French county décor. It was too cozy, too comfortable, and too goddamn kid-friendly.

Typical. She shook her head, thinking of Dominique.

Nothing here said sexy, mystique, arousing. Instead it said: leftovers, soccer meets, hair rollers, and there was no way in hell that Quinton ever got his dick sucked in this motherfucker.

Payton stepped into Quinton's and Dominique's Victorian-style bedroom, with rose wallpaper, matching rose bed linens, and a white wrought-iron headboard. Her eyes skipped around the room and landed on the family portraits on the walls.

For a moment Payton wondered what it would be like to live like this. To have babies without inducting them into her family business. But as quickly as the thought came was as fast as she dismissed it as bullshit. She wasn't someone's mama, her birth name was Deneen Tony, and then she became known as Erica Smite, and then Nora Danes, and Payton Anderson, now known as Payton Carrington . . . and Payton Carrington was far from naïve and knew that this motherfucker had to be made to sing the devil a lullaby. She placed her shoulder bag on the night-stand, and as Quinton licked between her ass, she squinted her eyes and enjoyed the chills he sent through her body.

"I'ma miss you," Quinton moaned as he tossed her salad.

"Not as much as I'ma miss you," she said, thrusting her ass into his face.

A few moments later Quinton lay down on the bed and Payton climbed on top of him. He slid both of her nipples into his mouth and said, "I don't know what I love most—you, or your nipples in my mouth."

Payton attempted to laugh and mush her breasts in his face the way he liked, but she wasn't in the mood to put her all into it, so instead she reached for her shoulder bag and pulled out a set of handcuffs, shackles, and the red leather noose. She swung them before Quinton's eyes. A smile ran across his lips and he said, "Look at you, freaky as fuckin' hell." He bit her breasts.

Payton turned around in a sixty-nine position and slid down Quinton's chest. He began to suck her clit, as she eased his dick between her expanding cheeks. She licked the bulging veins and thick ridges; the music from her lips made an alto smacking beat while she slurped him as if she were granting his last wish.

After sucking him off for a few moments she shackled his feet. Then she eased back around and cuffed his hands.

Payton kissed Quinton from the palm of his right hand to his chest, where she sucked his nipples and then moved back down to his dick and graced him with more neck. She could tell by his moaning and panting that he was almost where she needed him to be: comfortably weak so that she could tell him, without hesitation, that this would be the last fuckin' day on earth he'd see.

Instead of having him cum in her mouth Payton eased her creamy trenches onto Quinton's cock and she began to ride him. She flexed her inner walls, causing sugar to pour from within.

"Payton!" he moaned. "Oh my God, baby, put it around my neck now. Now, baby!"

"Certainly," she said evenly, slapping the noose on him and pulling it tight, but not too tight where he couldn't talk; after all, she did have some things she wanted him to take to his grave.

Quinton's chest heaved up and down as he bit into his bottom lip. Payton yanked the noose and he started to gag. "Now tell me," she said, "why the fuck would you launder money from my company?" She yanked his neck.

Quinton blinked repeatedly. "What?" he struggled to speak.

Payton wrapped the end of the noose around her fist tightly and yanked it as if she were rounding up cattle. She could see blood preparing to burst in his face. "I asked you a question. What the fuck made you steal my money? I mean, were you losing your fuckin' mind? Did you think I would never find out?" she spat. "Speak, motherfucker."

He couldn't speak but the look of his bulging eyes clearly said that he was scared. Buckets of sweat washed over his body.

"I asked you a question," she said to him, and slightly loosened her grip.

"Payton, baby . . . listen . . ." He paused. "I'll admit, okay, okay, that I put some accounts in Lyfe's name to help, you know, with the setup."

"I didn't need you to do that, I had that covered. But what I didn't have covered were the accounts in your name." She yanked his neck again.

He cried, "I swear to God I'll tell you where the money is."

"Oh please, I've already taken my money back. Do you think I would come here to kill you and not have my money first? Now, what I don't know is why the fuck you would steal from me. Tell me what possessed you to think that would work out for you. You need to learn," she yanked his neck, "who the fuck you're dealing with!"

"I'm sorry," he sobbed. "But please don't kill me. I ain't mean that shit. I'm so stupid."

"Umm-hmm."

"And I swear to God I'll never do it again."

"I know you won't."

"But I have kids, Payton. Two boys."

"I wouldn't give a shit, they'll kiss you at the casket."

"Payton—"

"You should've never tried to play me. You thought I was stupid, that you could simply run all over me and take every fuckin' thing I owned. Oh hell, no, honey. Not the way it works and not the way it's gon' work. I'm the judge, the jury, and my noose here is the justice department." She yanked it tightly around his neck and watched him gag to death.

Once Quinton's neck hung low and his eyes stood frozen, Payton placed her two fingers on his neck and checked his pulse. Nothing.

She thought of removing her trusted devices but then figured, fuck it. She decided to leave Dominique—who she was certain would be bringing her desperate ass back any day now—some souvenirs to keep.

Payton slid her trench coat on and stepped to the full-length mirror to ensure that she was as beautiful leaving as she'd been coming in. She turned back to Quinton and pressed her cherry Chanel—covered lips to his forehead. "Mother always said, 'Go hard or go to hell.' "

Dominique had driven around the southern coast of California, unsettled and uncomfortable for a week. She'd been from one five-star hotel suite to the next, trying to decide if she wanted to stay in California or attempt to strike out on her own again—take her twins, and move to another part of the earth. South of France, Morocco, Alpine, New Jersey . . . somewhere—anywhere—far away. She had enough stashed to make it happen and she desperately needed to live away from him, so that she could get to experience what normalcy would be like.

But then again, if she were to truly leave here and leave Quinton, how would she prove that she was truly the bitch he shouldn't have fucked over? She looked up the stretch of the freeway and peeped in her rearview mirror at her sleeping sons and thought: *What about all the work I've put into my marriage? Cooking for this motherfucker, accepting his cheap-ass ways, folding my pride and tucking it in my ass pocket to ask him for money—because he was too cheap to give me a dime.*

A life filled with nothing; but then again, it was filled with something: she had his demands:

Don't work—I want you home when I get here. Don't make too many friends—I want your focus on me. Don't have the house messy—you're home all day, you can keep it clean. Don't have my dinner

*ready one minute after six—I want it at six. And don't get pregnant
again—we have enough children with the twins.*

And yeah, her soul constantly craved, and complained, and
ached, but none of that meant that she should walk out on her
marriage and give her husband away to the next bitch. Not when
she'd borne two of his children at the same goddamn time. Not
when she'd disregarded her goals, given up her individuality to
become a part of him—getting in wherever she could fit in, fak-
ing the funk at public appearances, acting as if they had the perfect marriage, when the only vow still standing was "till death do
us part" (and even that was moments away from the inferno).

And definitely not when she had that shitty-ass prenuptial
agreement.

Fuck that.

Dominique pressed the accelerator to the floor of her Mercedes minivan and headed up the freeway toward Hollywood
Hills.

In thirty minutes flat she was pulling into her driveway.
"Josiah, Malachi," she looked into her rearview mirror at her
sleeping twins, "wake up, sweeties."

Josiah stretched and shook his brother's shoulder. "Where
are we, Mommy?" He wiped his eyes.

"We're home." Dominique hopped out of the van and pressed
the remote to open the doors.

"You said we weren't coming back," Malachi said.

"We'll, we're back. Mommy has some business to take care
of, and besides, I'm sure Daddy misses us."

"Okay, Mommy."

The boys ran to the front door and pushed it open.

Dominique shook her head. "Your father has a terrible habit
of leaving the door unlocked," she said, more to herself than to
them.

Dominique's heels clicked against the wood floor as she entered the foyer. She sent the boys to their rooms to change into their pajamas. "I'll be up there to read you a story in a minute," she yelled behind them, walking toward the ground-floor master suite. She approached the doorway and could tell by the reeking of perfume that Quinton had had his mistress here—or the bitch was still here, riding his dick at this very moment.

She shook her head in disbelief that he would be so fuckin' disrespectful as to have his mistress in her home and in her bed. For a moment she wondered if she needed to grab a knife and slice one of these bitches, but then she remembered the video camera she'd planted in her bedroom and figured she would have to kick ass with her bare hands. She pushed the double doors to their master suite open and immediately Dominique lost her breath. She knew she had to be mistaken, so instinctively she closed her eyes tight and opened them quickly. Nothing about the vision had changed and there lay Quinton—dead: handcuffed and shackled to the bed, a red leather noose pulled tight around his neck, and fresh cum covering his still dick.

Zurich, Switzerland

Arri's hair flowed over her shoulders as she sauntered across the cobblestone street in Zurich to the concrete steps of the Central Bank. Her Manolo heels clicked in rhythm as she opened the glass doors and walked into the bank's lobby. She caught a glimpse of herself dressed in her Dolce & Gabbana cream power suit and Louis Vuitton shoulder bag.

She passed Lyfe on the way into the bank. He sat in the lobby, leafing through the morning paper, and once her heels clicked past him, he looked up and nodded his head. Arri walked over to the customer service rep and smiled. "How are you today?"

"I'm fine." The rep smiled back at her. "How are you?"

"All is well."

"May I help you with anything?" the smiling representative asked her in a thick Swiss accent.

"Yes," Arri said, "I would like to transfer money from my account, please."

"Okay, I need to see your passport, please."

"No problem." Arri handed it to her and the representative quickly handed it back.

"May I have your account number and password?"

"Certainly—000678214, and the password is Smooth Operator."

The representative typed the information that Arri gave her

into the computer. "How much would you like to transfer?" she asked.

"All of it to these accounts." Arri waited patiently while the representative completed the transfers.

"Thank you very much." The teller handed Arri back her bankbook.

"Have a good day."

Arri smiled and walked toward the lobby, where she walked past Lyfe and out the front door. She slid into a taxi and rode to a small hangar on the outskirts of the city. She walked over to Lyfe, who'd arrived shortly before she did and was now waiting for her outside of the chartered plane. "It's done." She handed him the bankbook. "All transferred evenly into these accounts."

"Great."

"Where's Zion?" she asked.

"I sent him ahead with Khris: She and Tyree arrived here this morning. We'll meet them in the Caymans when we get there."

"We're going to the Cayman Islands?" She smiled.

"Yeah," he said. "You remember where I took you before."

"Yeah."

"Well, it's home now. We own it."

She kissed him passionately. "I love you."

"You better." Lyfe smiled. "Now, are you ready?"

"Yes."

"Well, let's go."

California

Dominique sat in the front pew of the church, gazing at Quinton's mahogany and brass casket. She stroked the arm of her older four-year-old twin and he placed his head on her lap and sobbed. The feeling in the center of her chest was one she'd never felt before: her husband dead at the hands of Payton was sweeter than she ever dreamed. She always knew that they wouldn't be together forever, but this ending deserved an Academy Award.

The California Mass Choir hummed "Nearer My God to Thee" as Quinton lay dressed in a tailor-made black Armani suit, with a soft pink rose pinned to his lapel. He looked well rested as he lay among a sea of bleeding heart wreaths, carnations, roses, and mountains and mountains of wildflowers.

Light sobs and cries could be heard throughout the church as the pastor invited Quinton's family, friends, and coworkers to speak their peace about how great of a man, father, and husband they thought he was.

"Sit up, baby," Dominique said to her son, kissing him on his forehead, as he leaned against the back of the pew. "Everything will be okay," she assured him.

Dominique rose to her feet and slowly made her way to the casket. She stood before Quinton and ran her soft, black satin gloves from the gathered silk lining that trimmed the edge of the casket to Quinton's still lips.

Her pearl bracelets draped on her wrist as she ran her hands over Quinton's face and wondered how many people—including her own family—had thought she was stupid, crazy, insane . . . and even pitied her. After all, it was one thing for your husband to cheat, but it was a whole other ball game for his mistress to kill his ass. A mistress that no one knew, not even Quinton, was your sister.

Dominique's veil swayed before her face like a netted shield as she lifted it and bent over into the casket. She looked at a still Quinton and said, "This is such a relief. You're dead and my sister did all the dirty work. Don't worry, I turned her ass in, because I got the murder on the surveillance camera. I thought that camera would just catch you cheating, but it served an even better purpose."

Her heated breath hit against his stone cheeks. "Oh," she giggled slightly, "wait, let me back up. You didn't know that Payton was my sister, did you? You thought little ole—wait, excuse me— allow me to use your words; you thought fat-ass Dominique was all alone in the world and needed you . . . because I didn't have anyone else. Well," she smirked, "obviously you were wrong. You were such," she paused, "a motherfucker to be married to." She stared at him and shook her head. A smile curled her lips. "You thought you were such a smooth operator," she whispered and arched her brow, "but here's the secret, I'm the smoothest of them all." She snickered. "Because no one ever saw me comin'.

"I knew you were fucking Payton—how stupid did you think I was; the bitch was far from subtle about it, and her perfume reeks—oh God, I hated that fuckin' smell. But do you think that bitch gave a damn about what she was doing to me? Hell, no. She never has. She and my mother thought that I was nothing. They made me the black sheep. All because I wanted to be conventional, because I wanted a family, because I wanted a man for more than money and dick, so they labeled me stupid and ridiculous. And they made my life," she paused, "a living hell. But what they didn't know is that I really held all the cards and that I was a bigger bitch than they could ever be.

"But one thing they were right about was you." She smirked. "They had your bald-headed-sweat-too-fuckin'-much ass pegged. And to think for years I really wanted our marriage to work, I didn't want to be like them—but you and my sister forced me to be. You two forced me to take matters into my own hands, because God knows that I never intended to be this chick. The chick that I am now."

The choir continued to sing in the background and Quinton's mother's cries rocked the air. "Oh God," Dominique snorted, "I wish she would shut the fuck up, because honestly, she's the real reason why you never grew up to be a man." Dominique shook her head. "I knew that you and Payton were stealing money from the onset. And I knew it because you were so dumb that you had the offshore account statements in your briefcase. Who does that? Didn't you know I searched through your things?" She cracked up, laughing so hard that her cackle resonated around the room as if she were wailing.

The usher walked up behind Dominique and rubbed her back. "I'm okay," Dominique sniffed. "Please, just give me a few more minutes with him."

"I understand," the usher said as she patted Dominique's back again and then walked away.

"It's amazing how many people think I'm distraught. They just don't realize that I'm celebrating." She clapped her hands together. "Hell, I stopped giving a fuck about you the night you came into the house and wouldn't make love to me. So, as far as I'm concerned, you've been dead. And so I'm going to take the twenty million dollars that my man—oh, wait, you didn't know that I had a man." Her face lit up. "Well, yes, I did, he started as a one-nighter, but the dick was too good to let go, so I hired him and had him join the private eye. I'd already put him on the case. And together they came up with the best plan ever. They acted like the FBI"—she cracked up laughing even more—"and they muscled Lyfe to steal a fortune from his wife. I hated I had to deceive Lyfe, someone who was innocent, but I count it a fair exchange: no robberies, because I'm the one who made sure he got the banking information he needed, and I knew he would use it, considering his prior history.

"Now it seems that Lyfe may have gotten away with more money than me, but I'm okay with that, because I'm going to take my money, and the boys and I are going to the South of France, to meet up with my man, Terrance aka Keenan. And Terrance and I are going to spread the money on the bed and fuck until the night cries out. So thank you. Thank you for being such an ass." She stroked the side of his face. "You can rest now, sweetness, and take your sleep. Because when you wake up in hell you will see why it knows no fury like a woman scorned."

Dominique turned toward her twins, "Come on, boys," she said, "kiss your father good-bye."

The boys walked to the casket and Dominique picked them up one by one. They kissed their father on the cheek and their tears wet Quinton's face.

"It's okay." Dominique fought like hell not to smile, but she couldn't resist holding it in, so she curled her lips and said, "In the end, sweetie, everyone gets their just due. Now, we have to go." She looked at Quinton's casket and gave him a soft wink. She grabbed her sons by the hands and proceeded out of the church and up the street to where a driver stood holding the back door to a stretched white Rolls-Royce open for them.

Acknowledgments

My Father, who art in Heaven, thank You for answering my prayers.

To my mother and father, thank you for always being there, for being the best parents in the world, and for always supporting me, my children, my husband, and my dreams. No girl could ever ask for more. I love you!

To my husband, thank you sooooooo much for listening to me every night go on and on about my characters as if they were real people.

To my children, thank you for making me laugh, for giving me precious memories, and for always interrupting me when I'm on a tight deadline.

To my family: my grandma, aunties, uncles, cousins, and in-laws, your support means everything to me. I thank you for always spreading the word, for buying my books, passing them around, and always being the best family anyone can have.

To my cousin Sharif, you are such an inspiration to me. I admire your determination, your strength, and your desire. I pray for you every day and I believe in everything that you dream. Remember that we have dominion and the ability to move mountains. I love you, my cousin!

To my friends, church family, and my co-workers, your support is immeasurable and for that I will never be able to thank you enough.

To my One World/Ballantine family, those seen and unseen, thank you for everything! I may have written the manuscript but together we made this a book!

Melody Guy, thank you for being one of the best editors an author could have, but most of all thank you for your patience, especially when I always seem to need another week . . . and another . . . and another . . .

Porscha, Porscha, Porscha, wow, here we are. You are so incredibly talented and you certainly outdid yourself with this project. You were so dedicated, so amazingly patient, so willing to always give support, ideas, and share what you thought was best. I really enjoyed working with you on this project and I sincerely hope that in the end I made you proud!

To my agent, Sarah Camilli, thank you so much for all that you do; and to think we're just getting started!

To Nakea Murray, my friend. Show me how to do it like you, show me how to do! You are so dedicated and you have such an amazing gift to see in others what they can't even see in themselves. Thank you so much! Who knew that all of this would come from you simply telling me, "Risqué don't go to church!"

Tiffany Smith, thanks for embracing me, for supporting my work, and for making me laugh! I'm elated and privileged to call you my friend.

And 3 Chicks On Lit, we're in the building, every Wednesday night @7 on blogtalk radio!

To Dywane Birch, thank you for always keeping it real, for staying positive, and for being a wonderful friend!

To Adrianne Byrd, thank you for always being there to answer the phone at two, three, and six o'clock in the morning when I was pulling my hair out! You are incredibly talented and I know without a doubt that *Hustlin' Divas* is gon' kill 'em!

To Danielle Santiago, you are so incredibly special and soooo gifted, believe me: the best is yet to come.

To my childhood friend Sharonda Smith: what has it been, close to thirty years that we've known each other? I want you to know that you are an amazingly strong woman. You deserve the best and it will come. Keep your head held high and know that no matter what, I will always be there for you! Love you, sis!

To my buddy AJ: one day we will write that script!

To Keisha, thanks for being my Thursday night reality show pot'nah! It's been six years and I've seen your life grow in so many different ways. I want you to know that any- and every- thing is possible, that dreams come true, and that anything you put your mind to will be conquered. And just as I said in the last book, one day all the checks will cash (inside joke) and we will finally get what we deserve . . . or they'll get it.

To K'wan and Charlotte, you guys are the best. Thanks for al- ways being there to read, to chat, or to come over for a party. Love you guys. And K'wan, thanks for always answering the phone when I had a crazy idea! You are an amazing and talented author and I wish you nothing but the best, my friend.

To my facebook friends—I promised you a line so here it is: to _____ (fill your name in here), as without you who knows where in na hell I would be—LOL.

Seriously, I thank everyone who has ever helped me, read my work, taken my calls, listened to my ideas . . . everyone who has ever supported me in my career, I thank you from the bottom of my heart.

And saving the best for last: my fans, readers, bookstores, Whatsdastory.proboards.com, and the message boards: without your support, none of this would be possible. Thank you so much for supporting me in all that I do! Please email me at *Risque 215@aol.com* or visit me on facebook: facebook.com/tushon-dawhitaker, twitter, or myspace, and let me know your thoughts.

One Love,
Risqué

About the Author

RISQUÉ is the erotic pseudonym of a #1 *Essence* bestselling author. Her previous works of urban erotica include *Red Light Special* and *The Sweetest Taboo*. She lives in New Jersey, where she is already at work on her next novel. Visit her online at www.myspace.com/risquetheauthor.